Jeffrey Manship

SMOKESCREEN

Limited Special Edition. No. 2 of 10 Hardbacks

The middle child of three, Jeffrey Manship was born in Winchester in 1957. The family settled in Worksop in his teens, where he completed his education at the local comprehensive. He spent 37 years as a postman in the town before taking early retirement to fulfil his lifelong ambition of becoming a published author. He has two sons with his wife, Jakki, and four children from a previous relationship. His other interests include football, cricket (well, most sports really) and the family Labrador.

For Jakki and Karina, thanks for being in my life.

Jeffrey Manship

SMOKESCREEN

For Jakki,

The best person I will
ever meet in my life

Love Jeff

x x
x x x
x x
x

AUSTIN MACAULEY PUBLISHERS™

LONDON • CAMBRIDGE • NEW YORK • SHARJAH

A CIP catalogue record for this title is available from the British Library.

ISBN 9781788489737 (Paperback)
ISBN 9781788489744 (Hardback)
ISBN 9781788489751 (E-Book)

www.austinmacauley.com

First Published (2019)
Austin Macauley Publishers Ltd
25 Canada Square
Canary Wharf
London
E14 5LQ

Chapter 1

"Jake, can I see you for a minute before you go out?" Barry Conlon, my boss (or Delivery Office Manager to give him his proper title) had a way of picking his moments.

"I'm really busy today. Can't you leave it 'til tomorrow?" I pleaded, knowing what the answer would be.

"My office in five minutes. It won't take long."

I knew this was coming but why do managers always pick the busiest times? Does it give them a sense of power? Still, I thought it best to get it over and done with.

I looked down at the pile of mail I'd still got to throw into my over-loaded frame. There was at least another twenty minutes of prep before I could start bundling, and I should have been out on delivery five minutes ago. Most of it was junk; I didn't want to deliver it, my customers didn't want it, but it 'pays the wages' as they're always telling me.

With a deep sigh, I dropped my handful of letters onto the bench and trudged my way to the manager's office, past the tut-tuts and witticisms. "Who's been a naughty boy then?" Gerard Duggens asked.

"Oh dear, someone's in trouble," from Emily Pancroft.

"Been nice knowing you, Jake," said Mahmood Sadik.

I ignored them all; it's only the sort of thing I would have done if it was someone else taking the walk of shame. Having avoided the piles of strategically strewn mailbags, the dampness from yesterday's downpour still evident by the musty cloying odour that clung to them, and the even bigger stacks of parcels and packages, I arrived at Conlon's shiny metal door with its toughened glass window and MANAGER emblazoned across it. I knocked firmly and entered without waiting for a response. It felt like going into the headmaster's office to get the cane or detention—whichever he felt would hurt you the most.

The image persisted as his waving hand beckoned me to take a seat at the opposite side of his document-littered desk. He continued with his phone call eking out the moment for me. At well over six feet tall, he would have had no trouble looking down on me, but, being seated, he still managed to achieve the same image, possibly because it also seemed that his chair was at least a couple of inches higher than mine.

The office was about four metres square with the door in the centre of one wall and the only desk directly opposite. It was more of a table with metallic-grey legs and matching grey plastic top. There was a laptop, printer and two metal trays containing various letters and papers; 'in-tray' and 'out-tray'. I wasn't sure, but if I was a betting man I'd say the one with the four times as high pile wasn't the latter. There were four five-drawer filing cabinets along each of the side walls. I wondered why so much filing space was needed now that we were in the age of the computer. Above these to my left was a notice board with insignificant messages in red, blue and black wipe-clean ink. Opposite to that was a staffing spreadsheet.

And still the phone call continued. I was sure he was doing this deliberately.

I was getting fed up with checking the place out now, and it was a really busy day. I could do without this waste of time.

I looked at my watch, trying to drop him a hint, then straight back at him. His over-sized oval face registered no change of expression as he just kept jabbering away on the telephone. A smile crossed my face as I recalled that scene from *Star Wars* with Jabba the Hutt. This had the desired effect as he promptly ended the call. I wasn't quite sure whether it was because I didn't appear to be taking the situation seriously or that managers just don't like to see us workers smiling or enjoying ourselves. Or maybe he felt he had made me suffer enough.

I took the lead, "Do I need the union in?"

"No, no, Jake. It's just an informal chat."

I knew how this is would go; I'd been here often enough in the past. 'Are you happy in your work? Is there anything bothering you? Is there anything you'd like to tell me?' Standard 'caring' questions from the 'caring' modern manager.

"Are you happy in your work? Is there anything bothering you?" he began.

"Shall we cut out the, erm, what's another word for crap? Oh yes, niceties, and get to the point. I told you I'm snowed under today. Unless, of course, you want to get me some assistance."

That seemed to do the trick.

He leaned his considerable bulk forward propping his chins on his knuckles. "You were late again this morning."

I cut him short, "Only a couple of minutes. You're being a bit picky." *Ironic*, I thought. I had been two minutes late and already we had wasted at least ten in here.

"Two minutes today, maybe, but it's the third time you've been late in a month."

I opened my mouth to again protest, but he raised his hand to stop me. I momentarily wondered if the one remaining arm would be able to sustain the weight of that head.

"And the quality of your work; that's gone downhill just lately. We've had at least four complaints of miss-delivery since…well, in the last few months."

"Since my wife threw me out you were going to say. No need to mince your words, Barry."

"Yes, well, it's just not good enough, Jake. Like I said at the start, this is just informal at the moment. We don't want it to go any further, do we? How long's it been now, three months?"

"Four actually, not that it's got anything to do with you," I said, raising my voice. I was starting to get annoyed.

"Either way, you've got to buck your ideas up. Get over it, move on." Conlon leaned back in his chair and looked at me as though he was assessing me. "You're not a bad looking chap, a touch of the Bruce Willis about you. You ought to find yourself another girl. You shouldn't have much trouble." He obviously thought he was trying to help.

But I didn't, "When you pay me for my private time, you can tell me what to do with it; until then, keep your nose out." Besides that, I thought, *Bruce Willis is at least fifteen years older than me.* Thanks for the compliment.

"I was just trying to help you, Jake. Like I said, it's just an informal chat at the moment. You've got to change, pull yourself together, because if you don't, your twenty odd years of service will count for very little."

I stood up, my chair screeching as it scraped across the tiled floor, "Are you done? Cos I've got work to do." I paused briefly and added, "Oh and I'll be on the docket now. At least half an hour."

His lack of response I took as a signal that we had indeed finished. I strutted out of the office and heard him say, "Take heed of my advice, Jake," just as I slammed the door.

There were no jibes or tuts as I strutted stone-faced back to my mail. My colleagues had almost certainly heard my raised tones in the manager's office, making the mood I was now in obvious.

An hour later, I was still seething as I shoved yet another piece of junk through yet another door, catching the end of my finger in the spring-loaded letterbox as I withdrew my hand. I waited a couple of seconds knowing the pain was coming, and when it did, I clenched my teeth tightly, tears welling up in my eyes. When the agony subsided, I looked furtively around to make sure no one was watching; the embarrassment would have hurt much more than the actual injury.

However, this did serve to bring me to my senses, at least a little bit. I knew I had to calm down. I had another four hours or so of delivery left, and I couldn't afford to waste energy on the likes of Barry Conlon. And besides, what really annoyed me was that Barry did have a point. He wasn't a bad bloke for a manager, but he had that really annoying habit of stating the obvious; home truths always hurt the most.

Right at that moment, I really needed a smoke. It's funny how the greatest trauma or the least little upset becomes an instant excuse for lighting up when you are trying to kick the habit.

I parked my trolley, took out my e-cigarette from my jacket pocket, but then thought better of it and put it away again. For this situation, a real smoke would be required. Vaping was all right most of the time but, occasionally, only the real thing would have the desired effect. There's that excuse again. I reached into the opposite inside pocket of my uniform jacket and extracted the already opened twenty pack and disposable lighter.

I lit up, took a deep drag and could immediately feel myself beginning to calm down. I blew the smoke out slowly and watched it twirl away upwards in the still morning air. I had been so wrapped up in the earlier events that I hadn't noticed what a nice, bright, sunny day it was; a little on the chilly side, but not bad for early April. The chattering of birds and the distant playful bark of a dog accentuated the ambience. I took another prolonged drag on the cigarette and held it for a couple of seconds with my eyes closed, savouring the moment.

"They'll be the death of you, Jake," a voice jolted me out of my own little world.

"Good morning, Mrs Clayworth. Not a bad day today, is it?" I cheerily remarked when I focused on the owner of the voice. I would see the sixty-something widow most days, making the same pilgrimage. In fact, being in the same places at similar times on most days, I generally met the same people and, like as not, generally had the same conversations. Most of us are creatures of habit to some extent.

I ignored her mock chastisement. "Just off to do a bit of shopping are we?"

"Yes, I just thought I'd see if there are any bargains in town today," she never broke her stride, adding, "If you've got any bills for me, put them in the bin, won't you, Jake."

I played along, "The one that matches your eyes. Blue for recycling that'll be then. Don't spend up." Although she had passed me by now and I could only see the back of her head, I could tell she was smiling at that one.

My customers always cheered me up. In those brief moments when we passed the time of day with each other our problems didn't exist. These moments were my sanctuary from the rest of the world and all its complications.

Returning to my cigarette, I took another long draw on it, but the effect was losing its potency. I was briefly lost in my own world again but was abruptly yanked out of it by a squeal of rubber on tarmac, followed by a deafening explosive bang. I thought for a split second a bomb had gone off.

I whipped my head from right to left, at first unable to pinpoint the direction from which the cacophony had come as the din reverberated off the surrounding houses. I found it just as Mrs Clayworth came back down to earth with a sickening thud like a sack of potatoes being dropped off the back of a lorry at the greengrocers.

She had been struck by a works van with 'Peeterson and Dawling, Painters and Decorators' emblazoned on it. And with some force, judging by the state of the van and its distance from Mrs Clayworth.

The vehicle had slewed sideways, flattening the railings that bordered a lazily flowing stream, straddling the demolished ironworks and at a right angle to the road. The contorted body of the driver had come to rest hanging half in and half out of the windscreen he had shattered on his way through it.

It had all happened in mere seconds, but it seemed like ages. It was as though time had briefly stood still; the barking of the dog and the singing of the birds momentarily disappearing.

I snapped out of my inert state, the half smoked cigarette falling from my hand as I started to run towards the accident. The nearer I got the more horrific the scene became. Mrs Clayworth had been almost cut in half by the force of the impact, her torso inseparable from her shopping trolley. One eye stared lifelessly straight at me, the other was flowing in her blood to a nearby drain about to disappear, her life having already done so. Her legs seemed at all the wrong angles so did her right arm; the left one was missing. For some reason, I looked around for it, but I knew it would be of no use to her now. The sight of her and the strong coppery stench of all that blood made me wretch and it was all I could do to stop myself from vomiting.

There was nothing I could do to help her now, so I staggered on in slow motion towards the van. The driver was motionless, the blood from his many lacerations running over the bonnet, dripping onto the partly crushed daffodils beneath, the deep red vividly mixing with the yellows, whites and greens in the bright spring sunshine.

I thought for a moment that he too was dead. How could anyone in that state possibly still be alive? I could see his exposed skull where his scalp had been ripped away. His right arm looked broken or at least dislocated; his left was deeply gashed, blood pumping copiously from it. His distorted, gore-reddened face a mask of a thousand slashes. There was so much blood! How could one body contain so much?

Then he groaned and started to haul himself out of the wreckage through what was left of the windscreen.

"No don't, don't move!" I yelled in panic, fearing he would only worsen his condition. I didn't know what to do, so I just stood there in shock, arms outstretched and face frozen in horror.

The driver hauled his broken body across the bonnet, slithering through his own life fluid. At last I shook off my stupor and stumbled to help him. Not quite sure where to grab hold of for fear of making his injuries worse or even fatal. I stuttered to a halt as he fell onto the ground.

With the amount of blood he had lost and the mangled state of his body, especially the top half, I was astounded that he could even move and yet he continued to drag himself away from the van and towards me.

"No, don't. Stay still; don't move! You're going to do more damage. Don't try to get up; don't!" I pleaded with him. But he didn't seem to hear me and carried on pulling himself up, grabbing hold of my coat and pulling me down towards him.

Unexpectedly, he didn't haul himself to his feet but dragged me onto the ground with him instead. His eyes were bulging, blood and spittle frothed from his lacerated mouth, through his broken teeth, splattering into my face.

I was stunned helpless as it dawned on me that he wasn't trying to get up but was actually attacking me! His one good hand gripped firmly onto my throat knocking me off-balance. We rolled through the busted railings, his grip tightening and his snarling becoming louder. I raised my head trying to pull it away from his vice-like hold. Out of the corner of my eye, I saw we were rolling towards the stream, its water level way above normal, swollen by the recent rains.

Chapter 2

Suddenly panic was really starting to clutch hold of me just as firmly as the van driver's hand. My mind instantly shot back to when I was only seven years, old and I had almost drowned in a Spanish pool on a family holiday.

Now, here I was thirty-odd years later facing the same fear but in totally different circumstances. I didn't know which to do first—try to release his stranglehold or stop myself being dragged into the life-taking water.

The van driver was on top of me now, and I couldn't shift his grip. I tried to over balance him. I half pushed, half slapped him hard in the cheek with the back of my hand, gashing it on his few remaining teeth. His head jerked sideways, but he didn't fall off or release his hold, only grunted more loudly and bled more profusely. His blood was now running into my eyes, mouth and nose and into the scratches and gouges he had made; his blood mingling with mine. And still we were slipping down the slope that was slicked by his blood, intermingling with the fluids from the wrecked vehicle, inevitably towards that dreaded water.

I punched him in the face as hard as I could, which wasn't very hard at all as my strength was vanishing as quickly as the little breath I had left.

The spring-cold stream was lapping against my hair; my arms had stopped flailing; my vision was blurred and all but gone. *This is the end*, I thought, as I could no longer feel anything, not even his hand around my windpipe.

Then, suddenly, his weight was gone from me; I could breathe again, although it was painful to do so, and I could see him tumbling off me as I opened my eyes. He fell sideways, not breathing, lifeless, onto the bank and slowly slipped head first into the water.

A small crowd, that must have come out of their houses to see what the commotion was, gathered above me. "You all right, lad?" I heard someone ask.

"Of course he's not, stupid. Someone just tried to drown him. Somebody call an ambulance." This one I recognised. It was Edith Braysher from number twenty-two.

"I'm on it," her son, Eric, was the next voice I heard. "Hello, c-c-can I h-h-have an ambulance p-p-p-please," he stammered.

"Give us it here," Edith again, "He'll be dead before you get the damn thing ordered."

I was confused and disorientated as hands were now grabbing hold of me, but this time they were friendly helping hands, hauling me back to my feet and towards the road, away from the water. I yelped in agony as an elderly man tugged on my left arm. The pain was almost unbearable; tears came to my eyes for the second time that morning. The arm definitely didn't feel right at all, as though it wasn't properly attached to my elbow. I knew it was almost certainly broken. I had broken bones before, as a child, and that feeling never really leaves you but just remains dormant until the next occasion it is awakened.

At the top, I turned and looked back down towards the stream and the dead van driver, the top half of his body under water, and thought how close it had come to that being me.

Edith's gentle gnarled hands led me slowly away, past the wrecked van. *P. D. Peetersen and Dawling, Painters and Decorators. P.D.—how symmetrical*, I thought, wondering, *is he Peetersen or Dawling; which one? P.D...P.D.*

"You'd better come indoors, Jake, while we wait for that ambulance," Edith said as she wrapped her coat around my shoulders and then behind her to Eric, "He's going into shock."

Like a child, I was led across the road to her front door. I could see a couple of people, maybe more, gathered around something on the road, covering it with a blanket or another coat; I couldn't really tell. It didn't register that it was Mrs Clayworth they were concealing.

By this time, I was visibly shaking with the cold but more so from the shock that had firmly gripped a hold of me. "Th-thank you M-M-Mrs B-Braysher," I said through chattering teeth.

Eric butted in, "Is he t-t-taking the p-p-."

But he was cut short by his mother. "Go and put the kettle on, lad, and less of your cheek."

I could vaguely hear the blaring and wailing of the sirens as the emergency vehicles began to arrive. I couldn't tell how many or of which type, but there seemed to be plenty of them.

I figured I was probably deemed to be in no fit state to be interviewed at that time as no police officer came to question me. There were still plenty of people milling about, so they probably had enough to be going on with. There would be ample witness statements to take before they got round to mine.

As I was helped towards the ambulance, I could see a young policewoman cordoning off the area with blue and white 'police' tape. An older male colleague of hers was removing the covering from Mrs Clayworth's body to replace it with an official one of their own. I wondered if that meant it was a more important job and therefore more befitting of a more senior officer, or was I still in shock and just over-complicating things.

The blood had stopped running from her body, and a dry film was beginning to form over the various wounds. By the look of the amount of red on the road she probably didn't have any more left to lose.

The pungent unique smell of blood still hung angrily over the whole area, but this time I didn't wretch. It didn't seem nearly as shocking as a mere few minutes previously. The whole dreadful incident and what I had just been through made this one small part of it all appear somehow less significant. The entire episode had detached me from reality, and it was as though I was watching it through someone else's eyes, sort of like some scene from a second-rate horror movie.

As the paramedic was closing the ambulance doors, I could see Mrs Clayworth's lifeless blue eyeball staring up at me from its resting place lodged in the drain; it had been too big to slip through the grate. I suspected that image would stay with me for a very long time.

We slowly pulled away from the kerbside, the blue flashing lights casting their glare on the surrounding houses, glinting back through the windscreen as they reflected off the windows. "Sit tight, mate. We'll be there in five minutes," the ambulance driver informed me.

I was glad my life didn't depend on this because it was a full fifteen before we rolled up to the Accident and Emergency Department entrance.

"No need for the sirens," the driver said, "As you're not actually dying."

I accepted this, but then felt a bit unnerved to think that he had been able to so quickly make such an informed diagnosis of my condition. Still, I couldn't be in that bad shape could I?

The paramedic opened the rear doors, "You sit there a minute, mate, while I fetch a wheelchair."

I was feeling much better by this point, having been forced to sit back, relax and regain my senses. The more mileage we had put between us and the incident, the more my shock diminished and the less real the whole thing seemed. "It's OK. I can walk," I said.

"'Fraid not; it's not allowed. Health and safety."

We entered through the half-cylinder shaped automatic glass doors into the holding area. To my right were double doors leading to various departments, most of which I couldn't even pronounce, let alone understand what was done in them. Some I did recognise; *fracture clinic* stood out in particular, along with *physiotherapy*; both of which, I reckoned, I would be using in the not too distant future.

To my left was the waiting area with about thirty identical plastics on metal grey chairs set out in four rows on sand coloured rubberised-plastic floor tiles. In the corner beyond these were two vending machines, one for drinks and the other for snacks.

Straight ahead of us were more double doors which led to wards 6–19. To the left of these doors was 'reception'. My 'driver' escorted me along the industrial grey carpet that cut through the area to the reception desk. This was another curved structure, some twenty feet long and more than three feet high. Adorning it were three computer monitors, a couple of telephones and a wooden date block that informed me today was the seventh of April. I supposed I had to work it out for myself that it was Thursday.

I was wheeled straight past this to a small enclosure I had failed to notice before. 'Triage', a plaque on the wall beside it said. A matronly looking woman took a seat opposite me and began questioning me whilst constantly referring to a computer beside her. It soon became obvious that she was following a list on the screen. Things had certainly changed since my last visit to A&E. It seemed a lot more impersonal now, but I guessed it made it less likely that anything was missed.

I had to recount my ordeal, give my medical history and provide anything else that may have been relevant, which in my case was nothing. My temperature was taken, as was my pulse rate and blood pressure. My actual injuries at this point seemed to be of secondary importance.

I presumed I had been assessed as not likely to die in the immediate future and was returned to the reception area where I was finally allowed to leave the wheelchair.

As I rose to my feet, I got a clearer view of the area behind the desk. Standing directly in front of me was a thirtyish, dark-rooted blonde studying a file. She was wearing plain black trousers and a cream blouse with blue trim. On this was a name badge in the same blue with 'Margaret' on it. Margaret was either totally oblivious to me or chose to ignore me. Either way, I would have to wait until she was ready.

I scanned the rest of the enclosed zone. Sitting at a computer to the left was an older looking woman with blonde flecked wavy brown hair, dressed as Margaret but with 'Sandra' on her badge, seemingly buried deep in her work. Next to her was a closed door marked 'office'.

I considered coughing to gain attention but thought better of it as my throat was still very sore.

At last, Margaret looked up at me, "Can I help you?" she asked abruptly. I thought my battered and bloodied appearance might have given her a clue—given her some idea that I needed to see a doctor—but considered it better not to come out with some smart remark, like *I hope so, that's why I'm here.*

"I've just arrived in the ambulance. I think I may have broken my arm," I said.

She looked me up and down. "I'll have to take some details," her bored monotone told me.

As it had been at least fifteen years since I had last set foot inside a hospital (as a patient, that is) my details had, not surprisingly, altered. Margaret's sigh at this almost made me feel sorry for having the audacity to get myself injured and interrupting her day.

Ten minutes later, paperwork completed, Margaret waved me towards the seating area to await my fate, and again, I thought it was a good job I hadn't got life-threatening injuries.

I scanned the rows of empty chairs and noted there were only half a dozen of the seats occupied raising my hopes that I wouldn't have long to wait until I was seen to. Just twenty minutes later, "Jake Kolman," was called out, and I was led through for treatment, or so I thought. But it was to another row of chairs in another waiting area.

My hopes were again raised as I was attended to by a young slightly-built nurse, with short blonde hair and a smile which I thought she could show Margaret on reception how to do. 'Lisa-Anne', her badge said. But again my hopes took a dive as she informed me, "I'm going to assess you."

Whatever that meant, it didn't mean treatment. As I had already been assessed in Triage, I supposed this was the next step along the way allowing hospital target times to be met. I thought it best just to go with the flow.

"What happened to you?" she began.

I explained everything to her, about the accident, the attack and my injuries. At intervals, she interrupted me with "Oh" or "Ugh ugh" or "Oh dear" showing professional concern while examining and cleaning my wounds.

After I had completed my tale she said, "We'll probably need that arm x-raying. We'll wait to see what doctor says first though. OK?"

I nodded my agreement but wondered what she would have done if I'd said no, it's not OK; why can't I get an x-ray now? But I knew this would be futile and wouldn't get me dealt with any quicker. So I said nothing.

When she had apparently finished with my wounds, she asked me to wait a moment and disappeared from view. She hadn't gone far because I overheard her talking to what I presumed was another nurse. "Looks like another rage attack," she said.

"This'll be the fourth, won't it?" her mate joined in.

"Yeah, and the first one happened right here in A&E and on *my* shift. There were loads of people hurt."

"Did they offer you counselling?"

But I missed the rest of their conversation as I tried to work out the implications of what they had said. I couldn't remember any of this being in the local paper.

I reckoned I would learn more if I waited and asked the doctor when I eventually got to see him.

Lisa-Anne returned and informed me, "Doctor will see you in a while," before sending me back to the original waiting area. I guessed I must have been assessed as non-priority, or non-critical, or non-important, whichever term they used these days. Although the hospital seemed a lot more user friendly and a lot easier on the eye than when I had last used it, in the important areas A&E hadn't appeared to have improved much at all. You can put a woolly coat on a dog and call it a sheep, but it's still a dog.

Seated back in the waiting area, my thoughts turned to work. I had assumed the police would have informed my employers of my situation but considered it best to give them a call myself, to give them an update, not that there was anything much to update them with at that moment. But at least it would break the monotony for a while.

I tapped in the number, listened to the dialling tone and wasn't at all surprised when it went to the answering machine. Ignoring the recorded request to leave a message I pleaded, "Pick up the phone. Someone pick up the phone! This is urgent, please pick up the phone. It's Jake Kolman here." I knew my pleas would be audible at the other end but couldn't be sure if there would be anyone within earshot to hear them.

My pleas were either ignored or not heard, so I had to leave a message after all. I knew there would be a fair chance this would not be dealt with before tomorrow, but there wasn't a lot I could about that. I had at least covered my back by following the correct procedure. I could do without any more work grief at the moment.

It seemed like I'd been there ages as I glanced down at my watch, but it was only half an hour. Apart from the nurse occasionally calling names through for more assessments, nobody uttered a word; each individual apparently wrapped up in their own little world.

My arm was really starting to ache by this time. To take my mind off it a little, I strolled around the waiting area until my attention settled on a rack containing numerous leaflets.

I read about contraception, HIV, women's well-being clinics, flu jabs, and many more mind-numbing bits of vitally important information. It's amazing what lengths one will go to in such situations.

And still I wasn't called for treatment.

I cast my mind back over the morning's extraordinary events, my memory regressing even further as I came to the part where I thought I was going to drown. A shudder enveloped my whole body as I went back all those years and became that happy seven year old on holiday.

It had been our first family holiday abroad. Salou, on the north east coast of Spain. The day had been hot, really stiflingly hot, and we were by the hotel pool. Mum and Dad had a beer each, resting on the low table next to their sun loungers. "Mum, Mum, can I have a cola? I'm really thirsty!" I begged.

"Yes, of course you can, darling. Go and get one from the nice man at the bar."

"Can I have some money then, please?" I had asked excitedly, not understanding then why they had both started laughing at me. How was a child of seven supposed to understand 'all-inclusive'?

So I had gone and got the drink from the nice man at the bar and was slowly making my way back to Mum and Dad, taking great care not to spill a drop from the plastic cup. I didn't even see them coming; the two teenagers chasing each other with water guns. One had shrieked dodging a blast from the other but barged full force into me, knocking me straight into the pool. For a second, I hadn't realised what had happened. My first thought was *where's my cola gone?* But I soon forgot all about that as my mouth began to fill with water. It had been then that I realised what had happened. I couldn't swim. *I can't swim!* My mind yelled out at me. "Help!" I attempted but just swallowed more water. I had started to thrash about wildly but was just sinking deeper and deeper, the playful poolside sounds muffled by the water and everything was going dark. I had lost consciousness. The next thing I knew, I was back on the poolside with a crowd of faces, including Mum and Dad, staring down at me and the nice man from the bar was pressing down on my chest, bringing me back to life as I coughed and spluttered the offensive chlorine tinged liquid from my lungs.

I forced my mind back to the present as another shudder engulfed me.

Again, I took a stroll, considered going outside for some fresh air and maybe a smoke, but decided against taking the risk as I was sure I would miss my name being called and be put to the bottom of the list.

I looked out of the window. The sun was still shining although there were now a few wispy clouds chugging lazily across the sky. An ambulance pulled slowly away, and an elderly couple headed for the outpatient department next door. I was thinking I would pretty quickly be out of patience if they didn't see to me soon—I still had my sense of humour, but only just.

Chapter 3

A Rolls Royce Phantom, about ten years old by my judgement considering its shape and general condition, pulled up onto the area marked 'ambulances only'. The passenger door opened, and a tall thin elderly gentleman got out. His black pinstriped suit looked expensive, if a little old-fashioned. He scanned the car park as if he was expecting someone, the sun glinting off his slicked back greying hair.

He appeared to have spotted whoever he sought as a smile suddenly lit up his face, and he strode purposefully forward towards the entrance to A&E, where he was joined by a woman, some thirty years his junior and smartly dressed in a business-like navy blue two-piece suit. They briefly embraced in that loving way which suggested they were more likely to be father and daughter than lovers.

Chatting, they strolled slowly into the A&E department, but I couldn't hear about what, as they lingered between the opened outer doors and still closed inner ones. They turned to look back towards the Rolls Royce. I followed their gaze as the passenger window rolled down. The driver's lips were moving, silently to me. The man and woman looked behind the car at an approaching ambulance.

He shouldn't have parked there in the first place, I thought, and now he would have to move. The driver must have noticed my gawping because he stared straight at me as he slowly moved the vehicle forward.

His shark-like black eyes cut right through me like a laser, causing me to catch my breath and sending a shiver down my spine. He was a well-groomed individual with inch long crew cut grey-flecked black hair and with that sort of self-assured aura about him that instantly demanded respect and commanded fear at the same time. If first impressions were anything to go by, I hoped I never had the misfortune to have to cross his path.

I tore my attention away from him and back to the couple, now standing just inside my waiting area and still deep in hushed conversation. I now had a better look at the woman, and she was stunning. She was, I'd say mid-to-late thirties, about an inch shorter than my five-foot-ten and with a slim, toned figure nicely hidden behind that expensive well-fitted suit.

As I ogled her, the older guy took a handkerchief from his trouser pocket. In doing so, he had also inadvertently pulled out what appeared to be a pill box, and this fell to the floor, unnoticed by either of them.

He pecked her on the cheek and turned to leave as I moved towards them. "Excuse me, I think you just dropped something," I called, stooping to pick up the item. They turned back to me, and I handed it over.

"You really must be more careful with your angina tablets. We can do without losing those," the woman chastised him.

"Thank you, Suzanne but don't fuss," he nodded a thank you to me and left to re-join his returning Rolls Royce. Shark-eyes again cut me in two with that stare of his.

"See you later. Bye, Dad," she called after him, then turning to me, "Thank you," she said, politely smiling; a smile to end all smiles.

I almost missed her words as, now close up, I got a good look at her striking features. Her full lips were immaculately made up with soft pink-red lipstick, curved slightly upwards at the corners and framed perfectly white teeth. A tanned complexion, attention-grabbing hazel eyes and well-conditioned expensively tousled black hair in a casual bob style completed the image. "You're welcome," I eventually managed to stutter out.

I just stood there for a second as she went over to reception, and thought perhaps Conlon was right. I should move on, forget my ex-wife and get myself a new girlfriend. My eyes followed the woman to the reception desk. I smiled to myself; the chance would be a fine thing, but she's way, way out of my league.

I took a seat, glanced at my watch for the umpteenth time, sat back, closed my eyes and sighed a resigned sigh, my aches and pains once more rising to the surface. Curiosity prised open my eyelids, and I glanced to my right again becoming aware of the woman's presence as her expensive aroma wafted towards me. The scent reminded me of that Ralph Lauren Romance perfume, but I suspected, like her, it was something from a more exclusive and expensive league. She took a seat near the end of my row. I closed my eyes slipping back into limbo mode while I awaited my turn.

My next excursion took me to the drinks machine. The warm dry atmosphere that comes with artificial heating had begun to dry my mouth. Not only that, but I had tried virtually everything else to pass the time and relieve the boredom.

I looked at the selection on offer. Latte, cappuccino, espresso, Americano, mocha and more, most of which I had no idea what they would taste like. Whatever happened to coffee, white or black, sugar or no sugar? I decided I would have to take pot luck. I put my hand into my pocket but found my luck had run out. I had no change at all, only a note. I pulled it out and looked at it as though willing it to turn into coinage.

The woman came over to the machine and smiled politely at me as I moved aside. She put her cash into the slot and chose a cappuccino.

"You couldn't change a fiver please, could you?" I asked, "For a coffee?"

Again that heart stopping smile, "Sorry I can't. But let me get you one. What would you like?"

Any chance of me trying to appear sophisticated, or to impress her, was dashed as I was clueless about what to select. I took the coward's way out, "Same as you will be fine, thank you."

She repeated the process and handed the drink to me. "Thanks again," now it was my turn to smile politely.

"Suzanne Deering," she introduced herself, holding out her right hand, completely ignoring my dishevelled state. Had I been in ordinary clothing, I suspected she might have been a bit more wary, but my postman's uniform probably put her at ease. If we can pigeonhole people, especially into trustworthy or reliable compartments, we tend to be reassured by this for some reason. I allowed the thought to dissipate and fumbled my cappuccino from one hand to the other before gently accepting her handshake, "Jake Kolman, pleased to meet you."

I put my hand out to offer her a seat which she accepted. "What happened to you then?" She got straight to the point.

I thought, *you don't mess about do you?* "There was an accident; well, I mean, I was attacked." I paused and then attempted to clarify myself, "Sorry I'm not coming across very clear, am I?"

Suzanne said nothing and allowed me to continue.

"Well, there was an accident, a car crash. And as I went to help, the driver of the van attacked me. The nurse," I gestured towards the other waiting area, "said, or rather, I overheard her saying to a colleague, that I was the latest victim of a series of rage attacks." I paused, expecting a reaction of horror or shock. Instead, Suzanne looked more intrigued. It seemed to me that she also knew about these attacks, or at least knew more than I did. I was puzzled; maybe I had missed something in the news after all.

"You don't seem that shocked?" As she hadn't minced her words I felt it would be all right to act likewise. "Do you—" I began but she had started to speak.

"Was, sorry," she apologised for her interruption.

"No, go on," I encouraged.

"I was about to ask how bad the crash was, if anyone else was injured?"

"It was pretty bad, well, very bad actually. A customer of mine, Mrs Clayworth, was killed, and the driver died of his injuries as he was trying to kill me."

Now Suzanne looked a lot more shocked as I paused to allow my revelation to sink in. She invited me to continue so I gave her the full story. By the time I had finished, she was visibly shaken. I somehow felt better for having talked about it but apologised to her for being so insensitive, "I'm sorry, a bit too much info there. You OK?"

"No, that's OK. I'm fine, thanks."

I thought it best to change the subject. Besides, there wasn't a lot more for me to say on the matter. "What are you here for, if it's not too much of a personal question? You don't look a lot like an accident or an emergency." I had immediately felt at ease talking to her, as though we could converse openly. Although she was undoubtedly stunning, she also seemed very down to earth. She gave the impression that she was actually interested in what

I was saying and not just in herself, as most girls who know they are good looking tend to be in my experience. She looked at me while I talked, acknowledged what I was telling her in the appropriate places and asked questions if she wasn't fully sure of anything I was saying.

"No, I'm neither. I'm here for a meeting, with management."

And here was me pouring out my troubles to her and still she had shown an interest, listened to what I had to say and seemed to care about what I was telling her. Yet she must have been preoccupied with her forthcoming meeting.

"The rage attacks you overheard the nurses talking about, well, I'm here about them." Suzanne informed me when I had finished relating my woes.

I was taken aback, "You're not press, are you?" I don't know why it should have bothered me if she was. Perhaps, I've watched too many films as that's the way they always seem to react in those.

"No," she smiled that smile of hers again, only this time her brow was furrowed with concern. "No, I'm here because of the first one, the incident here in A&E the nurses were on about, from three weeks ago? Carlos Mendes was his name. He was an employee of my father's company."

I cut in, "You say *was* an employee. Did he, err, was he…"

"Yes, I'm afraid he died."

It was my turn to look shocked.

"I'm here to try and find out what caused his condition, his rage."

There were a few seconds of shocked silence, and then it was my turn to continue with the questions. "Was anybody else hurt?"

"Yes, apparently he went absolutely berserk." Suzanne then gave me the full story of what had occurred that day. "He only came in because his mate had had an accident. You know, come with him for moral support. Well, they'd had to wait a while, not especially long; no longer than usual. Carlos was getting more and more agitated. He went to complain at reception, got no help from them. I mean, what could they do? His mate had to wait his turn like everyone else. He wasn't a priority, only had a dislocated finger.

"Well, Carlos started ranting, shouting abuse, and not just at the receptionist. Security was called, but before they arrived, another patient tried to reason with him, to calm him down.

"But he wouldn't calm down. He struck the man, knocking him across the front row of chairs." She gestured behind me, and I turned around trying to visualise the scene.

"Another guy tried to grab hold of Carlos but was hit with such force that his neck was broken. Carlos then dragged him up and started tearing at his face, spitting and frothing. He even bit through his own tongue but this didn't interrupt his frenzy."

My mind went back to my own attack and how the driver had seemed in a similar condition, frothing and spitting and raging.

"Two security guards, big guys, then arrived and tried to tackle the situation. It was busy that day, much busier than today. As the guards fought with Carlos, others waiting here were caught up in the mayhem. Three patients, two nurses and both security guards sustained injuries. The man with the broken neck is still in a coma."

"Besides the guy in the coma, how are the others?" I asked.

"I don't know at the moment. These were the only details I was given at my first meeting with management, and they were probably more than they wanted to tell me. And of course, this is only their version. I don't know if they're withholding anything, but I do know they have tried to suppress this thing— you know, keep it out of the papers. This would be bad publicity for the hospital; they don't want people thinking it's not safe to come here. It was lucky for them this happened on a Thursday evening, too late to hit that Friday's local weekly. And there were only a couple of paragraphs on page five or six in last week's edition."

"I must have missed that. You'd have thought something like this would have been front page in a town this size." I interrupted her flow.

"Yes you would, but they obviously wanted to play it down, believing it to be just a one off."

"But it wasn't, was it? Mine is the fourth incident according to those nurses. They won't be able to keep it quiet for much longer."

"No, not a one off. The Monday before last there were two more."

"What, nothing for over a week and then two on the same day? Bit odd that, don't you think? What happened to those two?" My concern was growing, and my questions were coming thick and fast. I had become involved in this through no fault of my own and needed to know where it was going.

"I don't know; they really clammed up after those two. Maybe the police have asked them to say nothing. I don't know, but there must be more to this, and like you said, they can't keep a lid on this much longer, can they?"

"So what happens next?" I asked, unsure of the way forward.

"I don't know. I'll see if I can find anything else out in my meeting."

"And I'll—" But I didn't have chance to finish the sentence, to tell Suzanne I would see if the doctor would tell me anything when I eventually got to see him.

"Miss Deering?" Sandra from reception called to Suzanne and continued when she gained her attention, "The board will see you now. Come this way please."

Suzanne stood, turned to me and said, "I hope everything goes OK for you." She handed me a business card and added, "Call me and let me know how you get on." She purposefully strode across to the reception desk, dumping her half full coffee cup in the bin next to it as she went.

"OK and thanks. For the coffee and everything," I called after her as she disappeared with Sandra through the double doors marked 'wards 6–19'.

Like I thought, she cared. I could tell, but I now knew she also had a mutual interest in my circumstances. I looked down at the white card. 'H.G. Tobacco Company' was printed at the top in bold black letters, followed by Suzanne Deering, a phone number and an e-mail address. Despite their different surnames, I deduced the old guy must be Henry Wilberforce Haines-Garland, the owner of the company on Suzanne's card. I had seen a Roller in the firm's car park on many occasions when I had delivered mail there. And like I had noted, their embrace at the entrance had not been one of lovers. 'Bye, Dad', she had said as he left her. I popped the card into my pocket.

I wondered how much she actually knew about this whole thing. She had been involved since the beginning so obviously knew more than I did. But was she telling me everything? She had been quick to come forward and open up to me about the attacks. Was she just trying to gain my confidence to see what I knew? She seemed genuinely concerned, but was she really; after all I didn't even know her or anything about her. I had so many questions but so few answers.

Chapter 4

And this series of attacks, what about that? At least four incidents resulting in at least two deaths, all with similar characteristics. I remained in my seat in the waiting area and pondered what Suzanne had told me, wondering how much this would involve me. Unanswered questions were growing at an alarming rate. I didn't have long for my cogitations as "Jake Kolman" was called through for treatment.

"Just take a seat. Doctor Kahn will be with you in a moment." The ever helpful and cheerful Lisa-Anne smiled before disappearing behind cream floral curtains into a nearby cubicle.

True to her word it was just a moment. I'd been in hospital for more than three hours, but this bit took just a minute.

"Good afternoon, Mr Kolman," the doctor greeted me, looking down at his notes, probably for confirmation of who I was. "I'm Doctor Kahn; what have we been up to today then?"

I didn't appreciate being spoken to like a child but let it pass. I thought, *I don't know what you've been up to but I've been attacked*, but again saw no point in following this line. I'd spent enough time here already without prolonging it unnecessarily.

I recounted my story yet again, carefully trying to gauge the doctor's reaction, especially when telling him about the driver's behaviour. At this point, I could see by the flicker in his eyes that this was familiar territory to him. I decided to allow the doctor to complete his examination before interrogating him.

Just like Lisa-Anne Doctor Kahn displayed that professional concern with the appropriate "Ugh ugh, I see" and "oh dear" when they were called for.

He pressed and pulled at my injured arm. I was sure he inflicted such pain just to punish me for visiting A&E and to discourage me from doing so again. I supposed they hoped it

31

would keep the cost down if they could deter people, considering the financial state of our National Health Service.

"Yes, this looks like it's broken. Seems like a simple fracture though; shouldn't be a lot of trouble. We'll get you x-rayed and if it's as I expect we'll get it potted for you."

"Well, we don't need any stitches in those cuts. That one on your hand is a little nasty though. A bite you say?" He didn't require an answer but added, "Tetanus jab?"

My hesitation was response enough for him, "I'll get nurse to give you one before you go."

Almost as an afterthought he asked, "And you say you got some of his blood in your cuts? Mmm, we'd better have some blood tests as well. Just as a precaution." He smiled.

I didn't like that knowing smile or the tone of that 'mmm' and wondered, *A precaution against what? Did I have anything to worry about or was I just being paranoid?* It was the not knowing that worried me the most; not knowing exactly where I stood.

"Any questions?" he finished.

Well, you have asked, I thought, *so here goes*. "What can you tell me about this series of rage attacks? Are they linked? Am I in any danger?" There was so much I wanted to ask, so much I needed to know, but I left it at that for the moment. I suppose I knew deep down that he would be unable to allay my fears, and that was why I was so fretful. But I knew, just the same, that I had to ask the questions.

"A series of attacks you say. We've found no evidence to suggest what happened to you is linked to any other, err, incident in any way, at this time. Your cuts are not that serious and shouldn't cause you any more problems. We'll just get your arm sorted and—"

I cut him short. I didn't like the no "evidence to suggest" and "shouldn't". That wasn't very convincing. I decided to lay my cards on the table.

"So you know nothing about Carlos Mendes or the other two 'incidents' as you call them. Three, with mine four, in less than a month? In the same town? A bit coincidental don't you think? And you're not concerned that they may be linked?"

He was at first unable to respond. He had that kid-caught-pinching-sweets look on his face when he realised how much I knew and wouldn't look me directly in the eye. But then, when I mentioned there were four attacks, his expression changed to one partly of relief and partly of having regained control. He now looked me straight in the eye and said with as much assertion as he could muster, "You know I can't discuss other patients' circumstances. You just concentrate on getting yourself better."

But I wasn't really listening to his standard get-out. All I could think about was why that look of relief? Then it dawned on me. "There've been more attacks, haven't there!"

Again he had that look of guilt and again took the easy way out, "Like I said, I can't discuss..."

"I know, I know, you can't discuss other patients. You won't be able to keep this hidden for much longer. You do know that, don't you?"

He was rescued by an elderly gentleman, a hospital volunteer, I presumed, butting in, "Is this the chap for the x-ray?"

"Yes, yes, you can take him now, Edward." A relieved Doctor Kahn allowed.

"What can you tell me about these rage attacks?" I asked my chaperon.

"Oh, I don't know anything. I just help people find where they're going. Pleasant day today, don't you think? Nice to see the sun out for a change."

I returned a little while later, x-rays in hand, expecting to grill Doctor Kahn some more. But Lisa-Anne relieved me of them, told me to take a seat and once again disappeared behind those floral curtains.

Minutes later, a Doctor Johnsen (his badge was black and white; must be a hierarchy thing) approached me, "Mr Kolman?"

I nodded, adding, "Where's Doctor Kahn. I thought he'd be dealing with me?"

"Oh he's busy. It's only a simple fracture," he said holding the x-ray up to the light, "We'll get nurse to pot it for you."

With that, he was gone. Doctor Kahn was obviously avoiding me which only added to the intrigue and to my feeling of foreboding. Having the amiable Lisa-Anne to see to my treatment was of little consolation.

"There, that's done." She smiled at me when she had finished applying the plaster of Paris. She then produced a large needle (and I mean LARGE like out of some Frankenstein film)

33

and proceeded to remove from my arm a vast quantity of my blood, for those tests Doctor Kahn had ordered.

"We'll just get you that tetanus jab now."

She again disappeared, briefly, returning with the promised inoculation which she stabbed, still smiling, into my good arm. Another NHS deterrent, I wondered.

"Are we all done now?" I asked returning her smile. I didn't bear her any ill feelings about all this; she was only doing her job.

"Yes, just make an appointment at reception for the outpatient department in a fortnight's time."

"Thanks," I said and headed back towards reception frustrated and disappointed.

Appointment made and my attention turned to getting home, I took out my mobile phone which informed me I had wasted more than four hours of my life that I would never get back.

"Hello? Can I have a taxi from the hospital please?"

But that more than four hours was about to be stretched to more than five. "We've nothing for another hour. Is that OK?" the voice at the other end told me.

Well, no, it's not OK, I thought, but I suppose it will have to do, so I accepted. "Yes, I suppose that will have to do. It's for Jake Kolman. Thank you."

I went outside to wait and the craving gripped me once more. I really needed another cigarette. Fate and circumstances certainly seemed to be ganging up on me and my attempts to kick the habit.

Edward, my x-ray chaperon, had been right though. It was a pleasant spring day weather-wise. I lit up, took a long drag and blew the smoke up into the clear blue sky and recalled the last time I had done this, realising how much my life had changed in those few short hours.

Adjacent to the car park, I found a low wall to sit on. I had no desire to go back inside and wait. The seating might have been more comfortable in there, but I had had enough of the place for one day. So I just parked myself on the cold, hard brick wall to finish my cigarette and pondered what Doctor hadn't said rather than what he had said. There was certainly more to this than meets the eye, and I knew this would not be the end of it for me.

Cigarette finished, I looked for a place to bin the remains. It would be most inappropriate to go and ask at reception. Beep-bip-beep, my phone rang solving my dilemma, and I dropped the stub on the ground and extinguished it with my shoe. The screen advised me that my ex-wife wanted to talk to me.

My finger automatically hovered over the 'accept' button. But I didn't want to talk to her; that was the last thing I needed after the day I'd just had, so my digit moved across and pressed 'cancel'.

A taxi pulled into the drop-off zone, but it wasn't for me. I'd have at least another forty minutes to wait. I sighed and sat back down on my wall. Next, an ambulance with blue flashing lights aglow pulled up. The paramedics pulled out a trolley with a man on it. He looked in a really bad way with his face covered in blood and his hair turned to a redhead by it. He looked as though he had maybe been in a road accident. I wondered if that was the case or was he another rage victim? If that was the case, then I had gotten off pretty lightly.

"Jake, how'd you get on?" A voice jolted me from my thoughts. I turned my attention away from the poor guy on the trolley and towards Suzanne as she exited the hospital, my eyes lighting up at the sight of her. *How'd you get on?* I wondered if she had gained any more information than I had.

"Well, my arm's broken as I suspected." I raised my potted limb to show her, as if it wasn't prominent enough and continued, "Apparently a simple break, although it aches enough. Otherwise, just cuts and bruises. Oh and the obligatory tetanus jab, of course."

"That's good then. Anything else?"

I wasn't sure if Suzanne was asking about my condition or what I had found out, so answered both possibilities, "They've also sent my blood away for tests—just routine, they said; to be on the safe side.

"As for info, Doctor Kahn was totally unhelpful. He wouldn't even admit or deny other attacks and hid behind the 'can't discuss other patients' excuse. In fact, after I'd been x-rayed he even had another doctor see to me so he wouldn't have to deal with my questions. But I could tell he knew more than he was letting on."

Suzanne didn't look at all surprised, "I didn't get very far either. I think it was more a damage limitation exercise on the hospital's part. They were pretty quick to emphasise how they had followed all the correct procedures and that the hospital couldn't be blamed in any way. All they gave me was Carlos' circumstances, most of which I already knew. However, what I found intriguing was the cause of death. Heart failure they said."

"And when I asked about the others injured by Carlos, they wouldn't discuss them at all this time. They were unsure why Carlos had behaved in the way that he had or why he had a heart attack. They said their investigation was still on-going. In fact, the whole meeting was a waste of time."

She had met the same barricade as I had.

I considered what she had said and added my own thoughts. "I think that's the most worrying aspect of all this. Because if this was just a one-off incident of a guy losing his rag, then there would be no need for all this closing ranks. They must know these can't be just isolated, unlinked occurrences, otherwise why was I there today, having sustained such a similar attack. Any reasonable person would have at least queried the similarities. And don't forget, mine was the fourth attack. In fact, judging by Doctor Kahn's expression, I think there may well have been even more."

Suzanne cut in, "So you think they are hiding something, too. The question is, what and why?"

"I don't know, but I think I need to find out. They won't just be hiding this for the sake of it. I need to know how this affects me; what is going to happen to me. Maybe the police can help."

"Have they interviewed you yet?" Suzanne queried.

"Not yet, but they will. And I want answers. I have a right to know what's happening."

"Try not to worry, Jake," Suzanne soothed, although she didn't sound very convincing.

"Thanks for your concern; for listening to me." I tried to calm down and changed the subject. "I'll let you get off now," I said and glanced at my watch. "My taxi shouldn't be much longer."

"I'll give you a lift if you like," Suzanne offered.

"Sorry, there's no need. I wasn't dropping hints."

"I know you weren't. You just cancel your taxi while I fetch my car."

At that, she turned and headed off into the car park leaving me with no option, not that I minded.

Moments later a shining silver Mercedes E-Class Cabriolet drew up alongside me. *Very, nice,* I thought. *Good looking, sleek and sporty, classy; suits her.*

"Up or down?" she asked as I got in next to her and, noting my puzzlement at the question, added, "The roof; up or down."

"As it is, down's fine. Nice car, a better one than I'm used to." A bit of small talk would help relieve the tension of our previous conversation.

"What've you got?"

I was pleased that she was obviously thinking along the same lines. "Mine's a Punto. About ten years older than this, I'd say." I looked around the pristine interior. "It's not a case of up or down with mine, more a will it or won't it. You know, will it start or won't it."

Suzanne smiled at this remark, "Still, as long as it does for you. Where are we heading for?"

I gave her my address and then continued with our conversation. "Yeah, it's OK. I don't use it much; don't really need it. It's just more convenient having one. I've been meaning to change it for a while, but I've got other priorities at present. Besides, I can't let my ex-wife get the impression that I have money."

"Divorced?"

"No, just separated at the moment. Been about four months since she chucked me out, swapped me for her fitness instructor. But you don't need to know all my problems."

"I'm sorry," She said, and I knew she meant it by the sympathetic smile she held.

"And you?" "

"Still single. Just haven't met Mister Right yet. Still, one day maybe. How long were you and—"

"Sharron," I interjected.

"How long were you together?"

"Twenty-two years, two grown up children and a Labrador. Half my life and all I had thrown away for a fitness instructor."

The last bit—fitness instructor—I said as if it were illegal or immoral, like prostitute or murderer.

"Any chance you'll get back together?"

"I don't think so. I really can't see it." My eyes started to mist over a little; it was still so raw even all these weeks later.

Suzanne could see my discomfort so didn't push it. "What number did you say?" she asked as we pulled into my street.

I was sure she hadn't forgotten but appreciated her breaking from the subject. I reminded her, forty-two, just as my phone rang. It was her, my ex, as though she had been listening to our chat and wouldn't let me put her out of my mind. Although *she* had told *me* to go, she still tried to control my life.

"It's her, Sharron," I said as I again chose not to accept the call. Suzanne said nothing.

Chapter 5

To a stranger, from the roadside, number forty-two would appear to be an impressively large house, but closer inspection would reveal it to be a recently built block of four two up and two downs, the sort builders seem to prefer these days. Maximum number of properties on the space available, as long as they look good on the brochure.

We pulled up at the kerbside.

No doubt, this would be well below what Suzanne was used to living in, but she didn't show any condescension. "Looks nice; cosy." She smiled approvingly. With expensive tastes in cars and attire, well-off she undoubtedly was, but never a snob. Perhaps her looks were clouding my judgement, but I didn't care.

"Thanks again," I said as I got out of her car, "You've saved me a lot of time and trouble." I paused, door still in hand and added, "That's a free coffee and ride home I've had from you. Maybe I can repay you with dinner out sometime?" *Well,* I thought, *you won't find out if you don't ask; in for a penny, in for a pound.*

This time she held that smile of hers for a fraction of a second longer than was necessary, her hazel eyes competing with her generous lips to show the most affection. "Maybe," she teased, "You've got my card, call me."

And with a wave, she was gone as the powerful motor shot away from the kerb, kicking up dust and gravel.

I hoped she couldn't see the demented grin on my face as I just stood there until the car had disappeared from sight, and for some seconds after, my left hand raised in a half-wave.

That sounded positive, I thought; *well, at least not negative.* She hadn't said 'no', and she had asked me to call her. I turned and breezed the dozen or so paces to my front door, head held high and still grinning manically.

Well, I pondered weighing things up, *it's not been such a bad day after all; started bad, got worse and then really brightened up at the end. It, sort of, balanced itself out, good and bad, the yin and the yang, or something like that, as the Chinese call it.*

Still daydreaming, I put the key into the Yale lock, turned it and with my other hand—the one on the broken arm—I turned the handle and pushed. The pain that shot all the way up to my elbow jolted me back to reality.

At last, back home in my sanctuary, I could relax and quietly ponder the events of that extraordinary Thursday. I put the kettle on and made myself a coffee—a proper one.

I took my elixir into the lounge, grabbing a packet of bourbon biscuits from a cupboard en route. I put both items on the pine coffee table before collapsing into, rather than sitting on, the sofa.

A wave of exhaustion overcame me. My arms felt heavy, as did my eyelids. It was all I could manage to pull myself forward and pick up the cup. I took a careful sip of the hot liquid but still managed to burn my lips.

Returning the offending object back to its coaster, I picked up the remote control, switched the TV on and selected the sports news channel—its default mode as far as I was concerned. But I didn't take in anything the blond reporter was telling me. I was too exhausted, mentally and physically. I closed my eyes, just for a second.

That second turned into minutes and then hours until I suddenly jerked awake. When my eyes began to focus on my surroundings, my first thought was that the blond girl had now turned into a dark haired man in a suit. The barely touched coffee and the unopened biscuits lay next to the TV remote on the low pine table in front of me. As I became more lucid, I realised by my shaded surroundings that daylight had succumbed to darkness; it was now night time.

I dragged my body off the sofa with every muscle fighting against the action and walked stiffly across to the window. The only light seeping in was from the distant street lamps. I tugged the curtains together to shut away the outside world, turned and crossed the cramped lounge (Suzanne would no doubt call it cosy) and entered the kitchen. The wall clock told me it was ten thirty; I had dozed for nearly four hours.

Suddenly feeling famished, I took a ready meal for one (my standard diet these days), a roast beef dinner, and popped it into the microwave. Taking a lager from the fridge, I returned to the lounge to await the ten minutes or so until the food would be ready to eat.

Quickly noting there was nothing of startling interest happening in the sports world, I switched channels and put on the news. Still in a half dazed state, I had partially forgotten the day's events. It felt as though it had all happened to someone else, and I was just an innocent bystander. Sleep had compartmentalised the events into the past and now was, well, now. But the amnesia and lethargy were clinically removed when the news reader started telling me about my day's proceedings, with our local hospital as a backdrop. This was just the local news, and they only had about a two-minute slot so they couldn't dwell on the story for very long. In fact, they told me no more than I already knew; there had been several of the attacks but, so far, they had been unable to establish a link. The police were still looking into things, further investigations were necessary, people shouldn't jump to conclusions etc. etc. However, the fact that it was there on TV, right before my very eyes, rammed home the reality of the situation.

I returned to my own cogitations and realised my prophesy had come true quicker than I had expected—I had told Doctor Kahn he couldn't keep this quiet for much longer—but gained no satisfaction from this realisation.

If this had been worthy of TV news coverage, then maybe my original fears were about to come to fruition. Maybe this was going to be as bad as I had at first dreaded.

My brain was working overtime, everything was starting to seem ten times worse than perhaps it should. I forced myself to mentally stand back from it all and take a more reasoned view. There was nothing I could do at this late hour; nobody had wanted to tell me anything earlier so they certainly wouldn't talk to me now. I didn't really know where to start, considered calling the number on Suzanne's business card but thought better of it.

I took a long deep draw from the can of lager, paused for breath and then finished it off, immediately feeling more relaxed.

Ping! Dinner was ready, and I welcomed the distraction.

Feeling much better after washing down the roast meal with another can of lager, I was able to concentrate more.

I had forgotten how little I had eaten that day, not realising the mental as well as physical effects such neglect can have.

The only conclusion I could reach was that there was nothing much constructive I could do that night and therefore the best course of action was to get a good night's sleep and be refreshed and raring to go the next day.

I also decided this would be best achieved with the assistance of another can of lager.

The drink was soon dispensed with, and as I was starting to doze on the sofa again, I thought it best to go to bed. I could do without waking cold and stiff in the middle of the night.

The alarm was set for its usual time of six o'clock. I considered switching it off as I had left a message earlier and surely work must know what had occurred, but decided to set it as normal. With the trouble I had been in that morning (wow was it just those few hours ago!) I thought it best to phone again tomorrow and follow official procedure. Deep down I knew they wouldn't actually do anything if I didn't call, considering the circumstances. I was just being paranoid, overthinking things again.

God! I really needed to get to sleep!

The day's events, fuelled by the alcohol soon worked their magic, and I couldn't even remember my head hitting the pillow.

Brrrring! Brrrring! What seemed like minutes but in fact had been almost seven hours passed in a flash. There had been none of the nightmares I expected (those notions films put in our minds again). In fact, I couldn't remember waking up at all during the night. I felt refreshed and ready to face the day, including anything it had to throw at me. That is until I tried to get out of bed.

Clearly my body didn't share my enthusiasm. Every muscle, every joint every limb and every digit seem to be screaming at me, pleading with me to stay where I was. With a great deal of effort, I managed to resist them and dragged myself off to the bathroom.

I pulled the light cord, turned on the taps and moved my attention to the cabinet which held my toothbrush. Staring back at me from its mirror was a face I could hardly recognise. I wasn't even entirely sure that it was human. The eyes were swollen and grazed, as was the top lip. Both cheeks were bruised, the left one had three scratch marks where fingers had raked across it and the right one had a three-inch diagonal cut. It was only when I looked it straight in the eyes that I knew it was me.

Brushing my teeth proved painful enough, so shaving was definitely a no-go area, at least for the morning. Getting dressed also proved to be a lengthy and cumbersome task, especially when it came to putting on my socks, my aching body complaining at each movement. Choice of shoes was therefore made easy; it had to be my brown slip-ons.

A proper breakfast would have to wait as I had so much to do. A coffee and a cigarette (the e-cigarette thing would also have to wait—just another excuse) supplemented by two paracetamol caplets would have to suffice. I switched on the TV, didn't even bother with the sports channels, but instead went straight to the news. There was nothing new on the attacks and it seemed to be virtually the same loop as the previous evening.

I again considered calling Suzanne but realised it would be too early for her to have any further information. There would be nothing to gain, except possibly a date. No, best left until later; I didn't want to appear too pushy or desperate. I called work again, got the answering machine again and decided against leaving a message as I really needed to discuss the whole episode face to face.

Breakfast completed, such as it was, my next port of call would therefore be work. They needed to be properly filled in on my situation and would also need a complete run-down of events. Not something I was looking forward to, but it had to be done. In large companies such as the one I worked for, proper paperwork was paramount.

Persistent drizzle had replaced the previous day's warm sunshine. The prospect of going out didn't bother me too much as a fifteen-minute stroll to the office was peanuts compared to the usual five to six hours I would have had to contend with if I was actually going out on delivery. However, the cold dreary rain, gusty wind rattling through the trees and depressingly dark clouds detracted from my complacency and from my earlier positivity.

Everything felt somehow different and it wasn't just the weather. It was still the same old houses, shops and parked vehicles I passed every day and pretty much the same people going about their daily routines. But this time, I felt edgy, uneasy and suspicious, carefully watching every person, every movement and every shadow. The events of the previous day had changed my perspective on things and maybe on life in general, at least for the time being. This made me feel very uncomfortable, and I hoped it wouldn't be too long before things returned to something akin to normal.

My head jerked to the right as I took a sharp breath at the sound of squealing tyres. That breath slowly drained from me as I realised it was only a learner driver reaching a junction too quickly. My reaction was equally as erratic as the oncoming white van's headlights flashed her out. For a split second, my eyes were transfixed on the driver of the van as I flashed back twenty-four hours.

I shivered, shook my head and mumbled to myself, "I really need to get a grip." Quickening my pace and fixing my eyes on the pavement a couple of yards in front of me, I continued the arduous trek.

"What the hell happened to you?" a shocked Gerard Duggens stuttered out as I entered my place of work.

"You should see the other guy," I responded without breaking step on the way to the manager's office and immediately thought this was perhaps a little inappropriate considering what had happened to that other guy.

Such ideas were pushed from my mind as I reached my destination. Through the window, I could see Barry Conlon on the telephone as usual, rocking his chair from side to side.

Chapter 6

I tapped firmly on the door but did not march straight in as I had done the previous day; instead, I awaited a reply. Without taking his attention from the phone, the manager beckoned me in with his free hand. I entered, quietly shut the door behind me and took a seat (the same one as twenty-four hours earlier) opposite him. This time, it felt different. The circumstances had changed and so had my attitude. I wasn't enraged as before, instead, a calmness had come over me. Work things had taken on a new perspective and didn't seem quite as important now. I hoped this serenity would last but doubted it.

Barry looked up from the phone as I dragged my chair a little closer to the desk to rest my potted arm for comfort. As his eyes moved from the limb upwards to my face his conversation faltered, "I'll call you back Joan. Something's come up," he stuttered before replacing the handset deliberately in its cradle.

He swiftly regained his composure, "Well, you didn't have to go to those lengths after our conversation yesterday. If you wanted some time off to sort yourself out, you only had to ask." He cautiously attempted a smile.

I was glad he had taken this approach. This was a different type of pressure from our previous meeting, for both of us. I responded with a similar smile, "Why, thank you, Barry. If I had known that, I wouldn't have gone to all this trouble."

His grin came more easily this time, "Seriously though, Jake, how are you? It must have been horrendous."

"I can definitely say I've had better days."

"The police called me and filled me in. Apparently, you're lucky to be alive? If there's anything we can do to help, you know? H.R. are always there for you. Shall I give them a call?"

"Thanks Barry. Thanks for your concern." I wasn't being sarcastic this time as I knew he meant it. He wasn't just following procedure. "That won't be necessary, not at the moment. But I shall bear it in mind for the future."

Barry bent to his right to get some paper from an out-of-sight drawer. He set the wad of A4 sheets down on the desk in front of him. "Right, we'd better get the official stuff out of the way," he said, taking a biro from the top pocket of his grey suit jacket. "I'll put it all on the computer later."

As an afterthought, he added, "Would you like a coffee before we start?"

"Yeah, that would be nice thanks, Barry," I responded as someone knocked at the door. I jumped at the sudden unexpected noise, quickly glancing over my shoulder

"Sorry," it was Emily Pancroft, "I'll be on the docket today, Barry; 'bout half an hour." She hesitated, only momentarily, as her eyes fell upon my disfigured features. She smiled nervously at me as she backed out of the office and closed the door to return to her work.

Barry stood up and gathered up his paperwork, "Come on, Jake, we'll get those coffees and take them upstairs where we won't be interrupted."

It was a bit of a struggle, what with his papers, two coffees and three sets of double doors to negotiate, and only three usable hands between us, but we managed it.

I filled Barry in on the events, ensuring my stated actions complied with official procedures and conveniently omitting irrelevant factors, like stopping for a smoke. Barry wrote furiously taking everything down, never looking up from his pen work, until I had finished.

"I'll read it back to you to make sure we've got it all. Make sure I've got it right," he said and this he did.

"Yep, that's fine," I confirmed when he had completed the task.

"OK thanks then, Jake. I'll get a copy printed up for you and send it out." He picked up the sheets, tapped them gently on the table to straighten them and then stood up.

Following his lead, I hesitated, "Oh and I'll be off for at least a fortnight," I said waving my potted limb in the air as if he needed a reminder of my affliction.

"You don't look that bad to me." He playfully grinned, "Just give it a couple of days then I'm sure we can find you something to do, nothing too strenuous. We won't send you out, nothing like that; we wouldn't want to scare the customers."

Once a manager always a manager. I smiled to myself. "Two weeks, Barry, at least." I said as I left the room. This time, he had been all right with me because he really had no alternative, but I knew all too well that wouldn't last very long and pressure would soon be exerted upon me to return to work, whether I was fit to do so or not. Friendly or not, likeable or not, managers had pressures put on them by their superiors just as they put similar pressures onto us.

"Oh, and don't forget we'll need a sick note from your doctor," Barry called after me as the fire door slowly clicked shut.

I took the stairs back down to the delivery office which I needed to pass through on my way out of the building. Virtually all of the fifty-odd delivery staff, save for a few stragglers, had already departed for their rounds. I was glad as I didn't feel much like making small talk. There were things I needed to find out, things I needed to do, but I wasn't exactly sure where to begin.

As my lack of an adequate breakfast was starting to have an effect, a café would be my next step where I could consider my options and plan my next moves. It's always easier to think on a full stomach, I find, without hunger tearing at your attention.

Toms Place was across the road from the office. A proper greasy spoon café for a proper filling meal—a Full English, with as much grease floating on the mug of tea as would be on the plate was the order of the day.

When the food arrived, I heartily tucked in and at first had a little trouble cutting up the bacon, but I soon got the hang of it, quickly downing every last morsel. The hot tea took a while longer to negotiate.

Plate cleared, mug emptied and plan of action formulated I once again felt ready to face the world. First, I would phone Suzanne to see if she had anything new for me and maybe see about that meal.

Taking her business card from my pocket, I copied the number onto my keypad. The phone rang three times and then went straight to voice mail; a fine start to my carefully made plans. I hadn't expected that and so didn't leave a message as I wasn't quite sure what I would say. Before I could decide what to do next, she rang me back.

"Hello, H.G. Tobacco Company, Suzanne Deering speaking. Sorry I just missed your call. How can I help you?"

The sound of her voice lifted my spirits immediately. "Hi, Suzanne, it's me, Jake. I-I was just wondering..." So much for planning. I still wasn't exactly sure what to say or how I expected her to help me. I just felt I had to do something, to start somewhere and Suzanne seemed a better place than most.

"Oh hiya, Jake. How are you feeling this morning?" Suzanne sounded similarly cheered.

"As well as can be expected, I think is the proper medical term. No, seriously, I ache a little but everything appears to be in working order. A bit of a headache but glad to be alive now I've had time to think, to reflect."

"Yes Jake, by the sounds of it things could have been a lot worse. I'm glad you're OK though."

"Thanks Suzanne," saying her name made me tingle a little, "And yourself? How are you?"

"I'm great, thanks for asking; very busy though."

"Oh, I'm really sorry; I didn't think," I apologised for interrupting her at work.

"It's OK. I didn't mean it like that. There's no need to apologise. Any particular reason you've called me?"

"Sorry, yes; I'll keep it short. Nobody's telling me anything; not the hospital and the police haven't even been in touch yet. There's nothing new on the news. I just wondered if you had heard anything more. Sorry, I don't know why you should have, but I'm feeling a bit helpless right now, and you were my last hope. I'm starting to get a little worried."

Suzanne attempted to lighten the situation, "I'm your *last* hope? I feel slightly hurt by that, Jake," she teased. "I rather hoped I'd be a bit further up your priority list than that."

"I'm-I'm sorry, I didn't mean that; of course you are," I blustered.

"I'm messing with you, Jake. And don't keep apologising. I'm glad to hear from you, and you're pretty high on my list at the moment."

"Sorry, er, sorry," I then regained my poise, "All these attacks are scaring me. They must be linked. It's too much of a coincidence. And I'm right in the middle of it all."

Again Suzanne tried to calm my anxiety, "Well, I am actually working on it at the moment. Because of Carlos, you know. I agree there's more to this than we've been told, and I rather think there's more to come yet."

This latest revelation sent a shiver down my spine. "What do you mean?"

"Like you said, there must be a link. There have already been too many of them for there not to be. The only thing that is clear is that all this started with Carlos and there's nothing to suggest it is about to stop. I really need to find out more and not just for the company's sake. This is people's lives we're dealing with, and if this firm can help in any way then we will."

My worry eased a little knowing that someone at least was trying to do something.

"It's a bit early yet, Jake, but I've got one or two ideas. In the past, I've found the press can be quite helpful in finding things out, if you know who to ask."

And I bet she, with her stunning looks and vibrant personality, would find it easier than most to prise such information from them, I thought.

Suzanne continued, "I could perhaps trade a little info with them. You know, maybe give them some background on Carlos, or something."

This seemed a good idea to me, and I was eager to help. At the moment, it appeared to me that I was leaving all the work to Suzanne.

"Yes and if it helps you can mention me. Tell them about what happened. If need be you can send them round, anything. Tell them anything you want about me; I don't care whose feathers it ruffles. If it stirs others into action, then all the better. Besides, what have we got to lose?"

"Thanks, Jake. I really appreciate that. I'll get straight onto it. Thanks again for your support in this."

"No, it is I who should thank you, Suzanne."

"OK, leave it with me. I'll give you a call tonight and let you know how I get on. Speak to you later."

"Bye," I said as she put the phone down, gladdened to some extent to see that things seemed to be moving forward. But I was also saddened a little because I had got carried away with it all and forgot to ask her about that meal. Still I would have other opportunities.

I left Toms Place in a far better mood and more positive frame of mind than I had entered. I could now see a way forward. But there was still that nagging at the back of my mind. It was as though Suzanne wasn't telling me everything, like she was holding something back, as though she was privy to something; just what I couldn't figure out. Maybe it was just me being paranoid again.

I would call in the newsagents on the way home and pick up the local weekly which would be out today and see if there were any further revelations.

As I retraced my earlier path to my home, I didn't feel quite so jittery, not as apprehensive as I had when I left the house that morning. Then, I was feeling a bit down, dispirited.

Now the rain had eased a bit as had the wind and the sun was battling with the clouds for supremacy, sparkling like jewels off the tarmac and roof tiles.

The sun was at its zenith as I entered number forty-two. The place was silent as expected; empty. What I hated most about my separation was coming home to this void, and I especially missed the eager paws padding excitedly across the wood flooring expectantly waiting to ambush me and smother me with slaver. I think maybe I missed Dave the Labrador more than anything else in the world. I suppose this says a lot about the state our marriage had gotten into. Perhaps Sharron had a point. The cow.

I automatically put the kettle on, then the television, then opened the fridge; one routine marriage breakdown had failed to ruin.

A quick run through the sports news again revealed nothing startling, so I switched over to the news channel, made my coffee and took it over to the sofa along with the papers and the obligatory packet of bourbons.

There was still nothing new on the TV news. I couldn't quite work out if this was a good thing or a bad one. On the one hand, no news is good news. On the other, what were they hiding? What, if anything, were they not telling us?

Sitting at home in my own little self-contained life, the paranoia was again beginning to get the upper hand. Such loneliness on its own, without all my other problems, could send me round the bend. Maybe I should get another dog, or another wife. If I couldn't decide which then neither was probably the best option for now. At least I still had my sense of humour. That's one thing the lovely Sharron hadn't robbed me of. The cow.

Turning my attention to the local paper, I took the unusual step, a conscious decision, of starting at the front and not the sports section at the back.

The attacks were unsurprisingly front page headlines now. "Fear grips rage epidemic town." It yelled, not giving a damn if that fear or worse was fuelled by the newspaper, as long as they sold their quota. "Turn to page four," it advised.

As I was in the process of taking this advice there was a sturdy rat-a-tat at the door. I could see two dark figures through the frosted glass panels above the letter box.

Not God-botherers again, I prayed as I went to open it.

"Good afternoon. Mr Kolman, is it?" the older male uniformed police officer asked and continued without waiting for a reply. "May we come inside, sir?"

"I've been expecting you, please do come in." I ushered them into the lounge, cleared the newspapers off the sofa and offered them a seat which they accepted.

The pale skinned older officer took off his helmet revealing a shock of orange hair and did the introductions. "I'm Police Constable Neil Hardingtone and this," he gestured towards the brown haired, blue eyed twenty-fiveish darker skinned woman sitting to his left, "Is Constable Myra Weismann. We're here to discuss your incident yesterday."

"Before we start, would you like a tea, coffee, or something?" I asked politely, figuring the friendly approach would give me more chance of obtaining the information I required.

"That would be nice, thank you. I'll have a coffee if it's not too much trouble. Myra?" Hardingtone answered. Myra nodded her agreement.

As I went to the kitchen, I could see the attacks were still on the news, only this time 'just in' flashed across the bottom of the screen. I hesitated and Hardingtone followed my eye line.

"Do you mind if we turn the TV off, sir?" he requested, "It's a little distracting."

So, I thought, *They're still trying to hide things.* I wondered what the update would be but felt obliged to do as the officer had asked.

Chapter 7

The kettle was still hot from the beverage I had recently made for myself, so it wasn't long before I re-joined them carrying a tray with a couple of steaming mugs, one stating 'keep calm and carry on', the other 's**t happens'. Both, I considered quite appropriate for my current predicament. A small half empty carton of semi-skimmed milk, a sugar bowl and teaspoon were the only other objects on the tray. I didn't think they had as yet earned the right to share my bourbons.

The TV now stood silent in the corner. "Tell us in your own words what happened yesterday, Mr Kolman," Hardingtone requested. His colleague still hadn't uttered a word. I was beginning to wonder if she could actually speak English, noting that she did have a slight Eastern European look about her.

As if on cue she said, in a broad Yorkshire accent, "Shall I take the notes, sir?"

"Yes, of course," he replied shaking his head and smiling the sought of smile that said *you can't get the staff these days.*

Again I ran through the previous day's events, pausing or slowing down when I could see Myra struggling to keep up.

When my recital was complete, I felt it was my turn to ask some questions. "So what about all these other attacks; are they linked?" I thought it best to get straight to the point.

"I'm sorry, sir. We can't discuss that," was Hardingtone's equally succinct reply.

Again no one was willing to tell me anything. I was frustrated and beginning to get a little irate. "I've been as helpful as possible. At least tell me if I have anything to worry about." I looked pleadingly from one to the other but just got blank stares back.

"How does this affect me? Am I in any danger?"

"Like I said, sir, we are unable to discuss an on-going investigation," was Hardingtone's deadpan response.

"Damn it man!" I thumped the coffee table causing the mugs to rattle on the tray. "People are getting killed out there, and all you can tell me is…well, zilch!"

"We understand your concern, sir. We are taking all the appropriate action necessary."

I opened my mouth for another rant but stopped myself, "What's the point!" is all I blurted out as I realised that I was only going to get stock robotic answers.

"I think we're done," I said through clenched teeth, moving towards the front door to show them out. At least I hadn't wasted any of my biscuits on them.

"Thank you for your assistance, sir. If you think of anything else that might be helpful just give us a call on this number," Hardingtone concluded on his way out, and handed me a business card. Silent Myra traipsed along behind him.

The glass panels rattled as I slammed the door behind them. I screwed up the card and threw it across the room, then punched the wall in frustration and anger. Taking a couple of deep breaths, I went straight for my jacket, took the cigarette packet from its pocket and lit up.

A couple of long drags calmed me sufficiently. I thought these may well eventually kill me but right now I could do without getting my other hand put into a plaster cast.

Emotionally, I felt like a ship at sea entering a storm, up one minute and down the next, my mood swinging hour to hour from one extreme to the other, the gale force wind of fate forever battering against me. The day had started on such a positive note, but yet again circumstances had sought to drag me down.

I finished the cigarette and lit another up straight after. I hadn't chain smoked like this since the birth of Joseph, our youngest, some eighteen years previously. *At this rate, I might as well give up giving up*, I thought.

I dropped back down on the sofa to consider my next move and remembered the 'just in' on the news. As I switched the TV back on, I found I had missed the latest update and would therefore have to wait perhaps another twenty minutes for the loop to come around again. More frustration!

Yet again, I picked up the cigarette packet but hesitated, threw it down on the coffee table and settled for strutting around the room; something else I hadn't done since that visit to maternity.

There was nothing much I could do until I had spoken to Suzanne again and that was hours away. The news update provided nothing new just a different, more senior policeman telling us there was nothing he could tell us at this time. I needed to calm down so forced myself to put on the sports news channel, knowing full well this would help numb my brain.

This distraction did the trick as I learned Van Gaal's sack was imminent for the umpteenth week running, Mourinho was still being vocal, and England's finest was feeling particularly unloved and would need an injection of a couple of hundred thousand pounds a week to reassert his loyalty.

It was somehow comforting to see such normality.

I must have dozed off as the telephone startled me back to the land of the living. I hadn't a clue what time it was but outside it was still daylight. I hoped it was Suzanne.

"You've had an accident in the last three years," the automated voice tried to convince me.

It would serve them right if I told them about yesterday. I considered it but decided not to waste my time and ended the call.

Now, fully awake, I actually heard my tummy rumble and realised that since my fry-up breakfast, I hadn't eaten anything substantial. Lunch had consisted of tea, biscuits and cigarettes and now I needed to eat something proper.

I took a roast chicken dinner from the freezer, popped it into the microwave and readied the necessities to go with it; plate, cutlery and can of lager. Pausing before closing the fridge door, I took a second can out as I would probably down the first while the food was cooking.

The phone rang again, and this time it was Suzanne. "Hi Jake, how are you doing?"

"I'm fine thanks, Suzanne, and you?"

"Yeah, me too."

Once the niceties were completed, I got straight to the point, "Did you find anything out? Did your press link tell you anything?"

I must have sounded nervous in my eagerness as Suzanne tried to placate me with her calmer tones, "Yes, Jake, they were really helpful. I feel we've got something to work with.

"Like I said, I had to give them info about Carlos. You know, the stuff they wouldn't be able to find easily elsewhere. And I got times and dates, names and addresses of victims back, but we can't tell anyone where we got this from."

"Great, that should be really helpful. Maybe now we can begin to find the links in all this and find out what the police are so eager to cover up," my mood had taken a swing for the better.

"I'm not sure they are actually hiding anything. I suspect they don't know a lot more than we do at present. But try not worry too much, Jake. We now have something to work with and can move this forward. We're sure to get answers."

"Thanks, I hope so. The police came and interviewed me this afternoon. They took my statement but wouldn't tell me anything. I'm afraid I lost my rag a bit with them."

"I understand your frustration, Jake. I tried speaking to them again, too, but got nothing. Same with the hospital. I'm afraid we're going to have to deal with this by ourselves. But, like I said, try not to worry too much. We've got plenty to work with and we *will* get this sorted." Yet again Suzanne's positivity was managing to hold me together.

"I can't thank you enough for what you are doing for me," I sighed feeling easier talking to her. "I don't know what I would do without you. I wouldn't even have known where to begin. I feel like I'm imposing on you, but you're the only hope I've got."

"You're not imposing at all. I'm glad I can help, and don't forget I need to do this because of Carlos. It's not just for you."

I had been getting ahead of myself. Maybe this wouldn't be the right time to ask her for the meal. "So what more have you got from your friends at the press?" I asked instead.

"As I told you, names addresses etc. I don't really want to do this over the phone, so why don't we go for that meal tomorrow? I can fill you in properly then; that's if you're free of course?"

Was I free? She had actually asked me out. Of course I was free and would have been even if she had nothing to tell me. Besides, I was always free these days.

"Yeah, I'm not doing anything special tomorrow—"

Suzanne cut me short, "Great. I'll pick you up at seven then. OK?"

Yet again her forthrightness had taken me aback, but I quickly pulled myself together, "Yeah, yes seven is fine. But I'm paying this time, no arguments, all right?"

"There's no need. I can put it on expenses—"

It was my turn to cut her short, "I said no arguments."

"We'll see." She had to have the last word, "Seven."

Suzanne was a very welcome distraction from my worries, and she always seemed to put me at ease.

Now she was gone, though, my fears and frustrations leapt back at me. I could once again feel the anger rising within. Suzanne was the only friend I had in all this, but still my suspicions kept nagging at me. I knew she was linked to the episode through work but she did seem to be putting in an awful lot of time and effort on the whole thing, especially considering she would also have her normal work to be getting on with. It just didn't quite seem to add up properly. But it was all I'd got.

I hoped more beer and cigarettes would help to dispel this increasing unease I was feeling, didn't really think they would, but had them anyway; at least half a dozen of each.

The following morning, the alarm clock woke me nice and early with a start. Realising I must have set it out of habit in my drunken state the previous night, I cursed under my breath.

There was no point in trying to go back to sleep because I knew this would be impossible as I had so much to do and so much running through my mind. Every waking moment this thing, these events, were weighing heavier and heavier on me. I somehow knew I only had a limited amount of time to sort this out. Something at the back of my mind convinced me of this, but I couldn't quite place what it was.

Besides, my mouth felt like a dozen monkeys had slept in it, and my head was pounding so much I had to check out the window that there were no roadworks going on in the street.

I half fell out of bed, stumbled down the stairs and groped blindly into the kitchen. A long glug of water made me gag and I was convinced my stomach was going to empty itself. But I successfully fought the urge.

I couldn't even face the thought of a cigarette yet, so I put the kettle on and then went to the fridge. At times like these, there was only one thing to do. It had to be bacon butties; kill or cure time.

My senses slowly returned, and my mood brightened considerably as I remembered my date for the evening. My happy thoughts and bacon butties did the trick to a large extent, but I knew from experience that fresh air would complete the treatment. Again a pang of regret hit me as I once more missed Dave and our weekend walks. I would go to the corner shop and get some supplies. This would have to do instead.

Chapter 8

As I went out the front door, the wailing of emergency sirens shattered the early morning peace. Two blue flashing lights shot past; one an ambulance, the other a police car. I stopped in my tracks to see where they might be going, but they quickly disappeared out of sight at the junction ahead.

Five minutes, later I saw them again as I approached Singh's Supplies. They were both parked outside the shop blue lights still flashing. The unmistakeable large and rotund figure of Mr Singh, the proprietor, lay at the front door, half inside and half out, in a pool of blood which had begun to lazily flow from beneath his body down the wheelchair ramp and onto the pavement. There was another person, looked like an elderly lady, also on the ground a few feet in front of him. The nearer I got to the shop, the more grotesque the scene appeared as they came more sharply into focus. Mr Singh was on his side his skull split completely open above his right eye, his blood covered large areas of his white grocer's smock. The woman was laid face down, no obvious injuries were revealed, but a large pool of blood was growing forever larger next to her, about to mingle with that of the shopkeeper.

I stood there, just yards from them. Tearing my attention away, I scanned the vicinity but couldn't see any police officers. In the background, I could hear the screech of more sirens rapidly approaching. This was all abruptly drowned out by a terrible, almost beast-like scream from inside the shop.

I walked slowly forward trying to make out what was happening inside, but my vision was impaired by the reflection of the flashing blue lights on the shop window.

Suddenly a policewoman staggered out, her face and head covered in blood, her uniform ripped and drenched. Her left hand held the doorframe, the right clutched a butchers' knife that was protruding from her left breast. She fell forward, her face striking the pavement with a sickening thud like a cricket bat striking the ball for six, and the knife blade, forced deeper by her weight, stuck out through her back.

Another crash from within the shop drew my attention back in that direction. A snarling, hideous, giant of a man came charging out with a meat cleaver in one hand and a severed arm in the other. I knew there was at least one more casualty inside as the limb didn't belong to anyone outside the shop.

For a split second, I thought the giant was going to go for me next but this was rendered impossible as an incoming police car struck him as he dashed out into the road and flung him into the air like a bag of rags. He came back to earth just in time for a third police car to trap his head under its front wheel where he twitched for a few seconds then moved no more.

A second ambulance pulled up and turned off its siren. Where seconds earlier there had been a cacophony of mayhem, now there was just a surreal silent scene bathed in blue light, the stillness appearing to suspend time.

I turned slowly back towards the shop wondering how many more bodies were inside.

These rages were clearly getting out of hand, expediting my need to deal with this whole situation and increasing my anxiety at least ten fold.

"Please stand back, sir," the shaky voice of an officer urged. It didn't sink in past my numbness, nevertheless, I automatically did as requested.

"Oh god, not another one," I heard a colleague of the officer exclaim, echoing my own thoughts, as I ambled away in zombie-like numbness.

I only walked about fifty yards down the road, not sure where I was going, just wanting to get away from that terrible scene. I halted, rubbed my brow with my good hand, and tried to pull my senses back together. I needed to go home, needed the sanctuary of familiar surroundings.

The shopping would have to wait. I turned around and headed back in the direction from which I had just come, crossing the street to get as far from that macabre sight as possible. I tried not to look but couldn't help myself, my attention magnetically drawn as if I couldn't quite believe, or didn't want to believe, what I had witnessed only moments earlier.

My pace slowed, but I forced my feet to keep moving, deliberately placing one in front of the other, *left, right, left, right, one, two, three, four,* all the time my eyes transfixed on the police officers, paramedics and bodies, especially the blood; there was so much blood. I didn't react but just stared and walked; *left, right, left, right, one, two, three, four.*

A couple of the officers were sobbing and nobody seemed to be taking the lead. They must have been just as stunned as I was. One male constable had his arm round a female colleague. A crowd started to gather, at first silent but gradually raising the volume as shock gave way to realisation and in a couple of cases hysteria.

Left, right, left, right, one, two, three, four. After I had passed the spectacle and my head wouldn't turn around any further, I tore my face away and kept my feet moving. And as it all disappeared into the distance, the sound diminished along with it, but I knew it would never totally vanish from my mind.

Before I knew, it I was back at my front door. I just stood there looking at it, not really seeing it, then automatically took the key from my pocket opened the door and entered. I went straight to the kitchen and put the kettle on, not moving or even reacting until minutes later as it whistled to signal it had reached boiling point.

But I didn't make a drink. I just turned around, went into the lounge and sat on the sofa. It was then that I was overcome by an uncontrollable sobbing which grew louder and louder, turning into an all-out howl. I buried my face in my hands until it subsided back into a sob. Finally taking my hands away, I remained stuck in oblivion staring at the floor.

I was awakened from the stupor by the ringing of the house phone piercing into my brain in my silent, stagnant house. There was no caller display on this so I answered it, for once hoping it was PPI or double glazing.

"We need to talk, Jake. It's urgent. I need to see you, today." It was Sharron.

My non-response allowed her to carry on.

"Can you come round tonight, about seven? Is that OK with you? It's really important."

I slowly dragged myself back to the land of the living, "Ugh, what, seven?"

"Yes, is that convenient?"

"Er, yes…well, no, I've got plans. What's it about? Are the kids all right? Can't it wait 'til tomorrow? Yes, tomorrow would be a lot better for me." I was bumbling almost incoherently.

"No, like I said it's urgent. Change your plans. I don't want to discuss it over the phone. I'll see you at seven."

Sharron would allow no further argument putting the phone down before I had a chance to respond further. I supposed I could have called her straight back but I knew this would be useless, and besides, I had very little fight in me at that moment.

Exhausted by the trauma, I remained where I was for quite a while longer, just sat there staring into space. Deliberately and with great difficulty, I shook myself back into action. I couldn't just cabbage there and give up. I had to put myself back together, stick the pieces into place. There would be ample time for falling apart later when this was all over. At least that is what I hoped. I daren't even contemplate the alternatives. Stick them to the back of my mind with the rest of the things I was unable to deal with for one reason or another.

My watch told me it was nearly four o'clock. I needed to call Suzanne and cancel our date—if that's what it could be called. Getting together to discuss dead people isn't really anybody's idea of any sort of date unless you're a mortician or the like.

Her mobile went straight to voice mail allowing me to take the coward's way out. This time I had no hesitation in leaving a message. "Hi, Suzanne, it's me, Jake. I'm really, really sorry but I'm going to have to cancel tonight. Something very urgent has come up with Sharron. She won't tell me what but she *must* see me tonight. I'm so sorry, I'll give you a call tomorrow."

Once again, that cow was controlling my life, I thought; it had better be as urgent as she says. I had probably blown it with Suzanne and also set myself back regarding the rage attacks. I really needed to get to grips with Sharron and stop her from still trying to control my life. She was the one who had chosen to be rid of me; the cow.

But I hoped everything was all right, especially the kids. Perhaps I should call them and check they were OK. No, I didn't want to worry them or make them think something was wrong.

There was no need for the problems between me and their mother to affect them any more than necessary. Besides, if something was wrong with one of our children, I was sure she would have told me there and then. Not even she would be that heartless. More problems, more questions, but no answers.

I turned the TV on and switched to 'Soccer Saturday' for score updates but also in an attempt to restore some sort of normality. I was now feeling quite hungry having again missed a meal. Again the change of environment had allowed me to compartmentalise the events in my life and leave the bad things outside when I had shut the front door.

The fridge reminded me I hadn't done the shopping but I decided to improvise with whatever I had in. I could call at the supermarket after I'd dealt with Sharron.

A dry and curling slice of corned beef between two slices of semi-stale white bread enhanced by a dollop of brown sauce and a cup of tea was followed by what was becoming the norm for dessert; a cigarette. I refrained from alcohol as I would be driving to my ex's. And I particularly wanted a clear head for that confrontation. I didn't need to give her any more reasons for having a go at me.

She was the one who had thrown me out. She was the one who had had the affair. So how had she managed to make me feel like the guilty party, as though it was somehow all my fault.

I lit another cigarette. I'd never give up at this rate, but right at that moment I didn't give a damn. At least I was getting angry for a good reason and Sharron was taking my attention away from my other problems. I suppose she'd say I ought to be grateful. The…

My Punto pulled up outside my old house at ten past seven, purposefully late to show her I controlled my life now; I was in charge. I avoided parking on the driveway as I didn't think it was my place to do this anymore. The gravel crunched under foot as I crossed the twenty-one paces to the front door, noting that most of the lights in the house were on and smiling to myself at that. At least the electricity bill wasn't my concern now. I rang the bell.

Sharron opened the door almost immediately, "You're late," she chastised, not even commenting on my battered appearance. "You'd better come in now that you're here." She left the white plastic door ajar, turned her back on me and went through the hall into the lounge.

"Sorry, traffic was bad," I lied; my brave, new self had soon capitulated.

I briefly scanned the room noting how little had changed since this was my home too. Apart from the photos. They were gone. The same brown leather three-piece suite stood unmoved opposite the same forty inch smart TV, the space between separated by the same glass topped oak coffee table.

I was pleased to see we were alone and that 'thing', the fitness instructor, was nowhere to be seen.

"Please take a seat. Would you like a coffee, or maybe a beer," Sharron's tone had softened considerably. This put me on my guard straight away; she must want something, I thought.

"No thanks, let's get to the point," I took the opportunity, as she appeared to have dropped her guard, to reassert control of my own destiny. "What's so important that I've had to cancel my date for tonight?" I couldn't resist the opportunity to make her feel jealous.

She smiled at this, knowing she still had control of me. "A date? Oh I am sorry," her apology was blatantly sarcastic.

"OK, we'll get straight down to business. I don't want to waste any more of your precious time than I have to. If you're reasonable you might still have time to see your floozy."

I ignored her insult towards Suzanne, as I didn't want to get drawn into a slanging match. And as for being reasonable, I wasn't the unreasonable one here. But I ignored that little dig as well. "Well?" is all I said.

"OK, if that's how you want to approach this. Money. Don't you think it's about time you started paying me maintenance?"

I just stood there open-mouthed. I couldn't believe she had the audacity to actually ask me for money, for me to finance her boyfriend. And I had cancelled Suzanne for this?

"I thought you said this was urgent!" I shouted. "Do you know what I've been through these past three days?" I didn't give her a chance to answer. "No, you don't, you haven't a clue. I come here all battered and bruised and you don't say a word; don't even notice. All you think about is yourself! All you've ever thought about is yourself!"

I was really starting to lose it now, not just because of her cheek but also because the week's events had cartwheeled my emotions. "Money? You want me to give you money? Well you won't get a penny. I won't give you one penny to keep that prick!"

I thumped the table so hard it was a wonder it didn't shatter and then jumped to my feet.

Sharron took a step away from me, the shock and horror etched on her face being quickly replaced by fear.

"I think we're done here," I spat as I roughly pushed her out of the way and headed for the exit.

Sharron quickly regained her composure, "I'm entitled. I want what I'm due."

Stopping in my tracks I spun round, "You want what you're due?" I took a menacing pace towards her and she took a scared one away. "If you got what you were due we'd all be fucking happy."

My breathing was quickening, my good hand clenched into a fist and unclenched. Four months of frustration and anger were welling up inside me. I could quite easily have throttled the life from her there and then. Somehow I managed to control the rage growing within me. I took a step back, regulated my breathing and said as calmly as I could muster, "Tell you what, you want money; you want what is due to you, then you get off down to the estate agent first thing Monday morning and put the house on the market. Our house. Then we can all get our dues."

Sharron was too stunned to respond and just stood there, eyes and mouth wide open.

"If anyone wants paying anything then it's me. You owe me. So leave me alone and pay for your own and that scumbag's upkeep yourself."

I turned away without waiting for a response, saying, "I think we're done now," and headed out the front door slamming it behind me.

I stormed off down the driveway, accidentally kicking gravel aside as I did so. I unlocked the car and climbed in, slammed the door and thumped the steering wheel, angry at Sharron's nerve but also at myself for losing control like that.

Chapter 9

Before firing up the engine, I took the small rumpled carton from my pocket, extracted the solitary remaining cigarette, lit it and screwed up the empty packet turning my good hand into a fist. I held the pose for some seconds crushing the life out of the cardboard packaging as though it was someone's neck, channelling the anger within me, allowing it to slowly ebb away. I was about to toss it over my shoulder onto the rear seat but hesitated. Instead, I wound the window down and threw the crumpled object onto the driveway. Petty, I knew but it made me feel better.

I needed that detour to the shop for definite now and thought I might as well replenish my alcohol stock while I was there. This week was certainly having its effects on my vices and my attempts to curb them.

My anger started to rise again as I recalled cancelling Suzanne for that rubbish. The car spun full circle in the road kicking up dust and debris as I rammed my foot down hard on the accelerator, yanked the steering wheel round and shot off in the direction of the twenty-four-hour supermarket.

What a waste of a Saturday night. By the time I finally arrived home, it was too late to actually do anything with what was left of it. I looked at the unopened packet of cigarettes I had just bought and just threw them down on the coffee table. I had puffed on so many over the past few days, I actually felt sick at the thought of another one. Oh, if only that feeling could last then quitting would be so easy. But I knew by the morning, the familiar craving would be needling at my brain.

It was too late to try and reignite my tryst with Suzanne. I channel-surfed the TV for a while. There was nothing new worth mentioning on the news except for a half minute report on the morning's attack at Singh's shop. The details given in that were very sketchy with no names given just the usual "the investigation was ongoing". It was a sad state of affairs if the press was now our most useful source of information. It seemed to me that all the official bodies were that scared of either being blamed, sued, or both.

The main match on TV was Manchester United in yet another boring goalless game. I thought I might as well have an early night. A day that had begun with such promise had yet again not just gone rapidly downhill but had fallen off a cliff.

I took a cuppa, tea this time, and a book (Neil Warnock, The Gaffer—that should help me drop off pretty quickly) up to my bedroom, stripped down to my boxers and settled down under the duvet. But I couldn't relax or concentrate on the book as all the day's events were whirling around inside my head. Poor Mr Singh and the others at the shop and those pitiable, distraught police officers and paramedics. And then there was that bitch of an ex-wife of mine…

After reading the same paragraph five times and still not knowing what it said, I tossed the book onto the floor, finished what was left of the now lukewarm tea and snuggled down pulling the duvet up to my chin as my head sank into the soft downy pillow.

But the sleep state was difficult to attain, and when I eventually arrived there, it was broken and fitful. I tossed and turned and each time I did so, my arm ached, and I woke up, and I tossed some more repeating the cycle until I didn't know if I was awake or asleep.

Suddenly, my eyes shot open, and I saw the light was still on. I sat bolt upright. There was no one in the room but I could hear noises—shuffling and muted tapping—downstairs. Quietly, I climbed out of bed, tip-toed across the bedroom and onto the landing. The noises were more distinct and light was emanating from the kitchen.

I crept down the stairs, and, although much of the kitchen itself was out of sight, I could see shadowy movements casting onto the lounge carpet. I advanced slowly, looking for something to use as a weapon, but cushions were all I could find and deemed these to probably be inadequate.

Then a huge bald man, as tall and as wide as the door frame, came rushing silently at me. The obscured kitchen light behind him rendered it impossible for me to make out his facial features, although he somehow seemed familiar. All of a sudden, he was almost upon me, a meat cleaver raised high, and at the last moment, I realised it was the man I had seen earlier rushing from Singh's shop.

It was too late to take evasive action, and the weapon caught me a glancing blow on the side of my head. I went down. Everything fogged around me. As I regained consciousness, the intruder was nowhere to be seen. I could feel my head throbbing where I had been hit. I automatically raised my hand to the wound. It was very tender and my hand came away dripping with blood.

My senses slowly returned, and I could see in the dim moonlight shining through the thin curtains that I was still on the floor. It was only when I staggered to my feet and switched the light on that I realised I must have fallen out of bed and banged my head on the side cabinet. My broken arm ached, and I guessed I must have banged it on my way down. The wetness from the wound that I had presumed to be blood, in fact, proved to be only sweat, which I also realised my body was drenched in.

I breathed a sigh of relief on realising it had only been a dream.

Nevertheless, I crept cautiously down stairs, all my senses on stand-by just in case the bald man had lingered down there from my dream. I flicked on the kitchen light and braced myself. It was, of course, empty. I retrieved a couple of aspirin from a drawer and washed them down with a glass of water. My sanity had returned to something akin to normal, as had my heart rate, and I retraced my path to the bedroom to attempt to get back to sleep.

The sound of torrential rain beating against the window woke me. Through the still closed curtains the clouds cast a darkness that made it impossible to figure out the time. The bedside clock revealed it to be only seven. Saturday night ruined and to bed early and up at the crack of dawn on Sunday, for the first time in I don't know how many years. This was turning out to be one disastrous weekend following on from one disastrous week. There seemed to be no let-up in the eternal downward spiral.

Resisting the temptation to go for the cigarette packet, I thought it best to at least get a substantial breakfast. Because the way the weekend had shaped up so far anything could be in store for me.

Tea with two sugars, eggs, bacon, black pudding and fried bread relaxed my resolve to quit smoking, and I opened the fresh packet and lit one up. Healthy breakfast at its finest. Live long or live happy; I knew which would be my choice.

Refocusing on the reality of my situation, I suspected this would be another traumatic day. Nothing had yet been resolved, but I had to keep ploughing on; I felt I had to get to the bottom of this thing. The unacceptable alternative was to give up. There was always that nagging feeling that there was more to come. If, as seemed inevitable, these attacks were connected then there was nothing to suggest they had finished, and I had to know what my position was in it all.

The first thing to be done would be to rebuild my position with Suzanne. It still seemed that she was the only doorway to the end of this dark passage. She was the only solid link in the chain of events so far. But it was much too early to call, especially on a Sunday. I would phone her later.

I could no longer hear the rain beating against the window and reasoned that it had either stopped or the wind had changed direction. As I looked out of the window it was no surprise that the street was empty at such an early hour. The rain had indeed finally stopped and the sun was fighting it's never ending battle with the clouds.

Waiting for others to do something, I felt I was treading water. I was helpless, my situation seemed hopeless. The most frustrating thing was that there wasn't actually anything I could do except wait, and hope. It was like being the man on death row waiting to see if his last minute reprieve had come through.

I craved a bit of normality and so decided to go for a walk, maybe fetch a paper and read the sports pages, check the football results. Anything to take my mind off my predicament and kill a few hours. The waiting was the worst; the waiting and the not knowing.

The hours dragged. I had taken that walk, bought the Sunday paper, read it from back cover to front and then front to back, and drank at least three cups of coffee. And still it wasn't even half past ten.

I should phone Suzanne and apologise for the previous evening, try and explain; and tell her about the attack at Mr Singh's shop. I should do it now.

Instead, I paced the room, back and forth, back and forth. Stopping abruptly, I said to myself, out loud, through gritted teeth, "This is stupid!"

My eyes fell onto my mobile phone looking up at me from the coffee table. I picked it up, hesitated, then searched contacts for Suzanne's number. But it wasn't in there as I had failed to enter it. "Agh!" I yelled in frustration and threw the thing onto the sofa.

Letting out a couple of huge sighs, I fetched her business card and retrieved the phone from under a cushion. I went to tap in Suzanne's number, again dithered and entered it into my contact list instead.

I knew I was just delaying things, not being quite sure where to begin, what to say or how she would react. "Damn that bitch of a wife of mine!" I mumbled under my breath recalling the reason for my dilemma, or maybe just looking for someone to blame.

Taking the easy way out, I decided to text her instead.

I'm really, really sorry about last night. That bitch of an ex of mine.

I paused, deleted the message and started again.

Suzanne I'm so sorry about last night. Turned out it wasn't important after all.

Again these didn't seem the rights words, and again I deleted the text.

After more floor pacing, I tried again.

Sorry about last night, maybe we can do it another time. Could you call when you've got a spare minute and update me on what you've found out. Thanks, Jake

I looked at what I had just written, and it seemed pathetically inadequate. But it was the best I could come up with, and so I decided to leave it at that, just adding *xxxx*. I wondered if that was too many—too intimate—and deleted three of them, hovered over 'send' but made it up to two *x*'s before finally sending it.

Such dithering over sending a mere text message. I really was losing it.

Within minutes my mobile pinged to signal her reply. *That's OK Jake I understand. I'll come round yours tonight, about 7 OK? Xxx.*

Three x's? That made me wonder, but I put it to the back of my mind and replied,

Great, see you then xx

Again hovering before adding the third *x* and pressing 'send'.

My mood lifted immediately. Among all the bad stuff going off, any plus was a massive positive.

A knock at the door came promptly at seven o'clock that evening. As expected, it was Suzanne. She pecked me on the cheek as I let her in.

"I hope you haven't eaten," she said, "'Cos I've brought a Chinese with me. I've been that busy I haven't had anything all day."

"As it happens, I haven't had any tea yet," I replied, feeling a little guilty at having left her to do all the work. "But you must let me pay for it." I took my wallet out of my trouser pocket but she put her hand on mine to stop me from opening it.

"Nonsense, it'll go on expenses. I hope you like what I've brought." She said as she took the two brown paper bags into my kitchen.

"Where'd you keep your things?" Suzanne asked as I followed her.

I took two plates from a top cupboard, salt and vinegar from an identical adjacent one and knives and forks from their drawer beside the sink.

"Sorry, I've only got lager, or lemonade. I wasn't expecting…" I allowed the sentence to trail off as I again apologised.

"Jake, you're really going to have to stop saying sorry all the time. There really isn't any need."

"Sorry," I said, and we both giggled like kids at that.

"I'll just have a shandy, please, as I'm driving. What would you like?" Suzanne asked as she began to plate up the food.

I looked over her shoulder, breathing in the succulent aromas, not just from the food but also her expensive perfume.

"A bit of everything will be fine," I responded as I got the drinks ready; shandy for Suzanne and lager for myself.

"Well, we've got sweet-and-sour chicken, beef in gravy, noodles, seaweed, spring rolls and chips. You like all those?"

"Yeah, that's great. You must have known Chinese is my favourite; I like anything from there."

"No, it was just on the way. If it had been an Indian, I passed instead then you'd have got that," she looked over her shoulder and smiled at me to show that she was only teasing.

"We can talk while we're eating, all right?" I called to her as I took the drinks and cutlery through to the lounge. "Do you want a tray to rest on?"

"No, it'll be fine on my lap," Suzanne responded as she brought the two plates of food through.

Mine was piled twice as high as hers, "Are you sure you've got enough?" I asked.

"Yeah, I've plenty here. Got to watch my figure, you know. You got enough?"

Your figure looks just perfect to me, I thought but just replied, "Yes, I'm fine thanks."

Nothing more was said for at least five minutes as we both tucked into the feast. My earlier down-mood had been considerably raised, not only by a bit of normality but also by the wonderful company.

"Well," Suzanne began, "And before I start I don't want to hear the word sorry, not at all. OK?"

I smiled and considered saying it but agreed, "OK, but can I begin by explaining about last night. Sharron said it was really serious, and it couldn't wait, but—"

Suzanne raised her hand to stop me, "There really is no need for you to explain. I knew it must have been necessary because I know how important *this* is to you. And besides, if I let you carry on, I know you'll end up saying sorry somewhere along the line."

"S—OK, I'll leave it there, and thanks."

"OK then that's that out of the way. Right, where to start." Suzanne paused to gather her thoughts and take another mouthful of the delicious cuisine.

My heap might have been bigger than hers to begin with, but I was that hungry and enjoying it so much that it was disappearing much faster, so I made a conscious effort to slow down and took a long swig of lager.

"Before you start can I just say thank you for all this work and effort you are putting in for me. I really appreciate it you know." I thought I had better get that out of the way first because when I again immersed myself in this I couldn't be sure I'd remember to do it afterwards.

"There's no need. Remember, I'm not just doing this for you. It's for Carlos and Dad's company. So I suppose it makes it my job really."

I knew she didn't see this just as her job, she had shown by her actions, way above and beyond the call of duty, how much she cared. And not just for me but also for her father and his company and Carlos; she cared about people. I recalled the affection she had shown towards her father back at the hospital and suspected he would always be the top of her list.

"And besides, I feel in some way responsible for what happened. It all began with one of our employees."

"You've nothing to be sorry about," I cut in, "None of this is in any way your fault."

"Well, maybe not actually responsible for what happened, but I feel I must get to the bottom of it all. You know, a sort of moral responsibility."

I could see where she was coming from as I would feel the same if I was in her shoes and so decided to leave it there. But there was still that feeling that there was more to this than meets the eye.

Supper was soon finished and we cleared things away to the kitchen before we actually began with the reason we were here.

"Right then, down to business." I said, "What have you got."

"OK, so, my friend at the Gazette, has a brother who is close mates with one of the coppers on the case; or should I say cases."

Looking up startled, I interrupted her, "So they have linked the attacks?"

"Well, not officially, but I think we knew that they would. Anyway, my reporter friend managed to get us some names and attack locations—although, as you will know from your own experience, these would have been pretty hard to hide. But further digging by the both of us produced some of the victims' addresses and even a couple of phone numbers."

Suzanne could see my puzzlement from the frown on my face and explained, "It's amazing what you find when you type a name into Facebook, or the other social media sites for that matter. You know, they reckon that ninety per cent of the world's population are linked by one continuous thread on Facebook."

The frown had fallen from my face at this revelation, and so Suzanne continued, "Anyway, like I said, at least we have something to work with. I printed out the info for you," she handed me a copy and paused again while I scanned the sheet.

Chapter 10

Suzanne leaned forward, that wonderful fragrance of hers wafting my way, forcing aside the almost equally delightful aroma of the food. She pointed to each item on the sheet as she explained its relevance, "You'll see I've listed them in chronological order of attack, followed by attack location and numbers of confirmed casualties, and lastly victims' home addresses."

I followed her finger, nodding my understanding as she went along.

"You'll also notice by the attack dates that they appear to happen in clusters. You know a few attacks in a couple of days then nothing for more than a week."

My head continued to nod slowly as my own fingers located the details on the sheet. I paused when I reached the last one on the list; Singh's Supplies.

Suzanne could see my digit resting on this most recent attack. "Yes that one happened just this morning. Not far from here isn't it?"

"I know I was there. I saw it."

Suzanne's shock was understandable and tangible, "Why…Why didn't you say something earlier? Why didn't you call me?"

"I…I don't know. I didn't want to worry you. I didn't really see the point as I wasn't actually involved, or in any real danger." I bent the truth a little with this because it all turned out well, for me at least, and I didn't want to contemplate what might have happened.

"It must have been horrible for you."

"It was but not as bad as it was for poor Mr Singh and his family." I sat back allowing it all to sink in, then added, "A week ago, I would have been absolutely mortified by it, but now I'm becoming anaesthetised to it all. My senses are dumbing down with all the horror." My voice had become hushed and I must have sounded defeated.

Suzanne dragged the attention back to the list. She would be able to see how horrendously this was all affecting me despite what I had just said. I wasn't very good at hiding my feelings at the best of times. "The apparent clustering?" She paused as my focus returned to the list. "I have one or two ideas on why this might be but I need to do further research on it."

"Ideas? What ideas. What's happening Suzanne?" I was again starting to raise my voice, again showing my frustration. "You have to tell me; I need to know. I have to know what's happening." My vocals cranked up even higher as the panic levels within me grew.

Suzanne was, in contrast, totally calm, "Look, I don't want to worry you unnecessarily any more than you already are. I'll get straight onto it first thing in the morning and let you know anything I find out," she leaned forward, took my hand in hers and looked me straight in the eye, "Everything I find out."

Those beautiful, assured, hazel eyes served to calm my frustration, somehow putting me at ease, but I would not be denied, "You must tell me what you think, Suzanne." I squeezed her hand a little tighter, not so as to hurt her but to convey my earnestness. "Tell me what you suspect."

"Well, OK, but remember this is just a guess, not fact, and even if I am right, we don't know the consequences."

"Just tell me Suzanne, please." I pleaded.

"It seems, and I stress seems, that this pattern is similar to what you would expect from the spread of a virus."

Still holding her hand, my mouth dropped open, and I sat up straight taking in a deep breath then letting it out with a sigh. I was strangely relieved, realising it all made sense. This *must* be what it is. I think the relief came because I could at last see a way forward. I daren't yet think what the final outcome of this could be, but at least I knew what we were dealing with. *Know thine enemy* as someone once said.

"Please try not to worry," it was Suzanne's turn to plead now, "We will sort this; I promise." She put her other hand on top of mine and squeezed it reassuringly.

"I think I need another drink," I said as I rose from the sofa and went to the fridge, "You?"

"No I'm fine, Jake. Thanks."

An awkward silence fell over us as we both contemplated our conversation. I had wanted things to move forward, and they certainly seemed to be doing that.

My mobile rang. It was *her* again. I really couldn't deal with her right now. I refused the call and switched the phone off.

"Sharron?" Suzanne asked. At least my ex had served to break the silence and allowed us to reconnect.

"Yeah, how'd you guess?" I smiled.

Suzanne patted the sofa, "Come and sit down," she said returning the smile, "We'll talk about something else for a while."

"So, how long have you been a postman, then?"

"Twenty-one, no, twenty-two years, it'll be. Great job if it weren't for the management." I laughed. It felt good to laugh, though it seemed an eternity since I had last done so.

"You enjoy it? I mean, I couldn't be doing with all the bad weather. I'm happier working indoors."

"You soon get used to it; either that or you leave. I much prefer the freedom. Once I'm out on my round, I'm my own boss; nobody there to tell me what to do."

"I bet dogs are a problem though?" It was Suzanne's turn to smile.

"Why does everyone think being harassed by dogs is funny? It's a really serious problem. A dog bite is very painful." I put on my most indignant face and Suzanne didn't appear to know quite how to react.

I smiled, "Got you there. No, it is a problem but you soon learn how to deal with it."

Suzanne relaxed a little. "It's good to see you laughing for a change. You've got a lovely smile, you ought to use more often."

"It enhances my good looks, does it?" I asked

"Something like that," she teased.

"And what about you?"

"What, my good looks or my smile?" She wasn't showing off, just playing along.

"No, your job. What does that entail?" I remembered from the business card she had given me that she was employed by the

H.G. Tobacco Company, and I knew roughly what they did—they made cigarettes and other tobacco products. But the card didn't tell me what Suzanne's position in the firm actually was.

"I'm a PA, Personal Assistant, to my father. It's his company."

I wondered why they had different last names but didn't think it right to ask. I hadn't known her long enough yet. "Yes, but what do you actually do? Sit there most of the day filing your nails and looking beautiful?"

Suzanne playfully slapped my hand, "I work very hard, I'll have you know. I do a lot of filing, but not my nails. And the other things, well, anything and everything my father asks me to do. So less of your cheek."

That was me put in my place. "I would say sorry, but you've banned me from apologising."

The banter continued a little longer. "Yes I did, didn't I? Well I'll let you off just this once."

"OK. Sorry then." I grinned, feeling a lot more relaxed. It felt good to take my mind of my problems, if only for a short while.

The light hearted conversation continued. I discovered her mother and father had never married, and her mother had died when Suzanne was very young. I told her about my two grown-up sons. She told me about her university background. I sketched over my pre-postman work days and she spoke of her brief relationship with Charles Bingam, the shark-eyed driver from our first meeting at the hospital. I didn't say much about my marriage as I still found it painful to talk about and she respected this by not pushing me on it. We spoke of many things but without going into anything too deeply; just got to know each other a little better.

Two fleeting hours disappeared before either of us realised it.

"Goodness! Look at the time," Suzanne exclaimed as she glanced at the wall clock. The evening had vanished as if it was in a time warp. Einstein's explanation for his theory of relativity leapt momentarily into my mind.

"I really ought to be getting off now."

"Thank you," I said with great sincerity, as the evening drew to a close.

"For what?"

"For a really pleasant evening and for taking my mind off all the other stuff. You've been a massive help; great therapy."

"You're welcome," She replied as she rose from the sofa. "I've really enjoyed tonight too. We must do it again, you know, when this is all over." She was still trying to reassure me.

We held hands as we went towards the front door. Suzanne opened it and said, "Try not to worry too much, Jake. We will sort this."

She put her arms around me in a comforting hug and then kissed me on the lips. Not a long lingering kiss, or a lover's kiss; more a friend's kiss from one who cared.

I stood, door ajar and watched as Suzanne receded down the path to her car. We swapped waves as she slowly drove off, and I just stood there for long moments after she had disappeared into the distance. The oppressive darkness from which her visit had dragged me again quickly began to envelop me.

The chill spring air crept into my bones forcing me back inside. I didn't bother with the usual quick night time tidy-up but went straight to bed instead, not expecting sleep to come easily. But thankfully, I was wrong; exhaustion and alcohol winning out over fret and depression.

The downside, I suppose, of a good uninterrupted night's slumber is that morning descends all too rapidly. So quickly in fact, that the residue of the previous night's black mood lingered on. Although things now seemed at last to be moving forward, there still appeared to be no end to the nightmare.

Ah well, things can only get better, I thought, trying to cheer myself up as I dragged my body out of bed to face whatever this new day would bring.

The rain battered against the kitchen window, obscuring the outside world but not so much as to hide the endless grey—black sky. It looked less like an April shower and more as though it was set in for the day.

I sat down on the sofa with my tea and toast, Suzanne's aroma from the previous evening diluted but still present. The TV remote was in my hand, and I looked at it as though it was a grenade, reluctant to pull the pin and let the latest news explode into my world once more.

But I couldn't not do it. Ignore it and it might go away wouldn't work in this case. No matter how bad the news was, I had to know; no matter how poisonous the drug was, I had to keep on taking it. So, I reluctantly switched it on, hoping that sometime in the next twenty-minute loop I would learn just how far things had moved forward.

I didn't have long to wait as our local series of attacks were now *the* main story and on every national news station I found as I quickly surfed from one to the next. Reporters from many different news agencies were now at various scenes of crime across the town.

I spent more than an hour taking in every detail from every news channel. They were reporting that there had been seven *incidents* (as they were calling them), sixteen victims (that had attended hospital) resulting in nine deaths which included all the attackers. They had as yet been unable to link the attackers. I picked up the A4 sheet that Suzanne had given me just a few hours previously, checked their figures against hers and found they corresponded exactly. The news teams, though, didn't supply any names or addresses. By the time I had completed my news harvesting, I realised they had nothing much to tell me that I didn't already know. In fact, I knew more than they were prepared to report.

However, seeing it so prominent somehow made it seem more serious, more real; more dangerous. Pacing the floor, tugging my bottom lip, the frustration and anger within me was once again growing. I had never had so much anger within me as I had experienced during these last few days. In fact, I had been quite proud that most people who knew me considered me to be pretty laid back. I wasn't used to dealing with all this wrath and this only served to add to my frustration and further fuel the fury within me; a vicious circle spiralling downwards to God only knows where.

But it wasn't only God that knew because, when I thought about it, I knew exactly where it would all end up. In the morgue is where it would lead me if Suzanne was right about her theory.

This realisation hit me like a jolt from a short-circuited plug, and I froze mid-stride with my hand slipping away from my lip. I slumped down slowly onto the sofa shock having replaced anger. And I stayed there staring at the TV but not seeing it. Not seeing anything, oblivious to my surroundings, to the reporter babbling on, to the weather trying to batter its way into my house, to the post dropping through the letter box and onto the mat.

Nine dead! And the promise of more to follow, for sure.

After I don't know how long, I was hauled from this state of inertia by the ringing of the telephone, but by the time it had registered on my consciousness and I had picked it up, the caller had become fed up with waiting for me.

Tapping in 1471 told me that I had missed Suzanne, but I didn't call her straight back. I was confused and didn't really want to hear what she would tell me. All along throughout this ordeal, I had pinned my hopes on finding out what I had to face and then dealing with it. But now my wish had been granted, I wanted to turn back the clock and retreat back into my ignorance. I'd be careful what I wished for in future, if I had a future.

That thing that had been nagging me, gnawing at the back of my mind since this had first started to develop; this was it. The realisation of where this inevitably had to lead. Maybe not the realisation, more the acceptance of it because I think I knew all along. Sixteen victims, nine deaths-so far! The odds didn't look very good. All the attackers, all those who raged, had died; and I could feel the anger growing within me, propelling me towards my fate.

Chapter 11

Again the telephone pulled me away from my thoughts. Again it was Suzanne and this time I answered it.

"Hi Jake, how are you this morning; still bearing up?"

After a long pause, I managed a response, "No, not really…" and just let it trail off.

"Why? Have you heard something new on the news? What's happened, Jake?" Suzanne sounded frantic.

I knew I had to pull myself together, for her sake, if for nothing else.

"No, no; I'm sorry. Just feeling a little down this morning. That's all." It wasn't actually a lie, more an omission. I had learned nothing new, and was only facing the facts.

As though she could read my mind, Suzanne, now in control of herself, responded, "Jake, nothing is inevitable about this you know. We will find a way through this for you."

She paused waiting for me to react, but I said nothing.

"We don't know all the facts yet, so you must remain positive, Jake; you must."

"I don't know. It's just…" it was just that I didn't really know what to say.

Suzanne continued, "Jake you have to pull yourself together. You're no use to anyone like this."

"Yes, OK," I feebly mumbled.

Now it was her turn to get angry, "No Jake, it's not OK. Now stop feeling sorry for yourself and man up. We can beat this but only if you're willing to try."

She sounded so upset, frustrated, and then hung up on me.

I sat there, phone in hand until I had come to accept what she had just said. Now I was angry with myself. I had never been a quitter in my life and now wasn't the time to start.

Suzanne answered on the first ring as I called her back. "I'm sorry I had a moment of weakness. It won't happen again."

Her tone had softened, "It had better not, Jake. You have to hang in there."

"I know, I know; and I will. I mean, I am doing."

"Do you want me to come round? I can drop everything right now and be with you in ten minutes."

Right at that moment, there was nothing I would have liked more in the world, but I said, "No, there's really no need. I was just being a wimp. I'm sorry it was just a blip, but thanks anyway." She was my rock in all this, but I couldn't tell her that. We hadn't known each other two minutes, not long enough for anything like that, not yet.

"Well, if you're sure you're OK…" Suzanne let the sentence trail off giving me a chance to change my mind.

I changed the subject instead, "How's the investigating going? Got anything new to tell me?"

"Slow but sure. I've nothing earth-shattering new to report yet, though." Then her tone changed to a more serious one, more assertive, "Look, Jake I know I can't worry you any more than you already are so I won't hide anything from you. But I won't just speculate either. When I know something so will you. OK?"

"Yes, I know; I get so frustrated sometimes. If there was just something I could do, then perhaps I wouldn't feel such a spare part. I just feel so helpless."

"That's OK then. I'll call you as soon as I find anything out. Meanwhile, stay positive. And that's an order."

I was pleased she had finished on a lighter note. It put me at ease a little. I suspected that is why she had done it and once again appreciated her concern. "Yes ma'am; anything you say ma'am."

"That's good then. I'll call you soon."

And then she was gone.

Yet again Suzanne had raised my spirits, strengthened my resolve and spurred me on. My problems were still there, just as strong, imminent, dangerous, but I now felt I could at least face them. It makes all the difference when you feel you have someone to lean on.

Phew, what a start to the week and it wasn't even Monday lunch yet. No wonder people generally think Mondays suck.

I turned the TV off. I wasn't learning anything only depressing myself further. The twenty-minute news loop was putting my life into a loop, and I didn't need that.

I spent the afternoon doing the housework. Cleaning where it wasn't needed, tidying things away and moving things around. In fact, anything that helped the time to pass and to take my mind off things. By early evening, there wasn't a thing left that hadn't been cleaned, moved or thrown out.

Also by this time, my patience had run out, the frustration and anger were again returning.

I yanked the fridge door open and took out a can of lager and slammed it shut causing its contents to rattle noisily. I looked at the can but didn't open it. I threw it against the wall instead, the force making it pop with a loud whoosh, spraying its contents around the lounge.

I left it lying in the corner, the last drops of fluid trickling out onto the carpet. "Damn it!" I yelled and punched the same wall. It was no good, try as I might I couldn't stop the anger growing within me. I had to do something, anything. Whether it proved relevant or not, helpful or not, didn't matter.

I lit a cigarette which calmed me enough to think reasonably straight and considered my options, quickly coming to the conclusion that I didn't have very many. It was, therefore, relatively easy to decide my next step. I picked up the list that Suzanne had supplied me with. I would visit the attack scenes, at least some of them, and talk to neighbours, witnesses; in fact, anyone who would talk to me. Although, I realised it was too late to do this today I felt galvanised at having a positive plan of action. I would start first thing in the morning. I picked up my phone and thought about calling Suzanne but decided against it. She had said she would update me if necessary, and I didn't want to keep bothering her needlessly.

In spite of the rain that had not ceased all day and was still hammering on the windows, I found sleep easy to attain that night, didn't stir once and awoke invigorated the next morning to the singing of birds and brilliant sunlight streaming through a chink in the curtains. The future seemed more positive already. It was as though I controlled the moods of the days. Or was it the other way round; were they controlling me?

I picked up the list of victims and took in their addresses and attack sites. My many years as a postman came in handy. I had delivered to virtually every house, shop, factory, office and whatever else had a letter box in the town at some time or other and could visualise each location and its proximity to the others. This allowed me to quickly formulate a plan and decide on the best route to follow.

Order of business calculated, I turned the sheet over and relisted them in my preferred sequence. One had occurred at the local supermarket in town, so Tesco would be my first port of call. The nearest one to that was the White Lion pub, but I would leave that until later as it wouldn't be open and the likelihood was that no one would be about until after lunch. So my second visit would be the B&Q store on the northern end of town. The other four locations were all on residential estates. I would have to take pot luck with those as to whether anyone was about, but I reckoned at least some of the neighbours could provide me with the information I wanted.

Those four, I listed in order of the shortest distance between them but left poor Mr Singh until the end. If what I had heard from the news, the hospital and Suzanne proved to be correct I didn't expect it would be necessary to visit every site as I would probably obtain a pretty similar picture from each. If this was the case, then I could at least leave the corner shop out altogether. I had no real desire to go back there just yet as the horrendous carnage was still so vividly etched into my brain.

As I set off for the supermarket, the earlier warm sunshine was already giving way to threatening dark clouds, the wind was picking up and the temperature was starting to fall. Hopefully, this was not a foreboding of the day ahead. On arrival, I turned up the collar of my black overcoat and fastened its buttons against the cold before making my way across the carpark to the entrance.

I went straight to 'Enquiries'. "Would it be possible to see the manager, if it's not too much trouble, please Wendy?" I put on my politest and friendliest voice and used the name I had taken from her badge thinking perhaps this familiarity would give me the greatest chance of success.

The receptionist looked me up and down, lingering on my bruised face and then my potted arm. "You'll have to phone in and make an appointment," was her robotic response.

My ghastly appearance had obviously beaten my charm hands down. Bruce Willis never seemed to have this problem. "Isn't there any possibility of seeing him today? Is there a way round this, perhaps a short cut?" The courteous attitude was just about holding out.

"Or you could go on-line and book." Her tone never altered.

OK, so I had tried the nice approach and that wasn't working. "Look, love, I'm not leaving here until I've seen him. So be a good girl and run along and get him."

Before she had a chance to again bat me down, I pointed to my face and said, "You can tell him it's about this."

That must have intrigued her enough because she picked up the telephone and said to me, "Err, just a minute, sir. I'll see what I can do."

Wendy returned her attention back to the telephone. "There's an, err, gentleman here insisting on seeing you, Miss Earlwright."

Miss Earlwright must have replied as Wendy paused before adding, "He says it's important. I think you ought to see him, miss."

Wendy put the phone down and turned back to face me, "The manager will be down to see you in a minute, sir."

"Thank you, Wendy," I smiled my smuggest most satisfied, dog-that-got-the-fireside-chair smile and went and browsed the nearby shelves while waiting.

Moments later, I swivelled round as Miss Earlwright, Manager Charlene, politely asked, "How can I help you sir?"

I was quicker than her and looked her up and down before she had the chance to do the same to me. She was about five-five, fortyish and a little overweight but carried it well. Her neatly cut navy blue suit-uniform was nicely complimented by her tidy shoulder-length wavy brown hair.

"Could we do this in your office, please?" I asked, adding, "It's about the incident, the attack, the other day."

Charlene, paused and considered my request. Wendy leaned a little closer so as not to miss a word. The manager glanced across at her and replied, "I really don't think I will be able to tell you very much, mister…"

"Kolman, Jake Kolman."

"Mr Kolman," Charlene again turned towards Wendy then added, "But yes, I think this will best be done in private." She raised the volume for those last two words, and Wendy turned away busying herself with something under the counter.

As the manager lead me to her office, she asked, "Would you like a drink, Mr Kolman; tea or perhaps coffee?"

"No, I'm fine thanks Miss Earlwright."

The office was tastefully decorated in cream with a slightly darker carpet. Vertical cream blinds were half open in front of the full length window which looked out across a small expanse of neatly manicured lawn. This was bordered on two sides by rose bushes, some white and some red, which trembled in the breeze. Beyond the lawn, a lorry was being unloaded at the goods inwards bay.

A swivel chair and oak effect desk stood between the window and two comfortable looking metal and fabric chairs. On top of the desk was a computer, telephone and a small and neat pile of papers. The tidiness was in complete contrast with my manager's place.

Miss Earlwright offered me a seat, which I took, then asked me, "How can we help you, Mr Kolman?"

"What can you tell me about the attack here?" I got straight to the point.

"You're not press are you?"

"No, I was a victim of a similar attack, by a different person." I hoped my candour would loosen her tongue.

"And you want to know because…?"

"Well, you'll have seen the news reports," I looked up at her and she nodded her agreement, "And obviously, you've talked to the police."

"Yes, but they wouldn't tell me anything, just took a statement from me. I didn't actually see the incident myself, but I personally took statements from all those involved." She explained.

"Doesn't surprise me; they wouldn't tell me anything either. Nor would the hospital. As you'll appreciate, I'm really rather worried, especially as the news is now linking these incidents."

"Yes, Mr Kolman, and I do sympathise with you, but I don't see how I can help."

"Well, I'm shooting in the dark here. I need to know what happens next as these incidents seem to be ongoing. I want to know what will happen to me next. Can you understand that?" My tone remained calm.

"Yes, I can see that, but…"

"Rumour has it that this may be a virus," not the official line as yet, but I thought if I told her something she couldn't already know, confided in her, then she might confide in me. "So you will see how serious this could be for me. I just thought if I talked to people, witnesses, about the other incidents then I might find out something that might help me. Some common ground, maybe."

I could see Charlene weighing up what I had told her. She appeared to have reached a decision and leaned forward, and speaking in hushed tones (I didn't know why this was as we were the only people in the room) said, "I really shouldn't say anything. I probably shouldn't even be talking to you, but…"

I breathed a sigh of relief as I realised, completely against my expectations, she was actually going to discuss this with me. I'd like to think it was my charm that pulled it off but knew it was just as likely to be fear considering my appearance. Or maybe she just felt sorry for me and wanted to help.

"This hasn't come from me; you understand? We haven't even spoken, OK?" Charlene raised her eyebrows in expectation awaiting confirmation that she had nothing to do with anything.

"It's just between the two of us," I assured her, "I'll never mention your name and no one will even know we've spoken," I lied. "As far as anyone is concerned, you took the official line and told me you couldn't speak to me."

This seemed to satisfy her as she began to recite her run-down of the events.

"I wasn't actually in store that particular day, but I was told it was quite horrendous. Thankfully, only one person was killed, but unfortunately, three others were injured including one of my staff."

"And it was the attacker who was killed?" I encouraged her.

"Yes and two lady customers were badly beaten, and my cashier was bitten and punched. I don't know what would have happened, how bad it would have got, if the guy hadn't keeled over and died."

"Go on," I urged.

"Well, I don't know what set him off. He hadn't had to queue particularly long. We have a policy of opening more tills if customer numbers require it, which we adhere to rigidly."

I didn't doubt this official line at all.

"There were just those two ladies in front of him, each with only a basket. It would have only taken a couple of minutes for him to get served, three at most."

"How was he prior to this? Had anyone noticed anything unusual about him before he went to the checkout?"

"Geraldine, my assistant, had noticed him behaving oddly in the biscuit aisle. And a customer complained that he had been very rude to her when he bumped into her trolley. He pushed her out of the way, nearly knocking her over and swore at her."

"Just pushed her but didn't attack her?"

"Pushed her and called her the 'c' word." Charlene continued.

"And how long was this before he went to the check out?"

"Only a couple of minutes. I've checked the CCTV."

"And did the CCTV show any more abnormal behaviour from the man?"

"Not really. We've run it all back to the moment he entered the shop. He looked a bit down, agitated; maybe a little pre-occupied, but nothing to suggest what was about to happen. And he was only in store for twelve minutes up to the incident at the till."

Twelve minutes! If this thing went belly up for me, was that all the warning I'd get; twelve minutes! Would I even know what was happening?

"Are you all right, Mr Kolman?" Miss Earlwright must have noticed my distress.

"Ugh? Yes, yes, I'm OK. Just a bit shocked. You know, by the suddenness of it all." I pulled myself together, "Please carry on Miss Earlwright. What happened at the till?"

"Like I said, he was a bit agitated but nothing to indicate what he was about to do. All of a sudden, he just started shouting, 'For f's sake'." Charlene lowered her voice to explain, "He actually used the word, but I won't be as crude. 'For f's sake get an effin' move on', then he pushed the lady in front of him. When she turned round to complain, he punched her, right in the face, twice. She went straight down then he dragged the lady in front of her out of the way and threw her to the ground.

"Jenny, on checkout, stood up and tried to intervene. Such a brave girl. Well, he just dragged her right over the conveyor belt."

I was shocked by the speed and violence of it all. My attacker had been dazed and injured, not at all like this. But I managed to hold myself together, "And she was bitten you say?"

"Yes, horrendous, it was so horrendous," I could see Charlene's eyes beginning to glaze over as she must have been visualising the CCTV footage.

"He started tearing at her, at her clothing, her face, pulling her hair, yanking it out in handfuls. And by this time, he was frothing at the mouth. She's lost an eye you know."

Obviously, I didn't know but allowed her to continue her flow.

"He bit her cheek, bit a chunk right out of it. She'll need plastic surgery—the company will pay, of course." The manager's eyes refocused on me as she made this point.

It wasn't much, I thought, but there wasn't a lot they could do or could have done to prevent it happening, I supposed. I smiled a comforting smile, "Good; that's good of them."

Charlene mentally returned to the crime scene, "Then he strangled her. Other shoppers were trying to stop him but he was totally unaware of them. All of a sudden, he just keeled over, on top of Jenny. He was dead at this point, so the police reckoned. Heart attack, apparently."

The manager stopped talking, her story finished. There was silence for a few seconds. I didn't know quite what to say.

Charlene broke it, "And you? Was this like your attack?"

Not exactly, I thought, but didn't want to talk about it. I needed to think and take in what I had just learned. So I said, "Yes, very similar," and abruptly ended our conversation, "Thank you, Miss Earlwright, Charlene. You've been very helpful."

I needed to get out into the fresh air. The atmosphere in that office had become oppressive, and I could feel my emotions welling up again. I stood and shook her hand, "Thank you again. I can find my own way out."

Before I knew it, I was back sitting in my car in the carpark having passed from the office to my vehicle totally oblivious to anything going off around me. I sat there for many minutes, the revelations churning over and over in my mind before coming to the conclusion that although the circumstances of the two attacks were completely different, they were in fact very similar in essence. *And only twelve minutes warning!* I shuddered at the thought. But at least, I had some idea of what to expect. The attackers so far wouldn't have had an inkling. Would this knowledge help me to avert the crisis? I had no way of knowing.

My shock at Charlene's vivid account soon subsided. It was just one more horror scene among many. I regained my focus and set off for my next destination. This time, I would be better prepared, I hoped.

I pulled the Punto out of its parking space and joined the queue for the exit to the main road. So much was going around inside my head, and I failed to notice the cars in front of me had driven away. I was jerked back to the present by the loud blare of a car horn. I looked in the rear view mirror and saw a large Mercedes, an AMG Edition 463, I reckoned—a beautiful car, if you liked that sort of thing. I had an interest in vehicles of the higher price range, often day-dreaming about which I would buy when I won the lottery. And as my job entailed me being out on my own for hours on end, I tended to do a lot of day-dreaming. It flashed its lights, and I got the message, my attention returning to the situation ahead of me.

I soon reached the junction leading to B&Q and pulled up at the traffic lights in the right hand lane. I glanced across to the left hand lane and saw the Mercedes was next to me. The driver was shielded from me by his tinted windows, but I could feel his glare piercing straight into my brain, sending shivers down my spine. *Get over it asshole,* I thought and continued on my trek. It was still bugging me as I parked up in the DIY store's carpark. The idiots who drive those type of vehicles, the four-by-fours and off-roaders, are all the same. They don't bother with indicators and think the rules of the road don't apply to them. They're just selfish gits. I thumped the steering wheel.

It was really getting to me but I believed, hoped, it was just the normal run-of-the-mill road rage, and not the other type of rage. I forced it from my mind, breathed deep and slow, compelling myself to calm down and concentrate on the task in hand.

I stared up at the entrance to the store, took another deep breath and said quietly to myself, "Here we go again."

The soft and gentle approach had worked at Tesco to some degree, especially with the manager, Charlene, and so I decided to try it for a second time.

"Excuse me," I said loudly, hoping that one of the three staff members huddled together in hushed conversation would notice me.

The lean twenty-something man on the left of the trio, Colin his badge called him, responded, "Yes, how can I help you?"

"Hi Colin, would it be possible to see the manager."

"Sorry but he's not here at the moment. Should be back at twoish. Is it something I can help you with?"

"Erm…" I was undecided what to do.

"If you tell me what it's about, then we'll see if I can help." I liked Colin's cheery, willing to help attitude and chose to take up his offer. After all, what did I have to lose?

Again, I got to the point, "It's about the incident that happened here. You know, where one of the customers went berserk." Before he could respond, I continued, "And before you ask, no, I'm not a reporter. I was a victim of a similar attack."

A shocked Colin asked, "What, by the same guy?"

"No, someone else. You'll have seen on the news that there's been a string of them."

Colin nodded thoughtfully and then drew back defensively, "What about the attack here? Why do you want to know?"

"Maybe, I should come back when the manager's here," I said and turned to leave. I only got a few paces.

"I saw it you know."

I hesitated and slowly turned back to face the staff member. He was determined to milk his fame and went straight into a graphic account of the incident. "It was incredible; like something from a horror movie."

"Tell me about it," I encouraged and added, "Please."

Colin came out from behind the sales station. "Come on, follow me," he said. "We'll walk down the aisles while I fill you in. It'll look like I'm working and you're a customer."

He led me towards the tool section. "This is where it happened. I was over there." He pointed towards where the wood, hardboard and chipboard panels were stacked.

"This guy, chuntering he was. I didn't take much notice at first, but as he got louder I looked across. He was comparing the chisels, as though trying to decide which one he wanted and started pacing back and forth along the section—like he was prowling. It was quite comical, so I chuckled to myself. I called Dean over, my mate, to come and have a look.

"Well, this guy must have heard as he got really confrontational and asked what I was laughing at. Before I could say anything, he threw one of the chisels straight at me. Luckily, it missed.

"But he doesn't give up and grabs an 'ammer and marches towards us. He's frothing at the mouth, shouting and spitting, but I couldn't tell what he was saying.

"Anyway, he drops the tools, doesn't he? Me and Dean were both relieved at that."

"What happened next?" I asked because I knew that wasn't the end of it. I knew from Suzanne's list and the news reports that the guy died and a customer was seriously injured.

"Dean, he's a big lad, six-four; rugby player. Don't get me wrong, he's a really nice lad, wouldn't hurt a fly; won customer service awards..."

I intervened before I got Dean's life story, "What did the guy do next?"

"Well, he's coming at us, at me, and Dean goes to step between us. At that very moment, an old chap comes round the corner and bumps into this guy. So he just grabs him by the throat and throws him against the plywood and the old guy goes down. But our frothing geezer hasn't done yet and jumps on the poor man, stamps on him with both feet.

"We was shocked, me and Dean; couldn't react; didn't know what to do.

"So the geezer drags the old man up by the hair and starts trying to tear his face off; and growling he was."

At this point, Colin pauses to catch his breath.

"And?" I wanted him to continue even though I knew how this would end.

"Dean's reacted by this point; me I'm still stood there like a dummy. He goes to drag them apart and the geezer turns on Dean. Well, as I said Dean can handle himself, but he's struggling here. Then suddenly the guy just drops down dead, just like that. So we…"

I'd heard enough by this point and turn to leave. "Thanks, Colin, You've been a great help." I saw nothing to be gained by hanging around any longer.

I returned to my car still in a daze. I thought I would have been better prepared that time, but I was wrong. I was in just as much shock as when I had come out of the supermarket. The attack had been just the same as the others; hardly any warning, agitation turning rapidly to outrageous violent anger and death.

The guy at B&Q, the one at Tesco, the painter and decorator who had attacked me, and Carlos at the hospital where it had all apparently began. All reacted virtually the same; and all were dead.

I wondered if it was worthwhile going to the other locations; wondered if I had the stomach for it. But I thought I must at least try. I felt I had to give it a go, even though I didn't now expect there would be any great differences in the other incidents. I suppose that I was just hoping that one of them might differ and give me a glimmer of hope. I would have grasped at anything at that moment.

The dashboard clock told me it was twelve thirty; probably still a bit early for the pub. One of the other addresses was in the opposite direction but only five minutes away in a block of flats on a council estate. This, I decided to take in next.

I was beginning to feel hungry but couldn't face the thought of eating, not until I'd got all this out of the way. I doubted I would feel like anything even by then. To some extent, I was starting to regret setting out on the course of action I was undertaking, but on the other hand, I didn't know what else I could have done. I had to do something. And I had learned from my task so far, learned the similarities in the cases and also the finality of them. But I wasn't sure if this had helped me or had the opposite effect.

In my yearning for the facts, for advancement, all I seemed to be proving was the inevitability of my own doom. Each door I passed through seemed to reduce my options. Soon there would be no doors left to open and I would end up with the black hand like in the maze in *Takeshi's Castle.*

I couldn't dwell on this, couldn't allow myself to think that way and that is exactly why I needed to do *something.*

Chapter 12

Arriving at the block of flats, my apprehension had grown. I eyed the drab grey imposing structure and determined there were three floors, nine flats to each; twenty-seven in all. With a landing running across each row of front doors, the whole place had the appearance of a block of prison cells. I remembered when I had, some years back, last delivered the post on this estate and the dread of having to knock on the doors with packages or the all too frequent summons that required a signature. I tried to push these thoughts to the back of my mind and to focus on the reason why I was there.

It took me a while to control my breathing and keep down the volcanic uprising of panic. But I compelled myself to get out of the car and forced one foot in front of the other.

I slowly climbed the communal stairs, like a death-row convict, to the first floor and proceeded to number thirteen where the incident had taken place. I paused at this momentarily but did not knock on it. Instead, I carried on to number eighteen at the end. I didn't even want to be there, so I certainly wasn't going to disturb the victim's family.

I knocked on eighteen's door, waited and knocked again. No reply. The same at the next two. Fifteen opened his door as far as the security chain would allow, looked me up and down, and then slammed it shut in my face before I had a chance to say a word. I stood there staring at the door for a few seconds then decided it best to move on to the next one.

At least the young, unshaven man with the tattooed face at fourteen spoke to me, if only to tell me to go away (with a few expletives thrown in for good measure). Again, I hesitated as I passed thirteen and paused, too, at twelve. But I am an optimist and so knocked firmly three times, sure I would be lucky this time. A woman (at first glance she looked fiftyish, on closer examination probably only mid-thirties) opened the door and eyed me suspiciously. From behind her, I heard the heavy plodding of bare feet. A man of roughly my height and as wide as he was tall peered around the woman. He too stared at me, with an attitude that said *well, what the f' do you want?*

As I began to explain to him my reasons for daring to disturb him, he pushed past the woman, hoisted me off my feet and half pushed, half threw me down the corridor back towards the staircase. In language similar to the man from number fourteen, he also told me to leave and went on to describe what he would do to my various body parts if I didn't take his advice. The likelihood of my impending death did not spur me on to unbridled bravery. Instead, I gave that one up as a bad job and set off for the White Lion.

I reasoned that there would probably be someone there by now but deep down hoped there wasn't. My resolve was weakening with every visit.

As I turned into the pub's empty carpark, I thought I saw the Mercedes in the rear view mirror, but as I did a double take, it had vanished. It was nowhere to be seen as I scanned up and down the road. I whispered under my breath "Get a grip", as it seemed I was becoming paranoid in my obsession with the vehicle.

The old fashioned, some would call it traditional, sooty-cream walled building looked as though it hadn't had a make-over since the eighties. The rusting pub sign squealed as it strained on its hinges against the wind. The place appeared to be deserted, maybe even derelict with its cracked and broken windows, but the front door was open. As I passed through it, the cool breeze caused me to shiver. The whole thing reminded me of those Dracula films from the sixties, where the innocent traveller enters the castle in search of refuge.

The bar maid was leaning across the bar, engrossed in the daily paper. She rhythmically tapped a pen against her teeth through blood red lipstick. I wondered if she could actually see all the crossword, with her more than ample cleavage bursting across it, trying to free itself from her pink partially buttoned blouse. Her dirty-blond, grey-brown rooted hair completed the thirtyish image she was presumably striving to attain. She would probably achieve it to some of her clientele by closing time (midnight, every night as the tattered hand-written sign at the back of the bar informed me) if they had consumed enough of the spirits at 'two for one, all day happy hour'. In truth, she must have been nearly twice that age.

"Pint of lager please, love," was my opening gambit as I assumed I would have more chance of a conversation if I passed money over the bar first.

"Carlin' OK?" she cheerfully asked, giving me her best professional come-on smile. *It pays to keep the punters interested*, I thought, but it was nowhere near midnight yet and her *charm* wasn't going to work on me. Still, if I played along her tongue might loosen enough to get this over with reasonably quickly.

She carefully placed the over-full glass on the bar towel in front of me and held out her other hand. "Three quid please, sweetheart," she requested, displaying as much of that ample bosom as possible.

As I handed over the three coins, it was as if she had read my mind, "And what brings you to a place like this? We only usually get the dolies, spending their hard unearned cash at this time of day. And I can tell, you're not one of them, in spite of your battered face. I hope the other guy looks worse."

"Yeah he does," I replied but didn't expand on that. "I was wondering if you were working when that attack happened the other evening."

"Yes, I was," the bar maid was equally short with her forthcomings.

"I got like this," I pointed to my face, "In a similar attack. Could you tell me about your incident?"

"I've already told the coppers all about that. I can see you're not one of them," she let the sentence hang there, encouraging me to explain.

"No, I'm a postman," I smiled trying to lighten the atmosphere and hoped that she would trade information.

"Post Office branching out into detective work now, is it?"

I couldn't help a small chuckle at that. "I just need to find out about this epidemic of attacks. See what it means for me."

"Epidemic? You don't want to believe everything you hear on the telly. They make half that up to keep the punters interested."

I knew better but chose not to argue with her. "All the same if you could just tell me about it. It would be a great help to me."

As she pondered this, I downed my drink in one and sought to influence her decision, "Same again please, love; and one for yourself."

"Thanks, I'll have the same," she said and began to fill the glasses. "Nothing much to tell, really. Normal busy, noisy Friday night. Tom, that's the guy who died, finishes his drink and is mumbling to himself as he comes to the bar for another."

"Mumbling?" I queried.

"Yeah, old Tom was always doing that. Well, as he gets to the bar Connor, one of the lads playing pool, bumps into him." She sees the look of concern on my face. "Oh no, it was nothing like that. Connor's a good boy; says sorry to Tom, even offers to get him a drink. Well, Tom's having none of it and starts ranting. You know, youth of today, no respect, that sort of thing."

"So, how'd it get so bad?"

"Connor just laughs at the old man, says 'keep your hair on grandad' and turns back to his game. Next thing, Tom's smashed his glass over the lad's head and starts strangling him. Now, Tom was a bit of a grumpy old git, but never anything like that. There was blood everywhere."

"What happened next?"

"Keith, that's Connor's mate whacks Tom over the head with a cue, breaks it clean in two! Has no effect on the old guy though. He just carries on at Connor.

"The place is in uproar now, isn't it? They're all trying to pull Tom off. All of a sudden, he lets go and falls on the floor stone dead. Just like that!"

"Just like that," I repeated, thinking just like all the others.

"Yeah. That's all there is to tell, really."

"Thanks, you've been very helpful." I took a final swig from my drink and turned to leave leaving the half-full glass on the bar.

"See you in here again, will we? At the weekend, maybe?"

"Maybe," I responded without looking back. We both knew that was unlikely.

"Thanks for the drink," the bar maid called to me as I returned to the carpark.

Sitting in the Punto, I looked at the list. I really couldn't stomach much more of this. I would only be reliving the nightmare. All my worst fears were being confirmed. If this really was a virus, then I was dead; no two ways about it.

I stared at the A4 sheet of paper. Three more addresses on three different housing estates. There really was absolutely no point in going any further. I couldn't do the others. I just wanted to go home, sit in a darkened room and wait for it all to go away. I knew it wouldn't but decided to go home anyway. There was nothing more to be gained by torturing myself further.

Despite my little excursion, I was still in the hands of Suzanne. She still somehow seemed my only hope. She had remained positive, was telling me not to give up hope, not to worry. Well, she could be like that, couldn't she? It wasn't her that was on death row. And I didn't really know what I expected her to do. Sure, she was gathering information, evidence, but practically speaking, what could she actually do that would make any difference? If you're in front of a firing squad it doesn't matter how innocent you are, the bullets will kill you just as surely as if you were guilty.

I tried to push those morose thoughts from my head as I fired up the Punto and headed for the exit. Today had seemed to be a procession of car parks, each one leading a step nearer to the cemetery. I physically shook my head rapidly from side to side to disperse the depressing horror of my situation.

There was only the solitary car, a red Fiesta, parked on the stretch of road outside the pub, and it had pulled right up to the exit obscuring my view as I attempted to join the main road. I wondered what sort of idiot had chosen to park there, so close to the entrance, when there was all the other space available. Whoever it was hadn't gone into the pub because I had been their only customer.

I eventually figured it was all right to pull out, and as I did so, I caught a glimpse of the driver as he leaned forward out of the shadow and stared straight at me. His face was expressionless and his eyes never left mine. He seemed familiar. I thought I recognised him from somewhere, but I couldn't quite remember from where. And I couldn't linger as approaching traffic forced my hand and determined my course of action.

As I drove, I racked my brains for who he was. It was really starting to irritate me. The more I thought about him, the more convinced I was that I knew him. This only served to add to the ever growing heap of frustrations.

When I arrived home, I breathed a sigh of relief, glad that the day's task had come to an end. But my sanctuary was anything but that. I had hoped that the change of scenery would bring a change of atmosphere. I didn't expect to spend the rest of the day laughing, but, well, had hoped the familiarity would be comforting. However, it was more like when you've got a raging tooth ache and go from one room to another expecting it to feel better for the change of surroundings.

But just like tooth ache, the mood wasn't going anywhere.

And the two cars were still playing on my mind. Did I recognise the driver of the Fiesta? Was the Mercedes following me? Or was paranoia merely the next stage of my demise? In the end, it probably wouldn't make a difference either way. Even though it wasn't yet four in the afternoon, I could feel the impenetrable darkness rapidly closing in on me again.

A text came through, one tiny chink of light in all the gloom,

Hi Jake. Nothing new to report yet. Don't worry, chin up. Love Suzanne xxx.

Even this didn't have quite the lift it would have done a day ago. I replied with only *xxx*.

I awoke early the next morning after an uncomfortable night's sleep that had been pock-marked with fragments of incomplete, half remembered dreams, leaving an uneasy and depressing imprint of unfinished business; a mental residue similar to the bad taste binge drinking usually leaves in the mouth.

It was Wednesday, and the attacks had already disappeared from the national news headlines. Less than a week, and I was already discarded ground sheets at the bottom of budgies' cages. It may be the way of the world these days, but it didn't help me. It sure as hell wasn't yesterday's news as far as I was concerned.

I flicked the TV over to the sports channels, then trawled through the menu, not really looking at it but doing it more out of habit. I still felt I had to be doing something. Even though the previous day had unearthed nothing unexpected, I still had to believe the answers were out there somewhere. It was just a case of finding them; finding the right path to take.

Everything I did just lead to more frustration which lead to more anger. But doing nothing only seemed to accelerate the process.

The only thing that might help, the only course of action open to me was another trip to the hospital. That is where it appeared to have all started and that is where each and every incident led. If anybody knew anything, then that is where I would find it. What did I have to lose, apart from my life?

As I entered the Accident and Emergency department, it looked exactly as it had done six days previously. Sandra and Margaret were on reception and half a dozen or so people were awaiting their turn for treatment; it might even have been the same people by the look of them, but reason told me otherwise.

It might have looked exactly the same, but my perception of it had altered dramatically. A week ago, I would have viewed such a place as a safe haven where you would get help, and all your physical problems would be resolved. But now, it was fraught with danger; suspicion and peril lurked in every shadow, hidden like landmines. Last week, I was wounded, battered and in shock but still I had faith in the place. Now my physical injuries were healing, but I had faith in nothing.

With a heavy sigh I approached Margaret, "Good morning. Do you remember me?" I asked trying to sound cheerful, but it came out more like sarcasm.

Margaret's blank expression answered my question, and I wondered if she could even remember getting up that morning.

Nevertheless, I ploughed onward. "I was a victim of the rage attacks?" I explained hoping that might jog her memory. Maybe it did or maybe it didn't. It was impossible to tell as her face retained the same impassive disinterest.

I felt like shaking her; the anger again beginning to surface. Maybe if I slapped her, I might get a reaction. It would certainly make me feel better. Another sigh forced itself from my lungs; this one as much from irritation as anything else. "Could I see someone then, please?"

"This is for accidents and emergencies only. If you want to make an appointment then you'll have to go to Outpatients," was her dead-pan response. Then she looked back down at the paperwork in front of her.

"I don't want an appointment. I want to see someone about what is going on, damn it!" I thumped my fist down on the counter in front of me, but even this didn't cause much of a stir in her.

"Accidents and emergencies only. And please don't do that again, or I will have to call security." Again, she returned to her paperwork.

Well, that was it; she had driven me over the edge, and I just lost control, "Damn you, woman! I *will* see someone!" Again, I thumped my fist down hard in front of her.

I spun around and marched across the waiting area towards where I had been treated the last time I was there. "Where's the doctor?" I shouted, "I want to see a doctor, now!"

Chapter 13

The six-six, twenty stone black-uniformed man I did get to see obviously wasn't the doctor I had requested, but he made it perfectly clear that he was the only person I would be seeing in there today.

"Come on, sir, you're going to have to leave," he said, calm as you like and wrapped both his arms around. He lifted me from the floor and carried me outside as easily as if I had been his shopping.

"I should get off home if I were you, sir." His calm tone was not at all threatening as we both knew it had no need to be. His suggestion was my only alternative, he had made that abundantly clear.

As he returned into the building, I sat on the low wall between the entrance and the carpark, head in hands, looking down at my feet. Frustration and anger had taken control of me as I hit yet another dead end.

"Mr Kolman?" a voice I recognised interrupted my world.

I looked up to see it belonged to Lisa-Anne, the nurse who had seen me the previous week. I remained seated, elbows resting on my knees, my face imploring her to help me.

"I shouldn't be talking to you. Nobody will see you. We've been told to say nothing to nobody." Her defeated expression showed me that she really wanted to help if she could. But she couldn't.

Her caring calmed me a little but didn't help me in any other way. I opened my mouth to say something, but nothing came out. There was nothing else to say. I stood and turned to leave, shaking my head.

"I shouldn't be telling you this, Mr Kolman, but the attacks are all linked and go back to the first incident here at the hospital."

I stopped in my tracks as what I had known all along was now confirmed as irrevocable fact. I turned slowly around, and said, "Thank you, thank you, nurse." As Lisa-Anne, head down, disappeared back into the abyss that was her place of work.

Sitting in my car, staring out of the window at the angry grey clouds, I had again attained one small step forward, one more piece in the puzzle. But like all the other hard earned victories, it wouldn't alter the outcome one bit. I felt how I imagined Spartacus must have felt.

I started the car and slowly drove towards the exit, not really knowing where I was going to next. As I pulled out into the flow of traffic, I saw the red Fiesta, same driver, same expression, same stare, in my rear view mirror. I stopped right there in the middle of the road, and cars began honking their horns at me as I got out to confront the man.

But he didn't stop, just pulled round me, still staring. I kicked out at the back of his car, scuffing the dark grey plastic bumper and shook my fist at him as he vanished into the distance.

"Get out the way, dick head!" the next driver shouted at me. I raised my potted arm, one finger sticking up then climbed back into the Punto. Well, I thought, that wasn't paranoia. He was definitely following me. I re-joined the traffic, still puzzling over who the man was. I was now absolutely certain that I had seen him before.

My phone went off, and it was her again, Sharron. It was one thing after another; everyone seemed to be conspiring to drive me over the edge. Well, if they continued like this, then I'd gladly go over for them. Once again, I ignored her.

As I pulled up outside my house, a text message came through. I had no doubt it would be her again, but at least I could read a text message without falling out with it. I could read it and ignore it or act upon it. But first, I was going to put the kettle on and have a cuppa; she could wait until I was ready.

The kettle was coming to the boil as I opened the message. *Dave's been run over* was all it said. I never got the cup of tea.

In panic, I punched her number into the phone, and she answered it on the second ring.

Before she could even say hello, I blurted out, "What's happened, Sharron? Is he OK? Is he alive?" All the questions tumbled out at once.

When I left a millisecond gap in my deluge, Sharron managed to squeeze a word in. "Whoa, slow down. Yes, he's alive but they've had to keep him in; X-ray him and see the extent of the damage."

"Oh God! Will he die? What've they said," I was still in panic; I really loved that dog.

"Calm down, Jake. Like I said they're treating him right now as I wait."

"You're at the vets now? I'm coming right over."

"OK, OK, Jake, but you really must try to calm down. I'll be waiting for you."

No more words were needed. I ended the call, grabbed my jacket and car keys and ran straight out of the door, ignoring the post on the mat that had arrived seconds earlier.

The vet was only a ten minute drive away—everything in a town of this size was no more than a ten-minute drive away. I pulled into the sparsely populated carpark and hurriedly parked up, just about keeping to a single marked bay but not quite at a square angle. I didn't care, I just wanted to see how Dave was.

As soon as I entered the building, I located Sharron, standing alone, staring out of a side window. "Sharron!" I called in one of those whispered shouts one uses in such situations.

She turned towards me, and I could see by the redness of her eyes that she had been crying. I put my arms around her and hugged her tightly. She didn't resist. If there's one thing that will bring warring factions together, then it's the love of a canine. Perhaps, a dog should be the international symbol for peace instead of a dove.

Her tears started to flow again, and she sobbed, "They've said nothing yet."

"It'll be OK," I tried to comfort her but couldn't know how OK it would be.

"Mrs Kolman?" the vet, a tall, under-fed looking red head who appeared to be straight out of college, came across to us.

"How is he?" I asked.

The vet addressed us both, "Well, he's got some broken bones, but as far as we can tell, at this time, there are no internal injuries. We've operated on him so he'll be quite traumatised. We're going to have to keep him in for a few days, just to be on the safe side, but you should soon have your bouncing bundle back to normal."

We both breathed a simultaneous sigh of relief. "Thank you, thank you," I blurted out.

"Can we see him?" Sharron asked.

"Yes, of course you can. He'll still be groggy though; from the anaesthetic."

We were led through one white door into an eight by eight room with an examination table, a small sink and a strong smell of disinfectant, and then through another identical one before emerging into a corridor. We followed this for about twenty feet and were then ushered into a larger room with cages, some containing dogs but most being empty. Dave was in the one at the far end. He couldn't even attempt to stand with both front legs potted. A large expanse of shaved skin revealed a zip of stitches on his side where they had put him back together.

Sharron and I automatically moved closer together. I put my arm around her, and she leaned against me, subconsciously comforting each other and giving each other strength.

Dave's tail feebly wagged as we cooed and comforted him for a few minutes before leaving him to rest. Sharron had calmed down considerably, and I felt much better now that I had seen him. I took my arm from around her waist as she removed her head from my shoulder, the invisible wedge reinserting itself between us, both of us feeling the awkwardness that hadn't existed only seconds earlier.

At reception, we were informed that with the treatment Dave had received so far, plus the necessary overnight stays and the drugs that had been administered, then the final bill would be pretty large.

"Do you have pet insurance?" The receptionist asked. We both shook our heads as this had been an expense we hadn't previously believed to be essential.

"We can sort you out a payment plan if you like, and you can pay, say, a hundred pounds today?"

It seemed wrong, somehow, bartering over the dog, a family member who we both loved deeply.

"That won't be necessary. I'll see to it," I said as I took my credit card from my wallet, playing the gallant hero.

"No, it's OK," Sharron curtly butted in, "He's my dog, and I'll pay the bills."

I opened my mouth to object but thought better of it as the anger within me began to rapidly rise to the surface. Instead, I turned around and marched out of the building.

Normal hostilities had quickly been resumed.

I lit a cigarette and waited for Sharron to emerge. As she did so, I went straight for her, "What the hell was that all about!"

Sharron remained calm, almost aloof, "Like I said, he's my dog, not yours, and I'll look after him."

"Huh, if you'd been doing that, we wouldn't be here in the first place."

"Don't you go blaming me for this. It was an accident. And besides, if you'd mended that hole in the fence I'd pestered you about for months then he wouldn't have got out."

Sharron certainly knew where to stick the knife, which nerves to tweak.

"Can't lover boy do such things now that it's his house? Or is he too busy standing in front of the mirror?" I fought back.

"What he gets up to is none of your business."

Sharron then attempted to take control of the exchange, swinging it around to the subject she wanted to talk about. She had always been good at that. "So you're willing to put up cash for a dog, pay whatever it takes, but you won't give me any. Typical; no wonder I wanted you out. You always thought more of that dog than you did of me."

"I thought more of stray dogs than I did of you," I knew it was a cheap, petty shot but it made me feel better, "And doesn't it tell you something about yourself?"

Before she could respond, I returned the subject back to Dave. "And he's not your dog he's our dog." Then I continued with the insults, "Perhaps, if you spent a little less time on your back with your legs in the air, then you'd be able to look after him properly."

I regretted it as soon as the words had tumbled out of my mouth. Even when we had been together Sharron was always able to bring out the worst in me; and she hadn't lost the knack.

She slapped me hard across the face causing a sharp crack like a gunshot, making the whole left side of my face tingle with hot pins and needles and temporarily disorientating me.

I dropped the half spent cigarette and, now seething, took a threatening pace towards her, my hands clenching and unclenching into fists. Right at that moment, I so much wanted to punch her, but I drew back because I was certain that if I did then I wouldn't stop.

Sharron took a step back, the fear etched across her face. I turned away from her, firmly believing that if I didn't, then I would have killed her. As I stalked back to my car, I spat through my teeth, "You'd better look after him properly or I'll come and take him off you."

Sharron was too shocked to respond. She just stood there in the middle of the carpark where she remained before disappearing from my rear view mirror.

I had just about managed to control the rage. But the episodes were becoming more frequent, and I was exploding more readily. How long would it be before I lost the ability to control them? It would only happen the once, I knew that; there would be no second chances. The inevitable was creeping forever closer, the unstoppable force appeared to have no immovable object to even threaten its progress.

Arriving home with no recollection of how I had actually got there, I trudged back up my path towards the front door, slowly slid the key into the lock and opened it. I picked up the mail from the mat before closing the door and shuffled through the array of advertising junk on the way to the kitchen. I switched the kettle on before extracting the only worthwhile item from the pile. The rest I put into the recycling bin.

This one letter was from my employers.

That's all I need, I thought as I stared at the envelope, knowing it would not be good news—experience told me these letters never were. It was hand written on official, headed paper. I scanned down it and learned that they wished to see me the following day and that the union would be present. That fact plus the urgency of the appointment—less than twenty-four hours' notice—confirmed my belief that they weren't calling me in for a bravery award or anything similar.

Ten o'clock the meeting was scheduled for. I considered calling and cancelling it as they hadn't followed proper procedures, or lying by claiming to have a hospital appointment, just to be awkward. But I had enough problems piling up without adding another loose end untied. Besides, if my rage attack was imminent, I couldn't think of a better place for it to happen.

I sat down in the lounge with my cup of tea, still staring at the letter as though this would reveal its secrets. *What could it be about,* I wondered. It had to have something to do with my absence, but what made it so important that the union had to be present?

Then it all came together, like when you've been staring at jigsaw pieces for ages and suddenly realise where they fit or when the lights come back on after a power cut.

Chapter 14

The man in the red Fiesta; I *had* seen him before, just the once, maybe a year or so earlier. He had entered the delivery office as we were about to go out on delivery. Postman Craig Joinerson was never seen again after that day; he was sacked. Fiesta man, Gerry or Graham Ibis, or something like that, was there to do the dirty work. He was from the Investigation Branch.

So that confirmed the seriousness of it all. But I wasn't frightened or worried. No, I was seething. *How dare they!* They knew I had been injured and had my sick note. Well, I was ready for them. Rage attack or not, I was ready to give them the full benefit of my recent tribulations.

I slammed the tea cup down onto the coffee table causing the dregs to slop onto its surface the liquid rapidly running to the edge before dripping onto the floral patterned carpet. My mind immediately shot back to the decorator's attack on me, with his blood cascading over his van's bonnet to mingle with the florae below, their colours as vivid then as the memory was now.

Well, they wouldn't be sacking me. I was ready for a fight. Tomorrow couldn't come quick enough. I snatched up the cup and took it into the kitchen. "How dare they!" I growled through gritted teeth and then threw the cup across the room with such force that it smashed against the wall spraying its fragments half way around the kitchen.

Clearing up the mess did not pacify my mood, not one bit. It was a good job it was too late to go down there now. There'd be no managers there at this time, just a few collection staff. If there had been somebody there for me to see, then I would definitely have done something worthy of getting myself sacked.

Damn them! Damn them all, I thought as I took a beer from the fridge, hesitated, then exchanged it for a four pack.

Damn them, I thought again as I lit up another cigarette.

Falling asleep on the sofa could easily become an awkward and uncomfortable habit, I pondered as the night's cold woke me from my stupor. But right at that moment, I wasn't in the mood for any lifestyle changes. I didn't really see the point as I probably didn't have much of a life left to style.

The mood had yet again lingered, dragging on into the next day; Thursday. How much my life had changed from one Thursday sunrise to the next. The dull thud at the back of my head would soon disappear, I hoped, once I got out into the fresh air. It wasn't a proper hangover. I'd only had the four cans of lager, but the events of the past week were bound to have added to the ache.

My temperament was again swinging from one extreme to the other. Happy to see the glorious early morning spring sunshine cascading through the kitchen window to dance upon the floor, furious when I thought of the meeting ahead, the dark shadows of foreboding trudging relentlessly through the graveyard within my mind. Still swinging but the pendulum had been tilted further to one side and the anger was becoming deeper and more frequent, any reverie diminishing towards the horizon.

The sunshine vanished too, as I set off for the inquisition, replaced by the all too familiar cold windy rain rattling through the trees, drenching me and washing away my hopes. Once again, I was towing the gloom around with me, like a ball and chain, affecting the mood all around me.

Well, damn them. If I'm going to go down, I'm not going down alone, I thought, as I marched purposefully towards my destination.

As I entered the delivery office, I was met by a man who introduced himself as my union representative. He was not a person whom I recognised, but he would be representing me, as he explained. "It's John's day off. I'll be standing in for him."

Kevin, I learned his name to be, hardly looked old enough to be a postman let alone someone supposedly looking after people's lives. *John's day off,* very convenient; what a stitch up. I again considered cancelling—hell, I knew I had plenty of grounds to do so—but no, I was more than ready to deal with this.

This time, I didn't bother with the customary knock on the half open door but just marched straight in and stopped in the middle of the room, glaring at my manager.

"Take a seat please, Jake." Barry, leaning back casually in his chair, was clearly undaunted by my demeanour.

I took a couple of deep breaths whilst pondering his request then took one of the two chairs directly across the desk from him. Kevin took the other one. Seated next to my manager, on his right was the man from the Fiesta.

Barry introduced him, "This is Jeremy, Jeremy Ides. He's with the Investigation Branch; the fraud division to be more specific."

I just sat there, silent, staring, lips pursed, my breathing rate increasing, the volcano within me priming itself for eruption. I gripped the sides of my seat to channel the anger and to stop me from leaping out of it.

"Jeremy's job is to ensure nobody is cheating the business. No one is making, shall we say, false claims. For example, claiming they are unable to work through sickness or injury. To this end he has, err, been checking up…"

"Stalking me! Victimising me!" I blurted out. I could contain myself no longer. I thumped my fist down on the desk, scattering papers into more of a mess than they originally had been.

"No, he's just doing his job. He checks up on many people." Barry was still remaining calm.

I was not, "This is Harassment! You've got my damn sick note; you know what happened to me and you get this, this piece of..." I looked the investigations' official up and down unsure of exactly what to call him.

"Now, now Jake there's no need to resort to name calling. Like I said, it's his job. He's just trying to make sure things are done properly."

"Properly? Properly? You call this properly? Right," I took another deep breath, trying to remain logical and as controlled as possible, "Where shall I start. One, insufficient time to consult with my union official; two, insufficient notice given and three," my voice had now become virtually a shout, "Three! Read the damn sick note! Are you a qualified doctor?"

I paused for a couple of seconds, glowering from one to the other, waiting for a reply. Of course none came.

And my representative just sat there, like a tailor's dummy, saying nothing.

I pushed my chair back sharply causing it to fall over. "We're done here," I said firmly with a little more self-control.

"Err, hang on…" Kevin was unsure what to say but must have known he ought to do something.

"Oh, you're still awake then? Fat lot of use you've been!"

"Now, let's calm down a minute. Why don't you come and sit back down, Jake?" Barry stuttered. He was struggling to keep the meeting under control, and he knew it.

I stopped where I was but didn't take my seat and looked him directly in the eye, "No, I won't. You don't realise what effect this is all having on me. You haven't got a clue." And with that I crossed purposefully to the door, pulled it open and turned back to face them.

"You've got my doctor's note. Any more of this, crap, and I won't be responsible for my actions. And if I so much as think I see him again," I pointed at Ides, and looked at him as if he were something the dog had deposited, "Then I'll be getting in touch with my solicitor. Do you understand?!"

There was no response, and I turned back towards the door and slammed it as I left. I knew there could be repercussions to my actions, but, right at that moment, I didn't care. If I had stopped in that room a moment longer, I would have exploded.

Seconds later Kevin came trotting out after me, "Jake, Jake, wait!"

I halted at the exit to the building, "Oh, you've decided to do something at last. You should have known they couldn't treat me like that, but you did nothing. You're a total waste of space."

"I…I…"

"Don't bother Kevin. You're as bad as they are!" I spun round and strutted out, the union rep. following in my wake.

"No, wait come back in," he called putting his hand on my shoulder.

I stopped abruptly and whirled around to face him, my nostrils flaring, "Take your greasy little paw off me," I spat, peeling his hand away and pushing him roughly back towards the doors. "Touch me again, and I'll break your arm!" My daggered blazing eyes got the message across more than the actual words.

Kevin didn't follow me as I left the premises.

I put one foot in front of the other, not sure exactly where I was heading, going over and over the brief meeting that had just taken place, trying but failing to control my emotions, clenching and unclenching my fists.

My phone buzzed in my pocket; it was Sharron, again. I was just in the mood for her, so this time I answered it, "What!"

Sharron knew me all too well and ignored my retort, "I was going to see how Dave's doing. If you'd like to come too…"

She allowed the sentence to trail off, not pressuring me, giving me time to make a decision. She knew how much I loved that Labrador, and I appreciated her offer. For once, for the first time since we had split, Sharron had actually had a calming influence on me. Realising that, shook me almost as much as my meeting had.

"Yeah, sorry, thanks," was all I could mutter.

"Shall I pick you up? Where are you?"

Pulling my thoughts together I managed a more asserted response, "No, that's OK, thanks. I've just left work. I'll meet you there."

"Twenty minutes?"

"Yeah, that's good for me," I paused before adding, "And thanks, Sharron." My helter-skelter mood swings taking another rapid undulation, the pressure relenting.

She didn't reply immediately, eventually saying in a softened tone, "You're welcome, Jake."

We arrived at the vets together, me on foot and her in what I presumed to be *his* Volkswagen.

"Hi, how are doing?" I greeted her and she allowed me to peck her on the cheek.

"I'm fine thanks. Shall we go and see how Dave's doing?"

Once more we left the awkwardness outside.

Dave was a lot livelier than when I had last seen him, and the vet's assistant, Patricia, told us everything was fine and Dave was responding as expected. "You should be able to take him home in a couple of days Mr and Mrs Kolman." Neither of us put her right on that one. I supposed, legally at least, that is who we still were.

After petting the dog for a while, we left, together and in a much more cordial mood than previously. "Can I give you a lift home?" Sharron offered.

This time I accepted wondering if this new-found civility would last. I hoped it would. Prior to the last couple of weeks, I was not the sort to feel at ease with confrontation.

As she drove we talked, like normal human beings. "We still have finances to discuss, you know." Sharron was calm and friendly, not demanding.

"I know, I know," I responded in a similar tone, "I can't deal with it right now, but I will see you right." I leaned across and squeezed her arm reassuringly.

She glanced over and smiled, "I know you will, Jake."

"It's just that I have so much going on at the moment, but I will be fair to you. Sorry for the way I've been a lately. You know what I'm like; you know me better than anyone."

"I know, Jake," she smiled, took her hand off the steering wheel and patted my arm, "I'm sorry too; for everything." And I could tell she meant it, as I knew her better than I had ever known anyone.

Silence then fell between us until we reached my house. "Do you want to come in for a cuppa?" I asked, not just out of politeness.

Sharron hesitated, thinking over the offer, before replying almost reluctantly, "Thanks, Jake, but I really ought to be getting off. Some other time," she held my arm a little longer than was necessary to show she really meant it, but that now was perhaps not the appropriate time.

I pecked her on the cheek and she smiled at me as I left the vehicle.

My emotions were up in the air yet again. I was all over the place, not knowing where I stood with anything. So much was spinning around in my head; Sharron, Dave, Suzanne, work and the attacks, always the attacks. The grim reaper, just taking a tea break, was forever waiting around the next corner.

As I entered the cold unwelcoming dwelling, a text message came through, from Suzanne. After my amiable afternoon with Sharron I was not quite as exhilarated as I otherwise might have been. Nevertheless, I was glad to hear from her and only hoped it would be good news. I hadn't had a lot of that lately.

It was only a short message,

I have an update. Hope it will help calm you. Will call you tonight. Try not to worry. Love Suzanne xxx.

Suzanne seemed to have this way of saying 'don't worry' in a way that always made me worry more. The fewer words she used, the more I dissected them, reading anything and everything into them. She had an update—what was that? She hoped it would calm me—why? Was it good news or was she just trying to stop me from fretting? The message seemed to say so little and yet so much.

I supposed, I would have to do as she said; wait and try not to worry. *OK xxx,* I replied before locking the front door to keep the outside world outside, along with mister Reaper.

The TV evening news dropped another bomb on my already fragmented life. Carmen Corradon, a national news reporter for the BBC, outside our hospital, stared straight into my eyes, and informed me, "Not only have the police confirmed the link between the recent spate of attacks in this normally quiet Midlands town, but they also believe they have found the origin."

What I already knew was only being publicly confirmed, but the real aftershock came with her confirmation of Suzanne's theory, "The first incident appears to have occurred at this very hospital," Carmen gestured over her shoulder to the building in her backdrop, "When a Carlos Mendes, for no apparent reason, went on a rampage. Mr Mendes had just returned from a holiday in Brazil, where it is believed he picked up a virus; a virus that was fatal to him and many others he came into contact with."

So there it was, emblazoned on national television in front of my eyes. The facts I knew to be true but had been trying to keep hidden from myself. There was no point in denial now.

Speculation had become fact. Like when you have all the lottery numbers, it doesn't really hit you until you have the cheque in your hand.

I was stunned at the sudden lurch forward in this whole saga. A virus, like Suzanne had suspected, had predicted; or had she known all along? And why had she not told me of Carlos' trip? Why had she not told me where this was all leading?

Suzanne always seemed so concerned, always willing to help in any way she could. But could I completely trust her? I hadn't known her long enough to make a calculated assessment. My intuition told me to have faith in her, but I couldn't rely on that, not at the moment. I'd always considered myself a pretty good judge of people, until Sharron's bombshell was dropped those few short months ago. I had had absolutely no idea about her and that thing she was carrying on with. The person I should have known best, thought I knew the best in the whole world, proved I knew nothing at all. My perceptions, discernment and opinions of people, especially those I knew well, was all over the place. I could quite easily become paranoid at times. For now, though, I felt I had no other options than to place my trust in her.

Carmen continued, not allowing me enough time to process the enormity of her words. "The hospital is working furiously to pinpoint the virus in order to formulate a cure and ask everyone to remain calm. The police say they are working closely with the hospital in order to contain the situation. I have here Chief Inspector..."

Her words shuffled into the back ground, not audible to me, drowned out by the cacophony of my thoughts.

Chapter 15

Don't worry? How could I not. I had so many questions, most of which, I dreaded the answers to.

I needed to hear from Suzanne. Her text said she would call me, but I found the waiting almost unbearable as the anxiety grew and grew.

I punched the 'off' button on the TV remote, unable and unwilling to take any more. I glared at my phone, not daring to pick it up from the coffee table, as though it was booby-trapped; scared what it might do to me.

Resisting the temptation to call Suzanne, like a junkie defying his next fix, I retreated into my usual safe haven—beer and cigarettes. Two of each. Later, I was still pacing the lounge, willing her to call, dreading it at the same time. I picked up one of the two remaining cans, stared at it for a few seconds before deciding something more was required. I put the can down on the table next to the phone, went into the kitchen and extracted my emergency bottle of vodka from the cupboard under the sink. Cracking the seal, I raised it to my lips, hesitated momentarily and then took two long gulps.

I choked and spluttered as the effect bit into the back of my throat, but it did the trick, quickly working its magic. I wobbled, feeling light-headed, and had to grab hold of the sink. It took a few seconds to steady myself, and then I raised the bottle again. But I stopped it at my lips and decided to get a glass instead. It just seemed a bit more civilised, more acceptable and created the illusion that I was in control of it. Taking them both back into the lounge, I half-filled the glass and waited, eyes transfixed on the telephone, eye lids feeling heavy and my vision blurring.

Beep-bip, beep-bip. I sat bolt upright, snorting myself awake, disturbed by the phone; but not with the expected call.

The tone informed me it was shutting down as the battery was dying.

I cursed under my breath, whipped it up off the table and went in search of the charger. Having plugged it in, a few seconds later, it told me I had missed a call, more than an hour ago; from Suzanne.

Under the alcohol-induced confusion, I hadn't realised I must have fallen asleep. Again I cursed, out loud this time, as I found it was gone midnight and too late to return Suzanne's call. Once more my weakness for the booze had let me down. I resolved that, in the unlikely event that I should survive all this, I would definitely quit the fags and drink; well, at least get them firmly under control.

I texted Suzanne an apology, telling her I would speak to her tomorrow before trudging up to the bedroom. My head was starting to pound, and I collapsed onto the bed quickly descending into a deep and uninterrupted sleep. Deep, but not very long, as it was still dark when my shivering body dragged consciousness back into me; and my head was still thumping away. "When the drumming stops, the danger begins," so those old westerns used to tell us.

Nevertheless, I opened a window for fresh air and took two aspirin in an attempt to banish the beat. Climbing under the duvet for warmth and comfort, I closed my eyes in the hope that sleep would again take me away. This time my slumber was neither deep nor uninterrupted, and I was glad when the sun's rays began forcing their way through the curtains.

Still angry with myself for the previous evening, I determined that today I would be much more positive. I would act instead of wimping out. If I was going down, it wouldn't be without a fight. I would call Suzanne as soon as I had had a cuppa and to hell with the consequences. I could hide from the truth no longer. The tide seemed to be flowing more rapidly now, and I had to go with it, even if it meant crashing onto the rapids.

I switched the TV news on while I drank my tea and munched on a stale piece of toast. The same report was still running and with no more details. It was as though my life was in a loop, just like the news, each new day the same as the previous.

As I finished the sparse breakfast, my attention turned towards the telephone. I sprang back and gasped as it rang. It was as though it could tell I was watching it, issuing a warning as a snake would with a hiss.

Plucking up the courage, I answered it on the fourth ring, my earlier determination was already starting to waver. It was Suzanne, "I've just seen the news." She said.

"Yeah me too. It's like you said." I knew I sounded defeated, but I didn't care; my life was in free fall, and I couldn't see any way of stopping it. "Look Suzanne, what's happening here? What am I missing? What aren't you telling me?" She was still my one and only hope.

"I think I might be onto something. I can't really explain over the phone. I've got one or two loose ends to tie up. Try not to worry; I'll call you later."

"Try not to worry," I couldn't hide the irony from my voice. "You keep saying that, but everything I hear is telling me the opposite. I'm drowning here, Suzanne."

"Oh, Jake there's always hope. You may not be as doomed as you seem determined to think you are. I can't go over it all now, but consider this. Not all the victims—those treated at hospital anyway—have gone on to attack people. Not all have gone on to rage. Some have recovered with absolutely no after effects."

I was totally stunned into silence by Suzanne's revelation.

"You still there, Jake? Hello?"

"Yeah, yes; how; what?" I was hardly able to put a sentence together, but eventually managed to shake myself back into some sort of order. "What have you found? Who hasn't raged? How...Suzanne?" I felt like I was pleading for my life.

"Jake, there's not been enough victims to reach a proper conclusion, but some have definitely not raged; in fact, two of the nine who were treated in hospital have totally recovered."

"But...how?" It was a lifeline for me; one small chink of light in the absolute darkness I had been descending into. It was the one and only sign that the tide might just possibly be turning. It was all I had to hang on to.

"Must dash, I'll call you later."

And with that, she had gone, leaving me hanging there alone with my thoughts. Again it seemed all I could do was to wait, while my life, my future, was decided by others, completely out of my control. It was not a feeling I wanted to get used to.

I sat there on the sofa, time was immaterial as I tried to work it all out. But I had insufficient information to reach any conclusion and just ended up going round in circles. Did I have a chance of survival; a future? How would I know? Would it all soon be over? Why do some go on to rage and others not? What was the deciding factor, the magic potion that would guarantee me life?

That last unanswered question was, of course, the vital one; the only one that really mattered and not only for me. But right at that moment, I didn't really care much what it meant for anyone else.

Things were certainly moving forward but still weren't producing any answers. I couldn't quite decide whether that bit of hope was a good thing or a bad one. I had begun to come to terms with my impending demise, but now what? Neither could I decide which was worse—the not knowing or the lack of control of the situation.

The post falling through the letterbox with a dull slap hoisted me away from my thoughts. I went and retrieved the familiar batch of junk which this time contained nothing of any interest, just bin-fodder.

I must have cogitated for quite some time because as I went into the kitchen to bin the unwanted items the wall clock told me it was lunch time. I couldn't eat, though, and settled for a coffee and a cigarette instead.

And I switched on the TV news. My life was becoming one endless cycle—cigarettes, cuppas, booze and TV news, always bad. This was no different as another grenade exploded at me, straight out from the High Definition screen. Another series of attacks had taken place and the news team were 'live' at one of these, in nearby Sheffield.

It was a scene of total carnage. There were at least half a dozen bodies strewn about the pavement on camera behind the reporter. At first, it looked like the aftermath of a terrorist attack, like a bombsite, except there was no debris, only bodies, bodies and rivers of blood. I could hear the wail of emergency vehicles arriving in the background.

What was equally as stunning was that the whole scenario was spreading—this was the first time an attack had been reported outside of our town. Sheffield was nearly twenty miles away and had a much larger capacity to propagate the virus and therefore a much smaller chance of containing it. It had mushroomed from looking for a needle in a hay—bale to one in a hay-field. A solution had to be found and quickly.

Ironically, I thought, it would pretty soon provide Suzanne with the additional data she required to fine-tune her theories. This gave me no comfort whatsoever.

I stayed glued to the news all afternoon, awaiting any new information, but none came. The same report just kept repeating over and over, looping three times each hour, hour after hour. It took me back to when I stumbled upon the live newscast of the 9/11 events, the thoughts making me shudder with shock and horror just as I had done then. Although, this was nowhere near as big as those tragic events (not yet anyway), it was a lot closer to home, and I was infinitely more personally involved. Then, after hours of time-freeze, things developed rapidly.

Seven fresh incidents had been reported by the time Suzanne called me to say she was on her way over. They included a couple more in Sheffield, one in Doncaster, another in Rotherham and the rest once again here in our town.

Yes, things were certainly moving forward now. After nearly a week of going round in circles and getting nowhere, treading water, waiting for something, anything. Waiting and hoping that something would turn up. Well, that something seemed to have, at last, arrived and with a colossal bang, and the shock waves would go on for some time, of this I was sure. Viruses don't just disappear.

A determined and frantic knocking at the front door drew me away from the news report. As I opened the door, Suzanne stood there her eyes glazed, her brow furrowed. I guessed she had been listening to the news on her car radio.

No words were spoken; she just gave me a long, lingering hug, as much for herself as for me.

"Come in, I'll put the kettle on," I said as I ushered her into the lounge, trying to at least sound calm and in control—it was the man's position to do this wasn't it? A role I had, so far, miserably failed to fulfil.

123

After what we had been through, dealing with this for the past week and more, we quickly became anaesthetised to the events on the screen. I turned the TV off, and we transferred our attention to our small segment in this horror story, knowing that we perhaps held the key to all this. We had been involved from the virtual outset and were therefore, way ahead of anybody else.

"So, what have you got?" I took the lead, desperate to know if I had a chance or not.

"You must bear in mind that we have only limited data; not all the facts. You must realise not all those who were attacked would have gone to hospital. Those with what they considered to be minor injuries and those who didn't want to be stuck in A&E for hours wouldn't have gone. Would you have gone had you not broken your arm or someone hadn't called an ambulance for you?"

She had a point. I probably wouldn't have, but I said nothing.

"As I told you earlier, two of the nine victims have fully recovered. I wasn't sure, obviously, if their injuries had involved blood contact with their attackers."

"And?" I was determined to hurry Suzanne along now, eager to know the truth.

"And yes, they both did. Both victims were badly bitten, needing stitches, and their attackers were a bloody mess at the time."

"But how can you tell? How can you be certain?"

"Well, when I pushed you off the phone this morning, I said I was in a rush. It was because I had arranged to go and see them. They were both happy to help, still a little traumatised, of course, but relieved to have survived."

I mulled this over for a while, considering these new facts. "How do we know that they won't go on to attack? They might just not have done so yet."

"Erm, that brings me to my second point. And you might not like this one, Jake. I'm sorry…"

"Please go on Suzanne. You must tell me. I need to know, whatever it is. I have to know everything."

"As you'll have seen, it appears that my theory about this being a virus is true. As we noted earlier, these attacks happened in clusters. There hasn't been enough data to be exact, but from what we have, it would seem that the incubation period is about ten days."

Suzanne allowed this to sink in while I worked out the maths; I could tell by the expression on her face that she had already done so.

I counted on my fingers, "…nine, ten." I ended as I ticked off the thumb on my right hand. "Saturday…Tomorrow…"

I looked up from my offending digits to Suzanne, her tight-lipped, down-turned mouth, furrowed brow and damp eyes betraying her knowledge of the inevitable.

"Well, at least we'll know by the end of the weekend, one way or another." My words may have been positive, cheery even, but it was not the way I was feeling; like when you're in the dentist, and you really want the toothache to go away and have the culprit removed—then they call out your name.

Suzanne leaned forward and took my hands in hers. I could see she was scared, for me—not as scared as I was—but I still wanted to somehow reassure her. All I could do was squeeze her hand in an affectionate comforting way and attempt some sort of smile.

"Why didn't they rage? You know, the two survivors." I broke the moment with the obvious question. Suzanne didn't know, I could tell, because she wouldn't have looked so crestfallen if she had the answer to that, the one question that really mattered.

"I don't know yet. But there must be a reason, I just haven't found it yet."

"We don't have a lot of time to solve this, you know." I stated the obvious.

"I know, I know." Suzanne took my hand in hers once more. "That's why, I thought we'd go over to the factory, tomorrow, early. All the stuff is on my work's computer. We could go over it together. You might see something I have missed."

"I'm not sure that's a good idea," I frowned, "If I'm going to go berserk, I don't want you anywhere near. Maybe we should just lock me up somewhere for the weekend and wait and see." It was not what I really wanted but thought it was perhaps the best solution for everyone.

"No, Jake. If there is just a glimmer of hope, I want you to be there with me; if we find the reason; if there is anything we can do to stop this happening to you. This started with our factory, and I'm staying on it until the end."

I didn't quite like the finality of her statement. "OK, we'll do as you say then." I gave in. "But if I start to go, if there is any sign that I'm losing it, then you must get as far away from me as possible."

I raised my eyebrows inviting a response from Suzanne, needing her agreement to this.

She considered this ultimatum for a few moments before reluctantly nodding her concurrence.

Chapter 16

My phone rang, and the display told me Sharron was calling. I couldn't deal with her now, whether it was good or bad news. I declined the call, and this time she didn't call back or text me, so it couldn't have been that important.

"Right, I'll pick you up at eight tomorrow morning," Suzanne rose to leave and we went to the front door hand in hand. "Try and get some sleep and try not—"

I cut her short, "Please don't tell me not to worry. Every time you say that, there always appears something new to worry about." I smiled and rested my forehead against hers, just for a few seconds.

Still holding hands, I opened the door for her. We stepped outside, hugged and she kissed me on the cheek. Emotions were running high, and we kissed, lips to lips, holding the moment for several seconds and enjoying the respite from the turmoil; it seemed the natural thing to do. She broke free from me, smiled and went to her car. We said nothing, and she turned and slowly waved before getting into the vehicle. As she drove off, I raised my hand, holding it in mid-wave as she disappeared into the cooling night.

All the downstairs lights were on in my house, but an impenetrable darkness descended on it as I closed the front door, retreating into my own diminishing world.

Sleep came surprisingly easily, and I awoke early and refreshed to the chatter of birds as the sun streamed through the curtains. I pushed the window open, allowing the florally fragranced clean spring air to circulate into the bedroom. Slowly drawing in the delightful freshness invigorated my mood and my face was overcome by a broad good-to-be-alive grin. The depth of my slumber had momentarily short-circuited my memory, like when the lights flash off and straight back on suggesting an imminent power cut that never materialises. Laying back down on the bed, atop the duvet, I drank in the whole blissful atmosphere.

As my brain, playing catch-up with my body, started to rouse the sledgehammer of my demise hit me, and it felt all the more brutal because of the brilliant mood I had awoken to. I lay there trying to find a way out of the bottomless pit I had been thrown into.

Eventually, I dragged my body off the bed unable to delay my fate any longer. This would be the day my destiny would be decided. It was no use trying to be positive or brave or, well, anything really. Everything was still completely out of my control, and fate would do what fate would do.

The only things I could influence were the practical ones, like getting showered and dressed, having breakfast, lighting a cigarette, drinking coffee. All these things I did, but in a trance-like robotic fashion. And then I waited for Suzanne.

Only the chatter of birds broke the weekend silence until my consciousness was invaded by the sound of a car drawing to a halt outside, followed by two short toots on its horn. I pulled the front curtains slightly apart and saw the silver Mercedes waiting kerbside. Suzanne had arrived, right on eight o'clock, just as she had promised.

As I grabbed my jacket the telephone rang. Of course it was Sharron. I let it continue, considering whether or not to answer it. I wouldn't be able to deal with whatever she might tell me, good or bad. And I didn't want to spoil the improvement in our relationship from the last time we had met. Sharron made the decision for me, and the phone stopped its pleading. A text message quickly followed,

Just to let you know, Dave is fine. Coming home Monday. Call me xx.

I stared at the message as it hit me that I might not even be here Monday. I didn't know what to text back—*OK*, or *fine, I'll call you later* or…what? Nothing seemed quite appropriate. So I didn't respond, but put the phone into my pocket and gathered up my cigarettes and door keys. As I went to exit the building, I paused and took the phone back out, hesitated, then threw it onto the sofa. That was one problem out of the way for now.

Climbing into the passenger seat beside Suzanne, I greeted her with a "Good morning" and a peck on the cheek. As always she looked and smelled immaculate. For some reason, I couldn't quite figure, this made what lay ahead seem a little less daunting. After all, it would have no bearing whatsoever on anything the day had in store for me; I could be dead and gone before the sun rose again.

The atmosphere within was strained as we both realised the enormous importance of what we might discover, even if it was nothing. No words were exchanged in the ten-minute trip to the factory, the radio remained switched off, the silence empathising with the ambiance, magnifying the apprehensive mood.

I passed the time staring out of the window, not really taking much in but noticing the contrast with a week day. Had this been a weekday, the streets would have been bustling with people going about their working lives, kids on the way to school, traffic choc-a-bloc as workers made their way to their places of employment. But today the town was almost deserted, like virtually every other Saturday at such an early hour. For most people, it was just another weekend; but not for me. The world didn't reflect this, was oblivious to my predicament and this just seemed wrong.

All too soon, we arrived at the factory gates. Suzanne wound down her window and flashed her security card against the pad at the automatic barrier causing it to dutifully raise for us to enter. She waved to the security guard seated at the window in his gatehouse. He returned the gesture and we proceeded.

Just like the town, the place was virtually deserted. There were only two vehicles occupying the twenty-odd carpark spaces at the front of the main entrance. I knew from my experience on the post that there was a similar sized parking area around the back, near to the goods inwards department, and that this would be similarly deserted.

Suzanne drew into the spot designated for her, marked S DEERING, some twenty metres from the front doors. We remained seated for a few seconds then looked at each other, smiled a tight lipped grin of resignation and simultaneously took a deep breath.

"Shall we go in then?" Suzanne was the first to speak, beating me to it with exactly the same words I was about to use.

As we walked towards the entrance, the early morning spring sunshine cast long shadows, ours eagerly leading us forwards.

Suzanne entered the revolving doors first, gently pushing them. They spun slowly, smoothly, silently with much practised ease. As I followed, I could see a tall man standing at the bottom of a staircase to our right across the high ceilinged, marble-floored entrance lobby. As we went in, our footfalls echoed around the cavernous space. We headed towards the stairs, but I wasn't sure if it was to ascend them or to talk to the tall man. I remained a few paces behind Suzanne, taking in the old fashioned but impressive hall. Directly opposite the entrance was a polished oak desk, some ten metres long. To the left of this were double doors marked STAFF ONLY, again made of oak, presumably, leading into the factory. To the right were those stairs, marble, sweeping round, anti-clockwise in a semicircle and onto a glass fronted corridor which ran above the main desk and out of sight beyond the hall below.

As we approached the man, I recognised him as the driver of the Rolls Royce who had taken Henry to the hospital on the day I had first met Suzanne.

He strode confidently towards us. He was holding what looked like a computer memory card which he slipped into his jacket pocket, freeing his hands to embrace Suzanne.

"Morning Chas," Suzanne politely greeted him, kissing him on the cheek. As they hugged, he fixed me with that shark-like stare of his, once more sending a shiver down my spine.

"Don't often see you here on a Saturday Suzanne." It was not exactly a question from Chas, but it invited an explanation nonetheless. His eyes never left me, holding me there, preventing me from moving.

"I'm just here to catch up on some work. This's Jake, he's helping me." Suzanne responded matter-of-factly.

"Pleased to meet you, Jake," his words were friendly but the feeling wasn't in them. Chas offered his hand which I took, gripping in a firm handshake. His grip was firmer, but controlled; not too tight as to hurt but tight enough to let me know who was in control. And all the time, those eyes.

"See you later," Suzanne ended the moment and set off up the stairs. Chas released his grip and strode across the lobby towards the doors that led into the factory. As we neared the top of the sweeping staircase, Chas paused before passing through his doors, half turned, and once again our eyes briefly met.

"I don't think he likes me," my whisper echoed around the hall, making me jump. I was pleased to see Chas had already gone through his doors, and that they had shut behind him.

Suzanne looked back over her shoulder. "It's just his way. We used to have a thing, briefly; a while back. He's OK really; harmless enough."

Well, she knew him better than me, but I wasn't at all convinced. I'd have to take her word for him being OK, but I'd reserve my judgement on the harmless bit.

"What happened?" I asked, as much to make conversation as gain knowledge, but it wouldn't do any harm to see how things are, how the land lies so to speak, should mine and Suzanne's, er, relationship go any further.

Chas didn't look like the sort of person I would want to have a misunderstanding with.

"We went out for a few weeks. He'd been pestering me for a while. Dad really likes him, so it seemed the natural thing to do."

So daddy approved of her going out with a mere chauffeur; there was hope for me yet.

It was as though Suzanne had read my thoughts as she felt it necessary to expand on dear old Chas. "He's Dad's right hand man. Been with the company for years. Started in security and worked his way up."

Not just a chauffeur then. *Most impressive,* I thought, a little sarcastically. Or was I jealous?

"He'll do anything for dad and this company. He really appreciates what dad has done for him, the trust he has shown in him. He's like the son dad never had. The love and respect is mutual."

"So what happened?" I went back to my original question, intrigued as to why she and the all-singing, all-dancing Chas had not worked out.

"It just didn't work out," was the only explanation Suzanne would offer, and I decided it was best to leave it at that. It probably wouldn't make any difference to my lack of future, but at least it had been a small interlude in my dilemma. I suppose Chas did have his uses then.

We reached the end of the corridor, and I pulled the door open for Suzanne to go through into another one. There were a number of glass windowed offices on either side of this one.

"Morning, Mary. Nearly done?" Suzanne greeted the cleaner, a diminutive rotund woman in her later middle age years, who was busily transferring waste paper into a black bin bag attached to her trolley.

"Morning Miss Deering. I'll be a few hours yet. You have a nice day, now."

"You too Mary," Suzanne offered as we continued. I had to avoid the selection of brushes and mops protruding from the end of the trolley. There were so many tools for what was traditionally a simple job, each with its own specific use. 'Health and safety' had a lot to answer for.

The corridor took a ninety degree turn to the right, immediately meeting another set of double doors. Beyond these were four more offices, two on each side, and a lift. This appeared to be a newer addition, probably put in for Henry because of his age and health—I recalled picking up his angina pills at the hospital.

The corridor ended abruptly at a brick wall. The last office on the left had H W HAINES-GARLAND etched into the window glass, the one opposite said S DEERING. Suzanne led us into this.

I briefly scanned around it. The wall on the left was brick from top to bottom with no windows, the other three walls being bottom half brick, top half glass allowing the occupants to see outside and into the adjoining offices. Sort of communal with a bit of built in privacy. The office was not quite square being in the region of seven metres long by six wide. Suzanne's desk, identified by her nameplate, sat upon it, standing a little away from the window parallel to the all-brick wall and had one wheeled office chair behind it. Next to it were a couple of the usual grey plastic and metal chairs. Opposite, under the window to the adjacent office and running the full length of this wall was a grey plastic-topped bench, under which was a series of filing cabinets. On top of it were a number of machines—a printer, a photo copier, a computer and a couple of others whose purpose I was unsure of. I did recognise the end one though; that was a coffee dispenser. There were two more office chairs of the wheeled variety in front of the bench.

Besides the nameplate, Suzanne's desk was sparsely populated with a computer, a telephone, a coaster and a photo of her father, Henry. All very neat, tidy and organised, exactly as I would expect of her.

"Pull a chair round," Suzanne gestured towards the two at the end of her desk as she took the swivel chair behind the computer.

"Right, I'll just briefly go over what you already know, from the beginning." Suzanne started as we waited for the computer to load up the appropriate programmes. "I know a lot of it will sound a bit obvious but when it's all laid out in front of us, something may jump out that hasn't occurred to us before; OK?"

I nodded my approval.

The damn thing seemed to be taking an eternity to load up. My apprehension was growing by the second as I realised this was perhaps my last chance. If we couldn't find that vital missing piece then my fate, my life would be left in the hands of destiny. Maybe not all the victims had gone on to attack people and maybe we didn't have much data to work with, but what we did have certainly indicated that by far the vast majority of victims were affected, and did go on to die. The odds didn't look very favourable at all.

I tried to push these thoughts to the back of my mind as the screen came to life and to concentrate on the information in front of us.

Chapter 17

The screen blinked as the file Suzanne selected popped up. It was headed CARLOS MENDES—DEATH OF. Short and to the point.

"I'll bring up the known victims first; you know, the ones who attended hospital," Suzanne said as she pressed the appropriate keys. A list of more than a dozen names, addresses and telephone numbers appeared on the screen. This brought it home to me that these were real people from our community, people we worked with, shopped and lived beside every day, not just statistics on a sheet of paper. I would probably have delivered mail to all of them at some time, bills, documents, junk and personal items involving loved ones—little windows into their lives. I would have even spoken to some of them in the course of my work. They were different ages, from different backgrounds and with different lives. *This virus was certainly indiscriminate,* I thought, but then that is the nature of viruses isn't it.

I noted the places I had visited, only a few days previously and recalled the people—Charlene the manager at Tesco, Colin at B&Q, the barmaid at the White Lion; and the altercation with the lovely people at the block of flats.

And then there were my details, a name on a list, a real person like all the others, standing to attention alongside the rest of the platoon, awaiting our instructions from our lieutenant, Suzanne.

What really hit me hard, causing me to sharply draw breath, was that which was written alongside each name—whether they were dead or not. I was relieved to see that mine did not as yet have the dreaded 'D' typed in. One small symbol denoting the end of a life.

An '*R*' also signified whether each individual had raged, instigating the various attacks or had been a victim of the violence. Except for Carlos, all the '*R*s' had also been victims but not all the victims had become '*R*s'. And not just because of the incubation period; some survivors of the earlier attacks had recovered with no other effects, just as Suzanne had said.

As much detail as seemed necessary was included—dates of birth, sex, medical histories, working or retired or unemployed. Everything had been cross-referenced giving age ranges, seriousness of injuries, which wave of attacks each fell into and many more connotations.

All of which came to the same conclusion—there was no conclusion.

From the information we had, there appeared to be no reason why some died but some survived.

All this was displayed in black and white in Suzanne's comprehensive file.

"Well?" Suzanne asked as I sat back from the screen.

"Well, we must be missing something. What possible data have we not included?" I deliberately used the term 'we' to show that this was in no way Suzanne's fault. "Where is the missing link that will make sense of all this?"

"If it is a virus, and we must assume that it is now, then it could be just down to natural immunity, random selection or something."

"I'm sorry, I don't buy that," I couldn't buy that, daren't even think about it, "It doesn't feel right. I know there is another reason, and we have to find it."

"I agree with you. Something is missing. What do you suggest?" Suzanne sounded as though she meant it and wasn't only trying to spare my feelings.

"Right—and I'm thinking on my feet here you understand."

Suzanne nodded and remained silent.

"We've looked at all the victims and their details and drawn a blank."

Again Suzanne silently nodded.

"So, as I see it we have to go back to the origin, the start of the whole thing. And that means Carlos."

Suzanne looked thoughtful and asked, "I can see that that seems the only course left to us, but I'm not sure what good it will do. Carlos died, remember?"

"Yes, I know, but we have to start somewhere, and the beginning is as good a place as any."

I could see Suzanne mulling this over until finally she nodded, slowly. She wasn't convinced.

"Right, show me all you've got on Carlos. Not just the stats we've already seen, but his whole story, right back through his past and up to the time he went on holiday to Brazil. And then to his death."

"OK then," Suzanne paused and I could tell she was formulating some kind of order to her information as her eyes narrowed and distanced themselves from the now and back into the past.

"Carlos came over to this country from his native Brazil about twenty years ago and started work with us a couple of years later."

I cut in, "How did he manage to get a work permit, or residency for that matter?"

Suzanne continued, "He married an English girl, Fiona. She died about seven years ago, long after he had completed all the paper work to stay here. A burst appendix."

It was my turn to nod my understanding.

"And that's about it really. No kids, no other major life events; nothing out of the ordinary. Hadn't even revisited his homeland. He was a conscientious worker and never gave us any trouble."

I pondered the information then asked, "So why did he all of a sudden take a holiday in Brazil, after all that time away?"

Suzanne paused then brought us up to the present. "Well, after Christmas we had a raffle, a reward for how well the workforce have been performing. It was Chas' idea. And Carlos won."

Now if Chas was involved in this, I suspected straight away that all might not be as it seemed. Was it just coincidence that Carlos won a trip to his homeland and inadvertently picked up a virus there or had he been able to choose the destination and decided to visit his family?

Suzanne answered my query before I could ask it. "The prize was a week in Brazil and would include a bit of promotional work, you know, to get us known over there and maybe allow us to expand our sales in that area. We thought he'd be able to visit his family there and asked him which area he'd like to go to. But he told us he had no family left after Fiona had died; there was just him now," Suzanne paused a moment, "I found it all rather sad. So we packed him off to Brasilia. He flew out on a Thursday and came back the following Thursday."

"And have you?" I asked.

"What?"

"Expanded the business over there?" My suspicions were making me sound a bit abrupt in my race to find the truth. But I noticed, the anger was not as yet rising within me; perhaps hope was keeping it at bay.

"It's too early to say yet."

I thought, *it would be wouldn't it.*

"But Chas is hopeful."

There's that man's involvement again. "And?"

Suzanne continued, "And, nothing, really. Carlos took the holiday, came back a week later and the rest we know."

The pieces didn't quite seem to go together. Something definitely didn't fit, but I couldn't place what it was. It was all too neat and tidy, too convenient. Too much of a coincidence.

"Shall I get us a coffee," Suzanne asked seeing my pensive expression as I thought things over. I nodded. "I'll have to get it from Dad's office, our machine isn't working." She rose to leave, adding as she exited, "Ironic, really. Carlos didn't even smoke and they sent him to do promotional work."

Irony? Coincidences? Conveniences? Things seemed to be stacking up in the unbelievable column.

Tugging at my bottom lip, I sat staring in thought at the desk in front of me. Suzanne returned with two coffees. "It'll stay that way if you keep pulling it like that," she smiled trying to relieve the tension.

I wasn't in the mood for smiling, "It doesn't add up, Suzanne."

"It was only a bit of promotional stuff; nothing much really."

"No, I don't mean that. The whole thing just doesn't seem right."

Suzanne looked at me thoughtfully, "I've never thought of it like that. I just assumed, well, nothing really. I didn't think anything of it."

"Have you got any documents on the raffle? There must be a paper trail, for tax purposes if nothing else."

"Yeah, OK…" Suzanne said, slowly, quizzically, "What are you thinking, Jake."

"I don't know…" maybe I was clutching at straws again or maybe there was something in it all. There was only one way to find out. "See if you can find that paperwork, please." I left it at that, still deep in thought, still tugging my lip.

"It'll be in Chas' office if it's anywhere," and she left for the office next door.

Chas, he's there again, I thought. His name was becoming linked to more and more coincidences. I didn't believe in these at the best of times, but with him involved, my disbelief became more persuasive.

Minutes later, Suzanne returned, "There's nothing on Chas' computer. No trace of the raffle, the cost of the trip, or anything."

"But there must be some record," I reasoned, "Perhaps your dad has something; you know, actual paperwork not on the computer. His generation are, how shall I put this, sometimes prone to distrusting computers."

"Mmm, you could be right. I'll have a look." Again she disappeared for what seemed like ages, ticking off more minutes of my limited life span.

"Found it," she re-entered her office waving a blue cardboard file, with *Brazil Trip,* hand written on the front. She lay the file down on the desk between us, opened it and withdrew the contents.

There was a long list of names (the workforce I assumed) on an A4 sheet of paper, details of the trip, and a plastic bag containing the individual raffle tickets, from which I guessed the raffle had been drawn. Out of curiosity, I unfolded one of these— C. Mendes was written on it in capital letters. *Wow!* Another massive coincidence.

I looked at Suzanne, questioningly, as she looked at me the same. "Well, that was a stroke of luck," I said and picked out another ticket.

C. Mendes was written on this one as well. We grabbed a handful each, rapidly unfolded them, finding the same name in the same hand writing on each.

We pulled away from the file as if it was booby-trapped and sat staring at it. I broke the silence, "Is that Chas' hand writing?"

Suzanne glanced at it, "It certainly looks like it! I...I don't understand..."

"I'd say the raffle was tilted a little in Carlos' favour, Wouldn't you?"

"Yes, but why?" Suzanne was totally unable to see why the man she thought she knew would want to do such a thing.

"Well because, for some reason, he wanted Carlos to win I would think,"

I examined the other items more closely. The sheet of names was dated January twelfth, "Is this the date of the raffle?"

Suzanne looked at the paper, "Yes, I think so."

Next, I scrutinised the travel documents, carrying Carlos' details, and they revealed the trip had been booked some two weeks earlier. "Well, I think that shows there was no error. Carlos was definitely intended to take that trip."

"Yes, but why? He didn't do much while he was out there. It was more of a holiday. It doesn't make any sense."

The final document was still stuffed in the blue folder. It was a small creased item, of thin paper that had roughly been shoved down to the bottom. I had almost missed it. I unfolded it, laid it on the desk in front of us and smoothed it out with my potted hand. It was a list of the inoculations given to Carlos and stated when they were given.

"But they only administered these the day before he went. Surely..." Suzanne was dumbfounded.

I finished her sentence, "That was too late." I went down the list—Hepatitis A, Yellow fever, combined Tetanus diphtheria and polio, Rabies, Typhoid and finally Malaria tablets.

"He should have had at least some of these, if not all, weeks before he travelled," now it was my turn for the unfinished question, "But why?"

Suzanne opened her mouth as if to attempt an explanation but could find no words.

"That is if he had been given them at all. Maybe this was just done to keep the paperwork in order. Again though, why?"

I couldn't figure out what all this meant, or how, if at all, it helped me. The deeper we dug, the more problems were thrown up and still no relevant answers.

Everything was still closing in on me, claustrophobia brought on by the ever tightening noose around my neck was taking hold. I pushed away from my seat in an attempt to deter this and paced the room, looking for the answers.

Why would a cigarette firm fix a raffle to send a Brazilian, with no contacts in his homeland, to that country? Why would they falsify his medical papers? What had the firm got to gain from all this? Why send a non-smoker to promote smoking?

It didn't make any sense; but it must have been planned. The jigsaw was still incomplete.

Unless, of course, it was all a smokescreen. Again though, for what. *More questions with no answers.*

I was pleased the rage was staying at bay. We were learning things so at least we were making headway. But it was like driving in dense fog, knowing we were getting forever closer to our destination but unable to see just where that would be.

I allowed myself an ironic chuckle.

"What?" Suzanne asked.

"Oh, I was just thinking, a smokescreen for a non-smoker," I smiled again, shaking my head, still pacing the floor, and returned to tugging my lip which was becoming a bit sore from carrying all the brain power.

Suzanne looked puzzled at my statement, obviously not knowing my thoughts on the subject. Her expression suddenly altered as if a light had been switched on in a darkened room. "Non-smoker," she repeated as she clicked onto the computer again and began typing feverishly at the keys.

I turned to the window as though the answers were perhaps out there somewhere. Maybe the gardener had cut them into the lawn. My eyes took me across the rear carpark. There were just three cars in it, all stationed together. My stare continued to the horizon and the gathering clouds.

Suddenly, I shot back to the parked vehicles, specifically the farthest one, a silver Mercedes AMG Edition 463. The same one that had been following me earlier in the week; the one I had assumed to be with the Post Office investigation branch.

"Whose is that?" I pointed to the car and turned towards Suzanne.

She paused her fervent attack on the computer and joined me at the window. Her eyes followed my line of indication. "That's Chas'. Why?"

I paused momentarily before responding, thinking there couldn't be two like that in this small town. It can't be another coincidence, then said, "He was following me earlier in the week."

"What Chas? Are you sure?"

"Well it was definitely that car, although I couldn't see the driver through the tinted windows."

We stood there, puzzled, for a few seconds until Suzanne snapped back to the job in hand. "I think I may have found something."

Chapter 18

She went back behind the desk to the computer, beckoning me to follow her and tapped a few keys bringing the screen back to life. "It hadn't occurred to me before. It may be nothing, but look…"

She pointed at the screen.

I looked. It was another list, of the victims. One I hadn't noticed before. This one listed their hobbies, dietary habits, social activities; personal details.

"And?" I asked as I couldn't see the relevance, couldn't see what Suzanne obviously had.

"You pointed it out." She said and continued seeing that I still hadn't got it, "Carlos was a non-smoker."

I shrugged my shoulders and held my hands out, palms up, still not getting any significance. That was until Suzanne moved her finger from one name to another. Each one who had raged had a D before their name (this was no surprise to us as we already knew this) but also an N/S at the end. Each attacker had been a Non-Smoker.

"Are—Are you sure?" This revelation hit me like a wrecking ball smashing confusion into my brain. I checked along each line once, twice, three times. There was no mistake. I felt like I had immediately grown six inches taller, as the weight of my dilemma started to vanish.

For the first time since that first day, I believed I was going to live. Non-smokers raged, smokers didn't.

I was a smoker! Smoking had saved my life!

I gasped for air, unable to control my breathing and unable to stop the sobs emanating from deep within me, caused by the sudden overwhelming feeling of relief. I put both hands up to cover my face, as Suzanne put an arm around me in a reassuring hug.

"Thank you, thank you," I sobbed through the tears as I lowered my shaking hands and took hold of hers.

It took me a while to pull myself together. I wiped away the tears as a grateful smile lit up my face. My head dropped, and I stared at the ground and took in a large quantity of air; air that all of a sudden tasted sweeter than any air had ever tasted before.

As my euphoria waned and my senses returned, I realised this was nowhere near over. I sat back in the chair, took a deep breath and said, "What now?"

"I still can't see why." Suzanne said, "This must have something to do with our factory, but what. It makes no sense." She drew the last two words out slowly as if something was formulating in her mind.

Thinking had become a lot easier now the weight of impending death had been lifted from my shoulders, and the time constraints had been relaxed, for me at least. "Well, if you look at this from a totally cynical, business point of view."

Suzanne looked at me expectantly.

"A cigarette company in a declining market wants to boost sales. A virus spreading like wildfire that is only curable by ingredients in cigarettes..." I left Suzanne to draw her own conclusions.

"But that means," she paused as the enormity of what I implied meant, "That means we've done this. We caused Carlos' infection, Carlos' death." Suzanne slumped back into her chair, "No, no; I don't believe it. There must be some other explanation. Dad would certainly not allow such a thing and neither...would Chas." Again the pause before she uttered the final two words.

She looked at me pleadingly, as if begging me to come up with an alternative answer.

"Are you sure? I mean I don't for a minute think your dad would, but Chas?" I left that to sink in for a few seconds. Suzanne's silence answered the question far better than any words could have.

"You said he loved this company; would do *anything* to help it..."

Suzanne was still unable to respond.

"How has business been of late?" I was trying to lead her to the obvious conclusion as gently as possible.

"Not good," she squeaked, cleared her throat and added, "Not good, but not that bad. We're holding our own. Not *that* bad." She stopped, sat upright and thrust her shoulders back and said defiantly, "No, I don't believe it. I don't believe any of it, Jake."

I could have shown her the demise of their rivals. I could have reminded her of our strict and over-demanding tax system strangling the life out of the British tobacco industry. I could have pointed out that virtually all other cigarette production in this country had ceased and the rest planned to do so within a couple of years. All this was common knowledge to anyone who read the papers.

But I didn't want her hurting inside any more than necessary. And not only because she had helped me so much but because I cared for her, *really* cared for her. She didn't need to hear it because she already knew all of this and, essentially, it was irrelevant. What was done couldn't be undone. You can't alter the past, only the future. So I said nothing.

An awkward silence prevailed for many seconds; seemed like many minutes.

Something else occurred to me as the new clarity in my thinking sharpened my logic, "Something else just came to me," I said sheepishly, almost apologetically. It must have seemed to Suzanne that I was deliberately torturing her. Nothing could have been further from the truth, but I had to be honest with her; she had to face the facts.

"What?" she asked sullenly, sounding almost broken.

"Carlos must have been infected before he went to Brazil." I left it at that allowing Suzanne to put the pieces together herself.

Again she cleared the taste of bewilderment from her throat as she stared down at the condemning paperwork on the desk in front of her, "Went to Brazil on the Thursday, died in hospital on Friday, eight days later."

She could have argued that the figures we had were incomplete; that there was insufficient data; that the ten days' incubation period wasn't set in stone. But she knew I was right. This was one probability too many.

Although I knew she couldn't have been involved in all this (*could she?* The back of my mind prodded at me, but I chose to ignore it), I could see from her lost and shattered disposition that she felt as guilty as if she had killed Carlos herself. It was her father's firm and she worked there, right at the top, alongside the other decision makers. It was *her* company.

I put my arm around her, to comfort her, to show her that I understood and that I was there for her as she had been for me. In a matter of minutes, the polarity of our situations had been reversed.

"So can we get a cure from this," I attempted to draw her attention away from her dilemma and back to the original problem. Although I had a stay of execution, the general crisis had not diminished at all. Although smokers may be immune to the virus, smoking did not make them bulletproof—if they were attacked, they would be injured or killed just like anyone else. This had to be stopped before it got too far out of control; I knew there was a chance we may already be too late.

It seemed to work, "How do you mean?" Suzanne asked.

"We know smokers have some sort of immunity to the virus, so can a cure be made from this, without getting everyone to take up smoking? I don't think the government would be too keen on that scenario, or anybody else for that matter."

"Well, yes, I suppose; eventually. It's not as easy as you might think, though."

"Why not?" I asked, "Does it depend on the type of tobacco, or the brand of cigarette? Even so, we know the source of the cure so it shouldn't be that hard, surely?"

"It's not as straight forward as the film world makes out. Remember the Ebola crisis? They had first-hand samples of that virus and look how long it took them to develop anything that was at all effective."

I thought about that point, "So what you're saying is that we are only on the first rung of a very long ladder?"

"Precisely. And it gets worse. Although the components of all cigarettes, no matter what the brand, are pretty much the same, it's pin-pointing the particular one, or combination of ingredients; that would be the problem initially. Then, if and when that is achieved, it's finding the right combination of products and how to administer them to counteract the virus. Unfortunately, even in this day and age this would involve a lot of trial and error."

"Yes, but surely that wouldn't take that long. We know exactly the thing that prevents the virus; the cigarette." I would not be deterred.

"I don't think you're grasping how big a task it would be. For instance, do you know how many ingredients there are in a cigarette?"

I tugged my sore lip mulling the question over. It would obviously be a lot more than I thought or Suzanne wouldn't be asking the question. "Fifty or sixty; maybe a hundred?" I was just plucking figures out of the air, because, like your average man in the street, I didn't have a clue.

Suzanne smiled at my ignorance, then said, "Not even close. There are over four thousand chemical compounds in each puff of cigarette smoke, coupled with this are up to six hundred permitted additives, all of which, incidentally, do not appear anywhere on the list of ingredients. Then there are flavourings and colourings."

"Wow!" I was blown away, finally grasping the immensity of the task. Suzanne certainly knew her industry.

"And there is ample opportunity to add other ingredients that may not be permitted or even known about."

I just sat there. I was stunned. "So it would be like looking for that needle in the haystack again."

"Well, not quite that bad," Suzanne continued, "There are standard procedures, short cuts, but it would still be an enormous and time consuming task."

We looked at each other, both thinking the same thing but it was I who voiced those thoughts, "Unless someone knows which ingredients; someone who knows what stops the virus; someone who was there at the beginning of this mess."

Once more, I allowed my statement to settle in Suzanne's mind. When I saw the realisation on her face, I uttered what I knew she was thinking but dare not admit to herself.

"Chas," I said.

Right or not we both recognised where our next step would be. We had to confront Chas, show him our findings and take it from there. I guessed Suzanne wouldn't be looking forward to that confrontation. I knew for sure that I wasn't.

I couldn't quite decide which I preferred—if we were correct in our assumption then we may have a short cut to a cure, but that raises the question as to what Chas would do. I might not have known him as long as Suzanne had, but I could be sure he wouldn't just put his hands up in surrender. On the other hand, if we were wrong, then what? Back to square one, I presumed, and everything that that would mean for everybody.

Like most people, I wasn't particularly fond of lose-lose situations, but the consequences of this dilemma would certainly be very serious for someone. I had just escaped one death sentence and didn't much fancy facing another one for quite a while.

The sound of a woman's voice singing along with the radio to The Beatles' *Yesterday* drifted into my consciousness. The clatter of cleaning utensils indicated that it was probably Mary, the cleaner we had bumped into on our way in. The double doors in the corridor whooshed open. Suzanne and I looked up simultaneously to see a dark-suited figure moving purposefully towards Suzanne's office.

It was Chas.

Chapter 19

I decided to let Suzanne to do the talking, at this stage. She would still be in denial to some extent about Chas' involvement and want to give him every chance to explain. Besides, I was not unafraid of tackling the guy, either verbally or physically.

"Hi, Chas," Suzanne greeted him, trying to sound cheerful, not succeeding in the slightest but coming across as fearful instead.

The man seemed to almost fill the doorway, not quite having to stoop as he passed through into the office. But he was not like the man with the meat cleaver from my nightmare. No, Chas was more muscular, toned, purposeful and, no doubt, could ultimately be more dangerous. "Not finished yet then, Suzanne?" His question was directed at her but his eyes fixed firmly on me. "What have you been up to?"

I assumed, hoped, he was still talking to Suzanne and remained silent, trying not to let my fear show. Experience had trained me well in this at work with my numerous confrontations with our canine friends.

Before she could respond, Chas continued, "What's your boyfriend been helping you with?"

Things hadn't started very well, and we hadn't even begun to ask our questions. Still, on the bright side Suzanne hadn't bothered to deny the boyfriend bit. I wasn't expecting many more bright points in the immediate future.

"We've—" Suzanne began feebly, cleared her throat and continued with a little more assertion, "We've been looking into the Carlos Mendes thing."

Still Chas' gaze didn't leave me. But I didn't look away either. I wanted to gauge his response when Suzanne lay the facts out in front of him. I would expect his words to plead innocence, but I wanted to know if his body language was in accordance.

"Jake, here," I saw Suzanne glance across at me in my peripheral vision, "He was one of the victims of the attacks. Not by Carlos but by a subsequent assailant."

Suzanne paused but Chas said nothing, so she continued, "He's been helping me with my research."

"I'll bet he has," Chas said vehemently, his obvious dislike for me worsening by the moment. "And what have you two detectives found, then?"

His tone was definitely intimidating and not meant in a jocular way at all.

And still we stared at each other. It was like the front-off between two boxers at a pre-fight weigh-in. Unfortunately, for me this bout would be between a heavyweight champion and a lightweight amateur.

There was silence as Suzanne seemed unsure where to begin.

"We think we've found the cause of the attacks," I took over from her.

Chas the shark did not flicker one bit, giving nothing away, and asked, "And what is that?"

Suzanne continued this time, and Chas' eyes left mine for hers, "They are caused by a virus," Suzanne inner strength was beginning to return, "A virus linked to smoking. More specifically, to this factory."

Chas did not respond; his features never altered, and he remained impassive. For me, this spoke volumes—surely anyone who didn't already know this would have shown some sign of amazement, of incredulity, at least some flicker of surprise.

But I wasn't yet ready to start accusing him. I wanted to see and hear more, to see if he would let on about anything he knew. Not only that, though; I hadn't quite built up the courage either.

Suzanne continued, "Carlos went to Brazil and when he got back he suffered a fatal, er, seizure. We think, no, we're sure, this was caused by a virus."

Chas smirked, "They've told us that much on the news. So the guy picked up a virus in Brazil. That's nothing unusual for those type of countries, but I don't see how you can blame us for that."

Suzanne had only said it was linked to the factory but not said in which way. Again, I thought Chas knew more than he was letting on. He was fishing for information as much as we were.

"He didn't pick up the virus in Brazil," Suzanne didn't waste any time, dropping the bomb straight away, "He had it before he went."

There was just a flicker in Chas eyes. If I had blinked I would have missed it. He tried to remain impassive, but I had seen the proof.

Chas knew.

I wasn't sure if Suzanne had noticed it. She said, "We think someone gave it to him deliberately; someone from this factory." This time the pause was more sustained, urging a response from Chas.

He took a step back, the smirk turning to laughter, "Don't be ridiculous. I can take a joke like the rest of them."

This I very much doubted.

"But that is out there with the best." Chas shook his head and turned to leave. He paused at the doorway and added, "It's good to see you haven't been wasting your time on this Suzanne," and continued on his way.

Before he got much further, Suzanne continued, now completely in control of herself, "Why was the raffle fixed, Chas?"

She certainly knows the show-stopper questions, I thought. She could be a reporter or a chat show host if she chose a change of profession.

This stopped Chas dead as though he had walked into an invisible barrier. Slowly turning back around, he re-entered the office, "I-I don't know what you mean." She had caught him off guard with the directness of her interrogation.

"Oh, I think you do Chas. The raffle was fixed; we've seen the file."

Chas offered no explanation. His gaze shifted to the blue file on the desk and its contents laid out next to it. Unhidden guilt was written across his face like a teenager caught watching the wrong TV channels.

"Why was Carlos only given his inoculations just before he went away? They should have been given weeks earlier. Why, Chas?"

"I don't know, I'm not a doctor…" was his feeble response. He wasn't going to give in easily.

"Or was he injected with something else?" In face of the onslaught of accusations Chas again found it difficult to find an answer. Suzanne glared at him, "Well?"

Silence prevailed; the shark had been confused by the course of the tide.

"Tell us we're wrong." I decided it was time for me to join in, to show solidarity with Suzanne. Twice the people, twice the strength.

Rather than weaken Chas, it had the opposite effect. He glared at me and took a step forward. I held my nerve with my dog-deterrent face just about holding out.

"I think, we had better call Henry," Suzanne this time, drawing Chas' focus back to her.

"And the police," I added.

Chas stood there, his hands twitching with intimidation, his attention alternating between Suzanne and me, like a beast wondering which one to devour first.

But he kept his self-control, and the smirk returned, "OK then, call Henry. I'm sure he'll be delighted to have his weekend interrupted by this drivel."

Suzanne took her mobile from her handbag, and quickly tapped in her father's number. I could hear the dial tone as it rang and briefly wondered what we would do next if Henry didn't answer it. The tone stopped as Henry must have finally responded.

"Hi Dad, sorry for disturbing you," Suzanne began, all the time keeping her eyes firmly fixed on Chas. She expressed no trace of the fear I was feeling. She knew him so much better than I did, and I prayed her confidence in his likely reactions, or lack of them, was well founded.

"I really need you to come to the office."

Henry's response was not discernible to me.

"Yes, right away. I'm really sorry Dad, but it's really important. It's about Carlos."

There was a pause as Henry must have been speaking.

"Yes, as soon as possible please, Dad."

Henry again.

"See you in twenty minutes then. Love you, Dad. Bye." Short and sweet, straight to the point. Suzanne was certainly a person of action, not one to dither and worry about the consequences. I hoped that, in this instance, this wasn't a bad trait; only time would tell.

As she ended the call, I picked up the office phone. "Do I have to enter anything for an outside line before I call the police?" My question was directed at Suzanne.

"Nine." She said.

I punched the numbers in and hovered over the call button momentarily.

Chas swiftly crossed the space between us and calmly took the handset from my grasp before I could complete the connection. "There's no need for that." The confidence blazed from his eyes.

I relinquished the phone but did not back away. I matched his stare, "I think you'd better start explaining," I said forcefully, surprising myself with the determined strength of my own voice.

Chas returned the phone to the desk and stood back in the middle of the room, obviously weighing up his options. He looked from me to Suzanne, from Suzanne back to me and took a deep breath, "Very well," He said without a trace of fear or apprehension in his voice.

He began to pace the room, his hands together as if in prayer under his chin. "I did it for the company," he eventually spoke, "For your father, Suzanne. You know I'd do anything for this company. Business, as you know is in decline. If I did nothing then your father, you, all of us would be ruined."

He moved towards the window and spread his arms wide, "All this would go; nearly fifty people would lose their jobs, their livelihoods. I couldn't just sit there and watch it happen."

"So you did it for all of us," Suzanne interrupted with disdain.

I chipped in, "Not for Carlos, though."

Chas turned and glared at me.

I didn't back down, "Why him? What made you chose Carlos," I was on a roll and leaned forward, "What made you think you had the right to decide whether Carlos lived or died?"

Chas looked down at the floor and seemed to shrink by a couple of inches, "It had to be somebody. It was the only solution I could see; the only way to save so many others." The poor dejected man was pleading for our understanding and sympathy.

I was buying none of it. *Don't judge by first impressions* people were always saying. Well, experience tells me that those first impressions nearly always have a lot of foundation in truth. And that first encounter with the shark, at the hospital, would always stay with me. "No, I'm sorry, Chas. That didn't give you the right to do what you did, to go to the lengths that you decided to go to; and you know it."

His mask of dejection slipped straight off and he drew himself up to his full height, the steely determination once more returning to his face.

Suzanne said nothing and just listened. Her illusion of this man had been well and truly broken, and I knew she would require time to adjust. Not too much time though, I believed, as she had already displayed on several occasions her strength of character and ability to adapt.

"We'd been experimenting with something our scientists had developed in the lab." Chas expanded on his explanation, "They had come up with, er, a substance—you'll have to forgive my terminology; I'm no physicist—a substance they believed could be used as, perhaps, a performance enhancer."

I sat upright, confused by this. I couldn't believe that he was claiming they planned to market cigarettes as a fitness aid, or anything similar. I glanced across at Suzanne and was further astounded to see that her face did not bear the same expression of incredulity that mine did. In fact, she looked barely even surprised—she must have known they had been experimenting in that area. I was lost for words.

Once more, it was brought home to me that I didn't really know this woman at all. I had suspected that she hadn't been telling me everything she knew, but I never for a second thought it might be anything as big as this. I couldn't be sure now if anything she had told me was truth or lies. In my confusion, I didn't know anything anymore.

Chapter 20

I sat there in stunned silence and eventually retuned into Chas' explanation.

"They did it with energy drinks; you know, Red Bull and the like."

Suzanne intervened, "Yes, but it didn't work for us. We binned the whole idea months ago. We couldn't control it."

"Hang on a minute," it was my turn to interrupt, "You knew about all this?"

My accusation clearly unsettled Suzanne as she stuttered, "Y-You don't understand, Jake…"

My anger was growing, "Then make me understand!" I glared at her.

Chas saw his chance to widen the rift between Suzanne and me, "You don't have to tell *him* anything." The 'him' he referred to me as made me feel like something he was trying to wipe off his shoe.

Suzanne ignored him and directed her words at me, "I didn't know much about it, just that we were experimenting with different uses for cigarettes, possible alternatives for selling our product. Like Chas said, we were in decline." She then reasserted herself, "But it wasn't viable and we stopped it, or so I thought; so I was told."

The onus was back with Chas, and he attempted to explain further, "Yes, you're right. It didn't work." He then turned to me, a lot calmer now, "You see one of our scientists came up with this, er, this stuff that would mimic the production of adrenalin in the body."

"This stuff you refer to, you mean the virus?" I asked, combating his attempt to make everything seem reasonable.

"I didn't know it was a virus, not then…"

"You're splitting hairs, Chas. It doesn't matter what you call it; you knew what it would do." I was getting angry again.

"Virus, whatever. Anyway, we could get the body to produce it but we couldn't regulate it. It killed the mice we experimented with; every one of them went into a frenzy and died. We tried different things, drugs, to try and control it. Some, for example ibuprofen, delayed the reaction."

"But none would stop it?" I asked.

"Well, not exactly. Don't forget we specialise in tobacco products and therefore our research is within that area. This virus evolved from our work with tobacco. And something within cigarettes prevented the virus from working."

"Hence smokers not being affected." I was beginning to grasp the reasoning behind it all.

"Exactly. We had hoped to control it with tobacco products, you know, control the production of the adrenalin. But we could only prevent it not control it—it was all or nothing. If we could have achieved that control then, bingo!—performance enhancing aid."

"Or legal cheating for athletes and the like."

"Sorry, Jake." Chas was being a lot friendlier towards me as the conversation went on, obviously trying to win me over. I played along to learn more but wasn't taken in by any of it. A shark doesn't change its spots, or something like that. "It's not for us to decide what athletes can put in their bodies or what the moral issues behind such things are."

"What the moral issues are." I repeated his words. "Funny you should bring that up."

Chas didn't respond to that one.

I finished his speech for him, "But you couldn't control it could you?" My question didn't require an answer, so I didn't wait for one. "If you used the virus then it would kill. And you saw this as an opportunity, didn't you?"

Chas just looked down at the floor.

I turned to Suzanne, "And all along you knew about all this!" I was still having trouble getting my head round Suzanne's involvement.

"I-I didn't know. I suspected. I couldn't find a link, couldn't find any proof. I thought we had ditched the programme. I…" She also looked to the floor, like a naughty school child as she knew her excuses were pathetically inadequate and said barely above a whisper, "I thought it must just be coincidence."

She was beaten, but I believed her, believed her naivety and trustfulness. Because, basically, I was sure she was a good person (those first impressions again). I didn't want to hurt her any further and so returned to Chas.

"Again, though, why Carlos?"

Chas slowly looked up and turned towards Suzanne, "Your comprehensive employee files helped tremendously there. You see, Carlos had no family ties, not in this country."

"Don't you try blaming any of this on her!" I was livid at his cowardly attempt to bring Suzanne into this, trying to spread the blame.

He ignored me, "No children, and his wife had died. He didn't have such a healthy lifestyle either—he was overweight, drank too much and probably wouldn't have reached retirement anyway. And he was a non-smoker."

The last sentence was uttered much more quietly, added almost as an afterthought.

He paused then continued to Suzanne, "You're too meticulous for your own good sometimes. You were right about the jab we gave him. It was the virus."

Neither Suzanne nor I had a response to this. We were too shocked by his abruptness and his total disregard for the consequences of his actions.

"No ties and, being from Brazil, it gave me an idea, allowed me to come up with a plan…" Chas let the sentence hang, maybe expecting applause for his ingenuity.

"Then you two came along and had to spoil it all." He was becoming menacing again. "You had to dig around," He was addressing Suzanne, "I just hope it's not too early. If you expose this now, the virus may not have had a chance to take hold, then all this will have been pointless, and Carlos will have died for nothing."

I couldn't believe he was still trying to carry this through. I just sat there, speechless.

He turned towards me, "And you should be grateful. As a smoker, you'll be all right."

"Why were you following me?" I changed the angle of the conversation, playing for time, trying to stall him until Henry arrived hoping that he would be able to make Chas see sense.

"It was quite amusing watching you running around in circles. I didn't really expect you to stumble across anything enlightening, but, well, you never know. It soon became obvious that you were getting nowhere though, so I gave up after a couple of days; after your pointless return to the hospital."

I opened my mouth to protest but couldn't think of anything to say as I knew he was right about that.

Chas shook his head and tut-tutted patronisingly, "What were you thinking, Jake."

The real Chas was surfacing more and more. I looked across to Suzanne, her mouth was wide open and her eyes were staring at Chas in disbelief. She clearly wasn't used to seeing that side of her ex-boyfriend.

The doors in the corridor whooshed open and Henry marched into the office. I could see by his stern expression that he wasn't happy at being called in at the weekend, "What's so important that I've got to come in today. Couldn't it have waited until Monday?"

The three of us looked straight at him, in silence.

"Well?" He was almost shouting, "Which one of you is going to start?"

Still the silence prevailed, none of us quite sure where to begin.

Chas finally spoke, "Calm down, Henry, your heart. You have to remain calm." He glared at Suzanne as if to say the shock of our revelations might kill the old man, then continued, "It's nothing really, Henry."

I was having none of it. Chas would not be allowed to get away with this. "That is if you can call murder nothing."

Henry looked confused, "What does he mean?" and added as an afterthought, "Who is he anyway? What's he doing here?"

Chas still attempted to control things, "Calm down Henry, it's OK. He's nobody. He doesn't know what he's talking about."

I had no chance of winning this one. Henry would never believe a stranger over his faithful, loyal, would-be son.

"Yes he does," Suzanne seethed.

Everyone's focus turned towards her, as she said, "Chas caused Carlos' death, Dad."

Henry looked puzzled, like he had just woken up and didn't know where he was. He slowly turned to face Chas, his furrowed brow begging an explanation, a denunciation from him. No words came from his protégé.

"He has been continuing with the adrenalin project, and he used Carlos," Suzanne said.

"But-but—" the bewildered head of the company stuttered trying to comprehend what he was hearing, "We stopped that. It-it killed the subjects. We couldn't use it…Chas?"

Chas couldn't look his father-figure in the eye and turned his head away as if the old man's gaze was burning into him like acid.

"We stopped it; he didn't, Dad. He carried on with it even though he knew it would kill," Suzanne corrected herself mid-sentence, "No, because it would kill."

Suzanne looked towards her father, tears welling up in her eyes as she knew how much this was hurting him, "He knew it would kill non-smokers and is using that to create an epidemic; an epidemic that will kill anyone who doesn't smoke."

Henry still couldn't take it all in, the confusion freezing on his face, unable or unwilling to accept what he was being told. But it was his daughter who was telling him this, and the realisation that it must therefore, be true, turned his bewildered expression to horror. "Chas?" He pleaded for an explanation, a justification.

"I did it for us, Henry; you have to see that. The business is going down; you can see that. All these people, who've devoted their lives to this firm, would have been finished. They don't deserve that, surely *you* can see that Henry?"

I wasn't sure which way Henry would go, whether he would see reason or be blinded by his love for Chas. I couldn't tell how concerned he would be by the deaths of innocent people; after all, he had devoted his life to an industry that he knew cost thousands of people their lives each year.

"No, no, Chas. This is so wrong…" The old man uttered, barely above a whisper.

But Chas would not give up, "And Suzanne what about her? You've worked all your life for her. She doesn't deserve it either, and nor do you Henry. A few lives would be lost, sacrificed for the greater good, but when they realised smoking could save everybody then we'd all gain."

I realised now no one would be taken in by Chas' pitiful pleading, not even Henry, and so I took the matter into my own hands. Suzanne and Henry were too close to Chas and didn't deserve the pain and anguish he was prepared to put them through. "This has gone far enough. You're pathetic, Chas. It's time the police were called." I searched my pockets for my mobile phone before remembering I had left it at home.

As I reached for the office telephone, Chas took a stride forward and beat me to it. "I don't think so," he said firmly.

"No, he's right, Chas," the defeated Henry said in a voice that was scarcely audible, "We must call them."

Still holding onto the phone, Chas turned to Henry, "We can't do that, Henry. We'll all be implicated—you, me and Suzanne. We'll go down for a long time."

Chas put the phone on the desk out of my reach and took hold of Henry, gently, by the arms. "Suzanne wouldn't last two minutes in prison, Henry. We can't do that to her."

I saw my opportunity as Chas was distracted and lunged forward grabbing the phone. Chas was quick, though and before I could dial, he wheeled around, reached inside his jacket and pulled out a gun.

I stopped, unblinking, frozen in time, the phone in my left hand out in front of me. I held my breath and stared at Chas.

My mouth became instantly dry, my heart pounded and, staring down the barrel of a gun, I was terrified, convinced I was going to die at any second. It wasn't like they make it out to be in the movies. Chas didn't have to ask for the telephone, it fell from my hand of its own free will.

Henry's shouted interruption startled everyone. I hoped it wouldn't cause Chas' finger to twitch. "My God, Chas! What are you doing?"

Suzanne's response was more measured, "Don't do it, Chas," she said firmly, "There are other people about; they will hear the gun. There's no point; it's over."

Chas appeared to be weighing up her words and finally lowered the gun. But I wasn't about to make any move towards the phone again.

Chas spoke, waving the firearm in Suzanne's direction, "I told you we shouldn't have involved her in this Henry. She's too thorough, doesn't let things go until she finds a solution. We should just have left the police to deal with Carlos' death, and nobody would have been any the wiser."

He turned away, shaking his head, "We're all in this together whether we like it or not." He instantly spun back around to me, "Except him, of course. He'll have to go."

The gun was once again trained right between my eyes. Again, I sat there not breathing, not moving, waiting to die.

Chas suddenly tilted it upwards and away from me, forcing the air from my lungs. "But you're right, Suzanne, not here."

"No Chas, not anywhere. It's done." Suzanne, the voice of reason, probably knew the best way to deal with Chas in such a situation, but I was far from convinced that it would do any good. She held out her hand for the gun.

Chas wasn't beaten yet, though. "Can't you see? We can't change what has been done. We're on damage limitation here. We can't alter the past, and we, you, can't go down for this. Nobody has to know…"

"The next wave of attacks is imminent. We have to inform the authorities," I tried to sound in control, reasoned, but I was fighting for my life and hoped I didn't just sound desperate. I was adding anything I could think of to tip the scales in my favour.

"Wave of attacks?" Henry didn't appear to understand. He had obviously only been thinking about Carlos and trying to come to terms with what Chas had done. He hadn't had the time to think of the consequences of Chas' plan.

"My God, yes," Suzanne urgently yelled, "I'd forgotten that."

She moved towards her father and gently took hold of him, "All these attacks on the news, they've happened because of the virus; because of what Chas has done." She allowed this to implant itself in her father's mind.

"Sit down, Suzanne," Chas' gun waved her towards a chair alongside me. He must have realised where this was now going; that he was losing.

As she slowly took her seat, he turned back to Henry, "Think of Suzanne, if nothing else, Henry."

"But we have to call the police, Chas. You must see that," Henry, tears in his eyes reached out and placed a hand on Chas' hand, the one holding the gun.

I saw a chance, perhaps my last chance. I nudged Suzanne to alert her to be ready but could only hope that she understood my intentions.

While the two men were emotionally and physically locked together, I acted. I sprung from my seat, picked up a spare chair and threw it in the direction of Chas.

He could easily have dodged it, but his instinct, borne of years of intimacy, forced him to protect Henry. The chair caught him off balance, knocking him to the floor, the gun spilling from his grasp.

Without a word, I raced through the door. Suzanne had understood my nudge, grabbed her handbag and was right there with me. Although I was obviously concerned for her safety, I firmly believed Chas would do nothing to harm Suzanne, and so I was *fairly* sure he wouldn't shoot at us.

Chapter 21

Barging through the double doors in the corridor, I pulled Suzanne with me and crashed straight into Mary's cleaning trolley.

Unbalanced and disorientated, I crashed into the wall but managed to stay on my feet. The smell of bleach cleared my head and heightened my senses. I could hear scrambling behind me back in the office as the doors swung shut. It was only a matter of seconds before Chas emerged into the corridor.

Suzanne was ahead of me now, and Chas and Henry were too close behind. I turned back towards our pursuers, realising I had to gain us some time, even if it was only a few seconds. I grabbed the nearest thing to hand—a mop from Mary's trolley and swiftly jammed it through the handles of the corridor doors.

Mary appeared in my peripheral vision in the adjacent office, duster in one hand and spray can in the other. She seemed unable to move her limbs, and her face was frozen in astonishment.

I couldn't be sure how long the mop would stall them as Chas was a big and powerful man. Thankfully, it didn't appear to be of the cheaper variety, and as Chas crashed into the doors, the handle held firm. I didn't wait for his second charge but tipped the cleaning trolley over as a further barricade, turned around and sprinted after Suzanne who had reached the second set of doors by this time.

As she held these open and waited for me to catch up, I heard Chas frantically yell, "The lift Henry, get into the lift."

Suzanne and I sped down the corridor towards the stairs. I knew from the factory layout the lift would come out somewhere in the factory further away from the main entrance than our stairs. I only hoped it would delay them long enough for us to make our escape.

As we began to descend the stairs my eyes focused on the doors at the end of the reception desk, the ones marked STAFF ONLY, expecting them to burst open at any second. We clattered down the marble steps, our footfalls echoing round the vast hall like gunfire in a shooting gallery.

Still the doors remained closed.

We crossed the hall in seconds, each one seeming to last forever, all of them extra seconds on my life. Suzanne reached the revolving doors first forcing her way straight into them. In the split second I had to wait to follow her, I again glanced towards the STAFF ONLY sign.

And still the doors remained closed.

Not for the first time that day, I felt the faint flicker of hope that I may yet see another sunrise.

The early morning sunshine had given way to an April shower, and as I took a sharp left turn on exiting the building towards Suzanne's car, my feet went from under me on the slick gleaming tarmac.

My shoes did a wheel spin as, in panic, I attempted to regain my footing and follow Suzanne.

Panting like an exercised Labrador, I finally reached her car. Suzanne was already in the driver's seat and not even out of breath. If I survived all this, I really would have to think seriously about my health and fitness.

Suzanne fired up the engine, engaged reverse gear and skewed out of her parking bay in an anti-clockwise arc. She switched to the forward gears even before we had come to a rest and gunned the car towards the exit barrier, tyres screeching and spraying water as they fought for grip.

From the passenger seat, I could see that still no one else had emerged from the building. Indeed, as yet nobody had even entered the entrance hall. I was puzzled by this; puzzled but relieved. Surely, it wouldn't take that long for them to use the lift and continue with their pursuit, unless of course, something had happened to Henry. Perhaps he had taken a turn for the worst. I hoped this wasn't the reason for their delay.

As the red and white barrier rose in front of us, my uncertainty was answered. Chas' car came squealing around the building from the rear carpark, and I realised they must have taken the back exit out of the factory.

Once clear of the barrier, our view to the right was obscured by a couple of parked trailers, empty and rested for the weekend awaiting their Monday morning work load. To turn that way would have meant crawling out slowly until we had a clear view of our way ahead and losing vital time to our hunters.

Suzanne remained calm, turned left out into the industrial estate and quickly ran up through the gears, ignoring the speed limit. For the first time in my life, I prayed for a police car to come and stop us for speeding. But I knew this wouldn't happen—there could be no reason for such a vehicle to be on an almost deserted industrial estate at this time on a Saturday.

As I looked behind us, I could see Chas' Mercedes was in hot pursuit about a hundred yards away. Suzanne's E-Class Cabriolet would have been slicker and faster on the open road than Chas' 4X4, but on the wet and winding industrial estate there would be little to choose between them.

Suzanne didn't let up. Factories, some disused, some derelict, many still with thriving businesses, shot past in a blur. There were parked vehicles aplenty in these, mostly lorries and vans, but very little weekend activity in any of them.

The rain still hammered down, bouncing off the tarmac, but the sun was battling to regain control and began to form a vivid rainbow. It all seemed somewhat surreal. In other circumstances, it would have been something to behold. But in the circumstance we found ourselves in, our breath was being taken away for quite a different reason.

Again, I looked behind us. Chas had perhaps gained a little on us, perhaps not. It was hard to tell accurately in the misting conditions. They were still too far away to tell whether Henry was all right. From our distance both driver and passenger were just tall, dark silhouettes.

It suddenly occurred to me that we were heading deeper into the estate. Had we turned right out of the factory we would have been heading towards town. However, if we followed our present course we would eventually reach a 'T' junction allowing us to take the town option. Otherwise, we would be encountering more and more disused units. The further we travelled into the bowels of this deserted area, the less I could recall about it as it had been years since my job had taken me so far in. I hoped Suzanne knew where she was going.

I was dragged from my thoughts by the high pitched wail of a mobile phone. It wasn't mine, the ring tone was different, and I had left mine at home anyway.

My eyes followed my ears to Suzanne's handbag on the floor at my feet.

"Get that, will you?" Suzanne asked, her sharp assured tone strengthening me.

I fumbled around in her bag for what seemed an eternity, wondering why women kept so much irrelevant rubbish in these things.

Suzanne looked down towards the bag, not letting up on the speed.

"For Christ's sake, watch where you're going," I yelled, the fear in my voice palpable.

"Pass the damn bag here," the calmness was quickly evaporating from her voice.

As she reached across, I found the offending object and pulled it clear allowing the bag to fall back into the foot well. But I didn't pass her the phone; instead, I pressed the accept button to take the call myself allowing Suzanne to concentrate on the driving and on not killing us.

"Hello?" I said.

"Suzanne! Suzanne! Please stop!" Henry's panic stricken voice pleaded.

I looked behind us trying to connect the face to the voice. They had closed on us but still not enough for me to make out any facial features.

"It's your dad," I said to Suzanne.

She looked across at me, her expression begging for more information. I returned to Henry's voice, "For God's sake, tell her to stop! She'll kill herself. Please. We can work this out. Don't let her die like her mother."

Back to Suzanne, "He wants us to stop; says we can work this out. Doesn't want you to die like your mother?" That last bit puzzled me.

Suzanne could see the confusion on my face and briefly explained, "My mother was killed in a car crash when I was eight." Her foot didn't even waver on the pedal as we continued to hurtle to our fate.

They were perhaps only sixty yards behind us now, and I could clearly see the anguished look on Henry's face. Chas on the other hand was calmness personified. The smirk had returned to his face and he seemed to be enjoying the whole thing.

The grin broadened as his eyes met mine, sending an electric impulse of fear down my spine. He held my gaze as his hand emerged out of the window, pointing the firearm directly at me. I froze in horror but managed to blurt out to Suzanne, "Faster, faster damn it; he's gaining on us."

Chas lowered the barrel of the gun a touch, and I realised he was pointing it at our wheels. He jerked the gun to the side and pulled the trigger. A loud explosion rung in my ears and the bullet smashed into the tarmac next to us with a dull thud—a warning shot.

Suzanne glanced into her mirror, "What the f—?" She exclaimed, momentarily losing her composure but not her control of the car.

"He's shooting at us!" I yelled. I was no longer quite so sure that Suzanne was as safe as I had previously reckoned.

Again Suzanne seemed to read my thoughts, "Don't worry, he's only trying to scare us."

Well, I thought, *he's certainly succeeding there.*

My attention returned to our foe. Chas was once again manoeuvring the gun in our direction.

"No, Chas, no!" I could hear Henry pleading. I had almost forgotten I still had Suzanne's phone in my hand.

Henry grabbed Chas by the shoulder to stop him or at least hinder his aim. Although the old man was no physical match for Chas, it did throw him off balance causing their car to veer about manically. Chas was forced to slow down, losing them valuable ground.

"They've dropped back! Faster, faster!" I yelled at Suzanne. I chose not to tell her why they had slowed as she would fear for her father and perhaps give up.

Suzanne slammed her foot down on the brake, and I was thrown back around, almost colliding with the windscreen. We had come to a bend and the 'T' junction was just ahead.

Chas was well back now but was once again gaining on us. However, I judged we should have ample time to negotiate the junction. It was unlikely there would be any need for us to stop, partly because of the lack of traffic, but also because to our left was virtually all empty and derelict premises; any vehicles would turn from the direction of town onto the road we were about to exit.

As I focused on the junction, my heart skipped several beats, and the optimism I had just obtained was flushed away with the rain water. There had been an accident right on the junction. Suzanne slowed down only as much as she needed to.

The nearer we got the clearer the picture became. A blue Ford Focus stood in the centre of the junction. Embedded in the driver's door was a black Volkswagen Golf. The driver of the Ford remained in his seat, his head at an odd angle; he was either unconscious or dead I surmised. That was horrendous enough, but the real horror was unfolding outside the vehicles, right in front of us.

The passenger from the Ford, a young woman of about twenty, blood streaming from a head wound and limping grotesquely with what appeared to be a broken ankle, was screaming and trying to shake off the man from the Volkswagen.

Everything was happening in slow-motion, but we dare not stop. There was nothing we could do and Chas was only seconds behind us.

Volkswagen man, covered head to waist in blood, would not be denied. He dragged the woman to the floor and ripped her blood-drenched white translucent blouse completely off revealing her black lacy underwear. In other circumstances, it may have been quite erotic, and this only served to heighten the horror.

Her screaming stopped abruptly turning to a gurgle. Her assailant had ripped out her throat. She must have been dead by this point but that didn't stop the man from pummelling her face into an unrecognisable pulp.

The next series of attacks was clearly under way.

Suzanne swerved around the bloodied pair, forcing our vehicle to turn left, away from town and further down the road of despair. As we gained speed, I dared a backward glance. Chas was almost at the junction.

But he was hardly slowed by it at all. The smirk never left his face, and he did not attempt to miss the people in the road. In fact, from my position, it looked as though he had deliberately swerved to hit them. The man was thrown straight into the side of his Volkswagen whilst Chas' car seemed to jump a little as his wheels ran right over the woman's head, bursting it like a water bomb and spraying blood and brain matter across the road.

My stomach lurched as it fought to retain its contents.

Suzanne, with her eyes fixed firmly on the road ahead had, thankfully, seen none of this. "You OK? You've gone a bit pale." she asked, realising something was wrong with me.

"Yeah, fine," I swallowed and managed to whisper.

Once more, we rapidly gained speed as the long straight road stretched out in front of us. There was mostly scrub land on our right. Long forgotten industry a distant memory among the weeds, rubble and broken, rusting fencing. Dumped rubbish was strewn about with several burnt out vehicles dotted around. Badly spelt graffiti adorned many of the walls. Apparently, 'kylie lovs Gery', *but not enough to get his name right,* I thought, and 'wensday rule' were a couple of the more identifiable and repeated ones.

On our left were brick built factories and warehouses, long ago abandoned and also covered in similar graffiti, with virtually all their windows smashed, apart from a few near the roofs—too high for most except those with a strong arm and good aim. There were many missing tiles atop these edifices, some of which bore the signs of fire damage. This was one area of our town the tourism industry wouldn't want to publicise.

Looking over my shoulder, I could see that Chas was at least a hundred yards behind and not gaining, perhaps slipping even further back. He didn't appear to be in quite as much of a hurry as previously. It was as though he knew something that we didn't and therefore had no reason to rush.

Suddenly, Suzanne jerked the steering wheel to the right, and I was again hurled around towards the windscreen, this time more forcibly, and my head made contact with the glass. Not hard enough to damage the window but enough to cause my head to spin and my vision to blur for a moment.

As I refocused, we came to a halt. The road had come to a sudden end; the canal was right in front of us, barring any further progress. We had barely managed to stop before plunging in. I quickly looked left, then right and behind us, searching for a means of escape. About twenty yards back, on Suzanne's side, was a narrow side road.

"Quick, reverse," I shouted, pointing out the escape route. Suzanne spotted it at virtually the same time as I had and forced the car into reverse gear, the tyres complaining and kicking up debris as we retraced our path.

Frantically, I looked behind us for Chas' car, expecting him to be upon us at any second. But he had come to a halt about fifty yards back.

This not only puzzled me but terrified me as well. Chas was in no rush, like a spider in the centre of its web and we were the fly, knowing that however much the fly struggled, it could not escape. He slowly began to move his car forwards as Suzanne completed her manoeuvre and sped into the side street.

Another dead end. High brick walls rose above us on both sides, blocking out most of the emerging sunshine. In front was a solid stone wall about three feet high. I couldn't see beyond this but knew the car would take us no further. The walls were so tall and the street so narrow it felt as though they were closing in on us, like the lid was coming down on our coffin. Chas had once more come to rest, at the entrance to the street. There was insufficient room for a three-point turn, the only possible way out was to reverse. But Chas had parked at such an angle as to deny us the space to pass him.

We sat there for what seemed like forever—*and probably was for me*, I thought. A stand-off that could only end in one way.

Chapter 22

"Come on," Suzanne pushed open her door, "We'll have to run for it."

I leapt from the car. Suzanne had already set off at speed in the only viable direction—forwards. She reached the waist high stone wall first which was low enough for us to climb over. As Suzanne scaled it, I looked back to see that Chas and Henry had left their vehicle. I was pleased that Henry was coming with Chas and not remaining behind. Not only might he be able to persuade Chas to let me live, but he would certainly slow them down.

Suzanne was quickly over the obstacle, and it was my turn. I turned to face the grey stone blockade and my heart sank again. Directly behind it, just a few feet away, was that damned canal. It had bent its way round deliberately to again block us and assist Chas.

I dropped down from the wall and stumbled on some rubble which liberally pock-marked the tow path and lost my balance. I fell over and rolled towards the dank stagnant water coming to rest staring into the quagmire but my image was not returning the look as the water was too polluted. Suspended in it were various food wrappings, carrier bags, disposable nappies and a myriad of other mostly unrecognisable items. The soup was neatly topped off with a quilt of green algae. The stench made me gag.

"For God's sake, come on," Suzanne pleaded for me to get a move on. Further encouragement was unnecessary as I climbed back to my feet and limped after her, ignoring the pain from the ankle I had just twisted that shot up my leg each time I put my foot down.

Water barred our way on the left and solid brick wall on the right. Our choice of direction had been halved to back or forth. Suzanne, a little ahead of me, chose the latter and set off running at a pace I would find difficult to keep up with, more so because of my complaining ankle. She suddenly skidded to a halt on the rain-slicked footway spraying water and dirt into the canal. I was puzzled as she seemed to be staring at the endless brick façade but as I neared her and followed her gaze a door appeared in it. Suzanne pushed at it. It creaked slightly but would not open. She took a step back and gave it a mighty kick.

The rusting metal object gave way just enough for us to squeeze through. Suzanne went in first, and as I entered, I looked back to see that Chas and Henry had not yet come into view. I forced the objecting door shut and hoped this would allow us to proceed undetected.

We stood there a few seconds while our eyes adjusted to our surroundings, the only source of light coming from a large gaping hole in the roof. I looked up, and rain water washed onto my face and clothes, its splashing echoing around the vast chasm as it hit the floor.

Soon accustomed to the light, I took in the remnant of a once thriving business. The ground was strewn with rubble, metal, and bits of broken machinery. Where the floor was revealed large puddles had gathered. The rain water had mingled with oil, grease, and who knows what other substances, forming a slick sludge. Where the light danced upon it multi-coloured patterns emanated like some sort of psychedelic pop art from the sixties. The surrounding walls were a slimy gun-metal grey which did nothing to improve the ambience.

Suzanne, being more practical than me, had not stopped to admire the scenery but had instead picked out a doorway at the far end of the reeking room. "Come on," she said tugging at my arm. We proceeded cautiously, our vision subdued by the half-light and unsure of what lay beneath the sludge.

As we approached the end of the room, I could see there was just a gap, not a door, leading through a short corridor and into and another room, roughly the same size as the first with the same depressing grey walls. Although the roof in this one was pretty much intact light cascaded in from the glassless windows that spread the length of the far wall. In the corner to the left of these windows was another door.

This time I didn't need urging onwards.

As we crossed the void, the stench within increased. Only this time, it wasn't just the rank odour of stagnant water, grease and rotting long dead industry. This smell was far more acrid and caused me to retch. As we neared the door I could see the origin of the offending stink.

Three bodies, human, or at least they had been, were entangled in a greasy puddle. Although obviously deceased, they appeared to be moving. Closer inspection, but not too close, showed this to be due to the maggots and insects that were crawling all over them, relishing their hearty meal.

We both recoiled simultaneously. I put my hand up to my gagging mouth and just managed to control myself, but Suzanne was unable to hold on to her breakfast. She turned to the side and released it to splash against the wall, her stomach heaving several times, even when it was empty.

I kept my hand over my mouth, pinched my nose and took a closer look at the bodies, intrigued as to why they lay there unmissed and undetected. Ignoring the living objects, it soon became apparent by their attire that they must have been homeless people. Multiple layers of old, worn, and ill-fitting garments were accompanied by lace-less, torn and holed footwear. Next to them were discarded spent cans of super-strength lager. Momentarily, I realised how much I would give for such a drink right at that moment.

What also soon became apparent was that these were victims of another rage attack. Two of the people, one male and one female—I thought but couldn't be certain due to their damaged and decaying state—wore the tell-tale marks of such an assault. Man-tramp had one eye missing and a deep raking gouge down his face. A piece of scrap metal, presumably acquired from their surroundings, was protruding from his skull.

Woman-tramp's head was twisted at a grotesque angle and her mouth gaped wide. Her tongue was missing. Next to her was a brick that size-wise appeared to match the large and gaping indentation in her forehead.

The third person was relatively unmarked save for a superficial four-finger scratch across his cheek and nothing that might be deemed the cause of death. He, I concluded, must have been the instigator of the attack. He seemed to have had a heart attack as his teeth were clenched together in a manic grin. Held firmly between them was tramp-woman's tongue.

These horror scenes were becoming all too familiar for me and were already starting to lose their shock-value. It's quite remarkable how quickly we adjust to our circumstances.

I was yanked from my ponderings by the squeal of rusty metal. We had not managed to give Chas the slip, I realised, as the outer door we had used moments earlier had just been forced open.

Suzanne had stopped retching and regained her composure. We held our breath to deter the stench as well as our pursuers and looked at each other and then towards the entrance gap to our room. The sound of splashing footsteps grew as they advanced towards us. We turned our attention towards the door next to the corpses. I prayed that it wasn't locked or rusted shut as I recalled Chas' words, "He has to go. But not here…" Well, the present *here* would be a lot more conducive to his plans.

We had no other means of escape and nowhere to hide. This was our one and only option and there was no point in trying to be quiet as they were heading our way.

I grabbed the metal knob and twisted. My hand turned round the greasy handle, unable to get a grip. I looked to Suzanne for something to wipe it with but could tell by her half-step back that she was unwilling to part with any of her clothing. Mine was too wet from where I had fallen over the wall, so I turned towards the bodies. Suzanne looked away as I peeled back the outer layers from the least dishevelled corpse and tore a sizeable piece from his shirt.

The splashing steps were closing and had almost reached the entrance to our room.

I quickly wiped the knob with the rag, then my hands and tried the handle. This time it gave in quite easily and smoothly rotated almost full circle allowing me to exhale in relief grateful that it wasn't locked. I gave the door a good yank but it wouldn't budge, rust doing the job that the lock had forgotten to do.

I looked at Suzanne and she looked at me; then we both glared in the direction of the foot-splashes.

Taking a step back, I raised my leg and kicked with all my might against the door hoping to dislodge enough rust to allow the two metal structures to be parted. The footfalls from the other room stopped abruptly. I twisted the handle, paused, took a deep breath and gave it a firm tug.

The splashing from behind restarted only this time more frantically.

But then the splashing was drowned out by the loud screech of complaining metal as the door gave in. We darted through as our hunters entered the room we had just vacated. Although the echoing effect of the building would hamper our detection, I knew it would only take Chas a matter of seconds to deduce our direction—this was the only other exit.

We emerged into a small courtyard surrounded on all sides by high walls of the same red brick as the rest of the edifice. The floor was, in keeping with the rest of the area we had encountered, dotted with rubble and metal. Weeds, grass and the like had forced their way through the tarmac ground in various places. In the centre of the wall opposite our doorway was a gap blocked by a decaying wooden double gate. A sturdy rusting metal bar was in place across these preventing them from being opened from the other side.

With a little effort, we managed to remove this and pull the gates open towards us. I was not surprised to be confronted by my old nemesis on the other side; the canal.

Once again, we chose to go right. The opposite direction would only have led us back towards where we had set out from, with the same problems as we had when we abandoned our transport.

The canal, still working against us, had now straightened, when I had really needed it to carry on curving to keep me away from Chas' line of fire.

"Give it up, Suzanne," I heard Chas shout as he and Henry came onto the canal towpath. "You know this is useless."

I looked back over my shoulder and saw they were only about fifty yards behind. But Henry looked distressed and was leaning against the wall. He was wheezing so loud, I could clearly hear him from as far away as we were and knew Suzanne must also have heard this and realised the distress he was in.

"Stop. Please stop, Suzanne. I'm sure…we can sort this out. Everything will be OK. No one has to die," he managed to gasp.

We halted and turned to face them. Chas' manic grin did not concur with Henry's words.

"Come on," I wheeled round and tugged on Suzanne's arm. She strained against me for a second, mentally being pulled back by her father. She gave in, and we began running again.

We were putting more distance between ourselves and our pursuers. Suzanne was barely breathing heavily at all but my lungs were fighting against me and burning with the unfamiliar usage. The only thing that spurred me on to more effort was knowing that Henry would be far worse than me and that would slow them down. Even so, I prayed he would be all right if only for Suzanne's sake.

Once more, I looked back confirming my suspicions. They were far behind now and we steadied the pace to a slow jog. My hopes were again raised as logic told me this wilderness couldn't go on for ever and sanctuary must be getting closer by the minute.

The wasteland on the other side of the canal had given way to a small housing estate. My attention was drawn to a young woman and a girl of about eleven or twelve. I couldn't make out what they were saying, but they were apparently having an altercation.

The woman had her arms outstretched with her hands raised in a defensive action. She was of sturdy build but was backing away from the girl who was at best half her weight and a good foot shorter.

As we got nearer to them, I could see the woman had been injured. Blood was flowing freely down her face from an eye wound onto her bright yellow jacket. I could also make out what she was saying now, "No, no, please Debbie no," her terrified words sent a shiver right through me.

The girl suddenly rushed at her screaming like a wild animal and knocked her to the ground. Suzanne and I came to a halt in disbelief as the brief but vicious attack unfolded before our eyes.

The girl was on top of the woman, tearing at her face like a wild dog. The woman's screams were quickly drowned out, turning to a gurgle as blood filled her airway. She fell silent, dead, either by her wounds or by drowning in her own life fluid. But the girl wasn't satisfied and turned her attention towards the woman's body. She tore at her clothes as if she were excitedly ripping open Christmas presents.

These were soon dispensed with and the child then started on the dead woman's flesh, still howling like an animal.

Suzanne gasped in astonishment and screamed just one long anguished word, "No!"

The girl stopped her onslaught and turned towards us. Her eyes met mine. They were staring wide with fury but showed no recognition of what was happening. She slowly climbed to her feet then suddenly rushed straight towards us, totally unaware of the expanse of water that stood in her way.

We instinctively took a step back as the girl flailed into the air and came splashing down into the canal. She went straight under, her eyes fixed on mine until they disappeared below the surface. I stood transfixed, frozen in time, looking into the murk expecting her to leap out at any second.

But she did not rise and only a steady stream of air bubbles broke the surface. Shock was replaced by relief and then by shame. I found it hard to accept that I could feel in any way pleased about the death of a young girl. But I knew there was nothing we could have done for her. She would have died from the virus and we were lucky to escape with our lives.

Three attacks, or at least the results of them, we had encountered already that day. All in such a small area and short period of time. We were either extraordinarily unlucky or Chas' mushroom effect was beginning to take place, and the virus was beginning to assert its stranglehold.

The idea that this, perhaps, made the need for him to kill me less pressing offered me no comfort whatsoever. I could not begin to comprehend what this would mean for our community, or indeed for the wider society.

"Come on, they're gaining," Suzanne urged me onwards.

I shook the images from my head and followed her. Up ahead the canal again began to curve away, hiding our course. But this mattered not one iota now as our only option was to continue.

Across the water, the small housing estate had been replaced by waste land with dense shrubbery reaching down to the canal, overgrown bushes appearing to stoop to drink the dank water. An expanse of reeds had taken a strong grip at the waters' edge, eating into the decaying bank. A family of coots, distinct with their white caps atop their jet black feathers, sheltered within.

On our side, the run of derelict warehouses and factories finally gave way to open space, with a low scalable wall as its only perimeter. But as we reached this, my hopes were dashed. The ground had inclined steeply away presenting us with a drop of at least twenty feet onto a surface strewn with rocks rusting metal and other debris. I didn't fancy our chances of surviving that, so we continued on our way parallel to the curving canal.

More red brick buildings soon removed any options we might have had—even if those only options had been as to which way to die.

Chas and Henry had dropped back quite a way, the latter seemed to be suffering greatly and even more distressed than before. He leaned against the younger man for support gasping for air.

A short distance ahead of me, Suzanne had rounded the bend but had slowed to a walk. As I caught up with her, she stopped completely. I peered around her and discovered why. Our path was blocked by a sturdy metal security fence, at least as high as a football goalpost. It jutted out over the canal and was topped by sharp spikes rendering it completely impassable. There was no way we could go any further in that direction.

We turned back, and I hoped Chas was far enough behind for us to reach the open space we had passed. A twenty-foot drop that would almost certainly maim or kill me didn't seem such a bad option after all.

Chapter 23

As they emerged into view, I could see they had already passed our only escape route and my heart sank. I bent down putting my hands on my knees, defeated both mentally and physically.

It wasn't a case of giving up more one of knowing that I was beaten, knowing when I had run out of time and alternatives.

Chas must have realised our predicament. Fifty yards stood between us and I could clearly make out his victory smirk. He held out a hand inviting Henry to remain where he was and rest. The older man leaned against the wall for support.

Chas advanced towards us with the gun in his hand hanging loosely by his side. "I told you to stop, told you it was no use; that I would win." He shook his head tutting, "But you wouldn't listen. You always have to find out things the hard way, Suzanne."

I looked at her, puzzled by his remark. She shook her head signalling to me that it was of no consequence.

Chas explained instead, relishing his moment of victory, "When she was mine, I told her I would always look after her. I always had her destiny in my hands."

"Look after me?" Suzanne laughed with disdain, "Control me more like."

Chas ignored the bait, "Like I said, you have to take the long route. I'll always win, Suzanne. You'll come to realise that fate will dictate that we were meant to be together."

Suzanne shook her head defiantly, "I'd rather die first."

I clenched my teeth, wondering why she had to bring up that subject. I was sort of hoping that killing someone might just have slipped Chas' mind.

As if reading my thoughts, Chas looked straight at me as he continued to approach, "Funny you should say that, the dying thing."

"Stop, wait!" Henry had regained some of his composure and was slowly catching up. "Don't do it, Chas! There's no need."

Taking up the argument I said, "Henry's right Chas. You've won. You saw the tramps in the warehouse. And the woman and girl over the canal. You've got your wish. This thing has grown out of control. It's too late to stop it now."

I wasn't only pleading for my life. I firmly believed my words were factual and it was too late for us to prevent the disaster that was unfolding.

Chas seemed to consider my words as he looked down and pursed his lips. "Good point, Jake."

He paused for a few seconds then added, "Shame, really. I was quite growing to like you, Jake. But you know too much. Sorry, but you're going to have to go." He raised the gun.

"No, stop, Chas," Henry, having now reached us, wheezed, tugging at Chas' sleeve, distracting him. Chas turned to placate the older man.

"Come on, Jake," Suzanne yelled, stripping off her jacket, "We can swim for it. It's your only chance."

She crouched down and pushed her arms behind herself in readiness to plunge into the stinking quagmire, then glanced in my direction and halted in mid pose.

Chas turned back in our direction and raised the gun, levelling it with my chest.

I looked down at my feet like a naughty child who'd been caught out lying. "I can't," I mumbled.

Suzanne dropped her arms and stood upright, confusion etched on her furrowed brow. She looked at me quizzically as I continued, "I can't swim…" My voice even quieter this time.

Chas lowered the firearm and burst out laughing, shaking his head, "The hero can't swim. He was going to save the world but it will have to look after itself, because of a bit of water. You couldn't make it up could you?"

Chas was genuinely amused by this but no one else was laughing. He strutted up to me, "Maybe I won't have to shoot you after all. I could just throw you into the canal, make out it was an accident."

I braced myself, ready to fight him.

"That way we wouldn't have to tell anybody anything." He turned towards Suzanne. "And you wouldn't have to go to prison. Everyone wins, except you of course, Jake. Still, you can go to meet the big guy in the sky happy in the knowledge that you have saved your girlfriend from a horrible fate."

He seemed quite pleased with himself at the way things were turning out.

"I'll tell them everything, Chas; everything. You won't get away with this." Suzanne spat through clenched teeth.

But Chas was still in control, "What and have your hero boyfriend die for nothing? That's not very gracious of you Suzanne. I thought you were better than that."

I was going to die, I knew, and could see his logic. I was about to try to convince Suzanne to do as he said when Henry again interrupted. "You can't, Chas. Please see sense. You've got to stop all this now."

The old man was getting more and more distressed, the anguish telling in his voice. "Please Chas, you've got..." he started to plead, but stopped mid-sentence.

I could see something was seriously wrong as he gasped for breath and clutched his chest, staggering backwards, only the brick wall keeping him on his feet.

"Your tablets, dad!" Suzanne yelled and took a step forwards to help her father.

Chas pointed the gun at her to warn her to keep back. Henry groped in his pocket for his tablets, eventually finding them. But as he pulled them out, they fell to the floor. Chas instinctively bent down to retrieve them for him.

And as he did so I saw my window of opportunity, probably my last one.

I threw myself at Chas with all the force I could muster, colliding with his midriff like a rugby player making a tackle. I caught him off-guard and off balance, knocking him to the ground. The gun slipped from his grasp and skidded along the wet gravel before plunging into the canal. I had no time to feel relief or anything at this as all my concentration went into trying to contain my larger adversary.

I was on top of him and swung my right arm in an arcing punch. Chas managed to fend off the blow, and I followed it up with another with my left hand. This connected with his cheek bone but caused me more pain than it did him—in the turmoil I had forgotten the arm was broken and in plaster.

The agony shot up to my elbow as if I had been struck with a cattle prod, and I yelled out, stopping the onslaught just long enough for Chas to regain his composure.

The bigger, fitter man quickly took advantage of my demise and rolled me onto my back. I resisted, but the desperate man did not have the strength of ten, and I was easily overpowered.

He sat astride me but didn't strike me, instead took great delight in practising his smirk and twisting my injured limb. The pain was like nothing I had ever felt before. It seemed as though the two parts of the broken bone were being ground together. While keeping the pressure on my arm he pressed his other forearm across my throat.

I started to feel dizzy, and I could feel consciousness beginning to slip away.

Chas suddenly released me, but I was too confused to react. In my semi-conscious state, I could feel myself being lifted from the ground. Shaking my head in an attempt to regain my senses, I was finally able to focus. What I saw brought me round quicker than any dose of smelling salts could have.

Chas had dragged me towards the canal's edge and was dangling my head over the water. I twisted and writhed, kicked and struggled as my aqua-fear hurtled my mind back to my near-drowning as a child.

My attempts to over balance him were useless. His grip was firm, and there was nothing I could do as the dank liquid got closer and closer. I could smell the rancid decaying soup as my head was almost touching it.

Chas suddenly raised me up completely off the ground preparing to throw me in. I still twisted and writhed but to no effect; his power and balance were far superior to anything I had to offer. I closed my eyes, accepting the inevitable, and took a last deep breath of precious air determined to hang onto every last second of my life

I could feel the air rushing past me as I plunged downwards, and then I heard the expected almighty splash, but I was confused. I didn't feel wet, and there was no sudden shock to the system as there should have been when my body came into contact with freezing cold water. It wasn't at all like I remembered the infant me sinking in that swimming pool.

But I still held my breath, not daring to let go of it, and slowly opened my eyes.

I was looking at blue sky, interspersed with grey angry clouds and the only liquid hitting my face was the last remnants of an April shower.

I swung my head round, and Suzanne entered my vision. She was looking down, but not at me. Her gaze was towards the canal. In her hand, raised above her head, was a half brick. It appeared to have rainwater dripping from it but as my eyes focused I could see this liquid was bright red and not water at all.

It was blood.

Pulling my aching body upright into a sitting position, I realised Suzanne must have struck Chas with the brick causing him to drop me on the tow path. And, as he was nowhere to be seen, it must have been him that had fallen into the canal causing the splash.

Dizziness was still my ruler, and I almost joined Chas as I attempted to stand. Suzanne dropped the brick, steadied me, and said, "No, stay down, Jake. Wait until you've come round. There's no rush, he's gone now."

As my senses returned, so did the excruciating burning agony within my broken limb. But I ignored it as much as I could, climbed to my feet and joined the others in their canal-side vigil.

"How long's he been under," I asked, unsure as I had lost track of time in my concussed state.

"Too long," is all Suzanne said.

"Is your father OK?" My senses were sharpening, and I remembered we were in the middle of nowhere.

"Yes, yes, I'll be fine," Henry said, sounding a little weak but perfectly coherent and no longer out of breath. "I've got my pills, so I'll be fine."

Suzanne cut in, "But you'll have to go to hospital, dad, just to be on the safe side."

He didn't argue.

"And so will you." She had turned her attention to me. "That arm must be in a bit of a mess," she said screwing her face up at the thought.

"Yes, it does sting a little," I responded making light of our predicament, just glad to be alive. These brushes with death were happening all too frequently for my liking.

"Have you still got my phone?" Suzanne held out her hand to me, "I'll call emergency services."

Chapter 24

We had a few minutes' rest while Suzanne explained our situation to the emergency call centre.

The threat to my life had severely diminished but this was somewhat balanced out as the pain and weariness of the whole episode hit me. There wasn't a single joint, muscle or bone in my entire body that wasn't screaming out at me. I slid down the wall into a sitting position. The effort high-lighted the injury to my leg, the pain jostling for prime position with that from my damaged arm.

When the call was over, Suzanne said, "We'll have to make our way back; the ambulance won't be able to reach us here."

Turning to her father she asked, "You up to this, dad?"

Henry wearily nodded his agreement, probably realising as I had that there was no alternative. He did look all right though, considering the exertion he had put his body through, now that his pills were working.

With much effort and groaning, I hauled myself off the ground, and we began to make our way back alongside the canal. The arm pain quickly won its battle as my leg resorted to a semi-numbness.

We came to the place where the trees came down to meet the water. They seemed to be bowing in sympathy with the plight that had befallen us. The encroaching reeds rustled their empathy in the gentle breeze and the coots, disturbed, took off together as if performing a fly past.

Adjacent to this was the spot where the raging girl had plunged into the murky water and we could see her body had since come to the surface. She was floating face down like a rag doll among the rest of the debris, looking so peaceful now, her flowery summer dress bringing a sort of innocence to the whole picture; the tranquillity directly contrasting with what had happened to the poor child. Her victim was a crumpled bloodied mess equally peaceful on the grass verge only yards away. A slight hum arose from her as the gathering flies harmonised with the soothing spring breeze.

We trudged on.

Next, I glanced at the wooden gates we had come through only minutes earlier. In some ways, it all seemed like a lifetime ago. I recalled the horrors that lay within that derelict and forgotten building. It seemed as though death and destruction lay hidden round every corner; and this would only be the beginning.

And still we trudged on, our pace steady but unwavering.

Finally, we reached the low wall where we had entered the tow path. Suzanne easily skipped over it first, turned, and held out a hand to help her father. I steadied him from behind, and followed them once he was safely on the other side. This time it was much more difficult as the pain from my injured arm rendered it almost unusable. As I stumbled over the brick barrier, out of the corner of my eye I glimpsed movement in the distance back along the canal. I got the impression that someone was climbing out of it.

Once on the other side, I took a longer look back in the direction from which we had come, screwing up my eyes in an attempt to better focus them. But no one was there, just the greenery waving in the wind. My imagination must have been playing tricks on me. Chas had had a profound effect on me, and we hadn't found his body. I stood there a moment longer, staring, then shook my head to dispel the paranoia.

An ambulance, blue lights flashing, was the first to arrive on the scene as we made our way along the narrow street. It came to a halt some distance behind Chas' car. The driver climbed out and came towards us as his mate opened up the back of the ambulance.

"Everyone OK here?" The driver asked, "Walking wounded only? That's good."

"My father has had an angina attack," Suzanne offered, understandably more concerned for Henry than she was for me and my injuries.

"Don't fuss, Suzanne. I'm all right. I've had my pills."

"Better safe than sorry, sir. Come on, in we get," the paramedic said, taking hold of the old man's arm and helping him into the vehicle.

His mate offered to do the same for me, but I declined his assistance and tried to persuade him to wait for the police to arrive. "None of us have life-threatening injuries here and we really need to talk to them. There have been murders committed here."

The older of the two green-uniformed men considered my request, nodded his agreement and said, "We can give you a few minutes, I suppose, while we turn the ambulance round. It's been manic this morning, what with more of those attacks happening."

I looked at Suzanne and her at me, recognising that our suspicions had been confirmed. Things were rapidly moving forward.

The blast of a police siren drew our attention, and we turned to the approaching car.

A female constable, whom I recognised as P.C. Weismann (the officer who had been at my interview after my attack), got out of the driver's side. An older male colleague, whom I hadn't seen before, came from the other side.

Suzanne explained the whole situation to P.C. Weismann; about the girl's body, and Chas, and the three corpses in the warehouse.

I spoke with the other police officer. "Could you give me a hand to shift the four by four so Suzanne can get her car out? We'll have to shove it as we haven't got the keys."

It was part of the scene of a crime, but I thought it would do no harm to ask as it was the only solution to freeing Suzanne's car.

"Under normal circumstances, I'd have to make you leave it. But things are getting so much out of control today..." The officer let his statement hang.

"More attacks; how many?" I asked.

He paused, knowing protocol should have prevented him from saying anything further, but it was clear to see by his state of semi-shock that he was getting out of his depth, "At least four, besides those your friend reported."

I didn't push the issue, and said, "Come on let's shift the car," giving him something practical to concentrate on.

The officer went in front of the vehicle while I got into the driving seat. I took the handbrake off and knocked it into neutral gear. Guiding the heavy car was difficult enough with one hand but it was made even more so because the power steering couldn't be engaged with the ignition not being switched on. It was a good job I only had to turn the wheel a half rotation while the officer moved us backwards, just far enough to allow Suzanne to get her car out.

"We need to be getting off," the paramedic said as I climbed gingerly out of Chas' Mercedes. "If you're coming with us, sir, you'd better be getting in."

I turned to Suzanne as Weismann was handing her a card.

"You can reach me on this number if you think of anything else you want to tell me. We'll be in touch," the officer said.

Suzanne smiled and nodded a thank you.

She turned her attention to me and said. "Go on, you go with dad, and I'll follow on behind."

I was reluctant to leave her on her own but what she said made sense, so I complied with her request and climbed into the ambulance.

Lights flashing and sirens wailing, we were soon breaking the speed limit again. I glanced over at Henry. He looked so tired, almost broken. He had dealt with so much that day, seeing his whole life falling apart before his eyes. I felt so sorry for him and opened my mouth to ask him if he was all right.

But I thought better of it and left him in peace to deal with his thoughts. After all, I barely knew the man and had hardly spoken to him. It would feel like I was intruding. Any conversation on the subject really ought to be between him and his daughter.

I sat back, exhausted myself, and attempted to arrange my own thoughts. The tiredness and relief had caused me to lose my focus and something was nagging at the back of my mind; something I couldn't quite put my finger on.

We raced through the industrial estate, retracing our path at a similar speed to earlier, past the derelict warehouses and sparsely populated factories, past the weeds, debris and broken down fences. It looked exactly the same as before, but felt so different. The estate hadn't been changed by the day's events but

I had. I felt a kind of numbness as though my brain had been anaesthetised.

As the ambulance pulled into the hospital, it came to me, that thing that had been gnawing away at the back of my mind.

We knew smoking stopped the virus and we would tell the police so. But from what Chas had told us back at the factory, there could be an anti-virus. If this was the case, it would save so much time and so many lives. Science would take weeks, perhaps months, developing their own anti-virus; time that people didn't have. The spread of the virus was already rapidly gathering pace. Chas hadn't actually said there was a cure but admitted their experiments had continued and implied there might be an anti-virus. I couldn't properly recall what was said, and maybe I was just clutching at straws but at the very least there should be information that would speed along the process of obtaining a solution.

Our driver turned off his flashing lights and sirens as he parked up at the emergency entrance. His colleague opened the rear doors to help us out. I could see Suzanne's car pulling in through the entrance. I had a decision to make.

Could I afford to linger in the hospital for hours, waiting for treatment, doing nothing, while the virus took a stronger and deeper hold on society? Of course I couldn't, so the dilemma was solved immediately. I reckoned if there was an anti-virus or anything to help us at all it would be back at Henry's factory and probably on Chas' computer.

I stepped off the back of the ambulance, and as Suzanne's car approached, I beckoned for her to pull over. I didn't want her to waste time parking up; every minute lost could mean another life gone.

She drew up alongside me and wound down the electronic passenger window, "What is it, Jake?" she asked.

I was abrupt, "We need to go."

"But my father; what about Henry?" she pleaded.

"I'm OK. I told you not to fuss. I don't even know why you made me come here," the old man complained as he was helped from the emergency vehicle.

"You've been through so much today, Dad. You really need to get yourself checked out," Suzanne argued as she got out of her car.

"The young lady's right. Best to be on the safe side," the older paramedic intervened.

Suzanne turned to me, "I can't just leave him here on his own. What's so important that we have to rush off anyway?"

"We need to go back to the factory. Chas' work should be on his computer."

"Yes, it is, but why? Why such a rush?" Her concern for her father had clouded her thinking.

"We need to find the anti-virus if there is one, or at least get all the information to the police. The next wave of this thing is happening right now as we speak."

Suzanne paused, considering my statement.

"The man's right, Suzanne," Henry interrupted, "You two get off. I'll be all right. I'll probably still be waiting to be seen when you get back."

Suzanne opened her mouth to protest but Henry waved her away.

"You can't leave that there," a security guard gestured towards Suzanne's Mercedes making her mind up for her.

"OK, Dad. We shouldn't be too long. We'll see you back here. Take care." She kissed her father on the cheek, gave him a hug and turned back to her car. "Come on then, Jake. Let's get this over with."

I had barely engaged my seat belt before we were pulling out of the hospital and into the stream of lazily moving traffic— Saturday shoppers going steadily about their business, oblivious to the horrors that were unfolding around them, about to explode into their lives.

Once we were away from the town centre, the traffic quickly thinned out, and we soon reached the cigarette factory.

The barrier came up allowing us entry, and the security guard in his office waved to us. Suzanne was fully focused on the job in hand and didn't return his gesture. She would want to complete our work as quickly as possible and get back to her father.

She pulled the car into the same space as that morning. We walked hurriedly towards the entrance, our shortened shadows behind us this time, pushing us onwards. It was as though we were reliving the day over.

This time, there was no Chas to greet us. Our footfalls echoed around the vast hall as we made our way upstairs to the offices. Mary and her cleaning utensils had disappeared, leaving no trace of the mess my actions had caused. This time we entered the office marked C. BINGAM. MANAGER.

Chas' office was similar to Suzanne's but not quite as orderly. An unwashed coffee cup stood on the desk next to his computer; some papers were strewn around it. I thought this a bit odd, expecting Mary to have tidied things away. Perhaps Chas didn't like people interfering with his work. Perhaps he always left things like that. It didn't seem to matter anyway.

Suzanne sat behind Chas' desk and adjusted the taller man's chair so that she didn't look like a little schoolgirl in the headmaster's office.

She fired up the computer.

It took her a few minutes to locate the relevant files. Eventually, she found them, or at least what was left of them. "They're gone!" she exclaimed, sitting back away from the offensive computer.

"What do you mean, they're gone? They can't be."

"Well, they have. Chas has downloaded everything onto an external memory device and erased the lot from his computer. There's the title still there 'Sport Enhancement and Tobacco Products', but nothing else. It just says, 'see storage options'."

"But why? He couldn't have known we were that near to him. We didn't even know ourselves 'til today. When did he do it?" I was intrigued. Things didn't add up.

Suzanne shuffled back to the computer and said, "He copied it all this morning before we arrived."

"Yes," I recalled, "He was putting what looked like a memory stick into his pocket when we met him on the way in this morning."

"And…" She didn't finish the sentence, just let out a short, sharp gasp.

"What?"

"It doesn't make sense. It says he last logged on less than half an hour ago. That's when he erased everything. But that's impossible."

I stood there with my mouth open, not knowing what to do or say.

"Let's have a look," I eventually came out with, hoping she had made a mistake.

But there was no error. "And nobody else could have done this? Nobody else has his password?" I was searching for an explanation.

"No; only me and Henry."

We both knew it couldn't possibly have been any of us.

I suddenly recalled climbing over the wall at the canal and how I thought I had seen someone getting out of the water. I had dismissed it as a trick of the mind at the time, but…

"I-I thought I saw somebody climb out of the canal," I half whispered.

Suzanne stared at me, mouth and eyes agog. Her eyebrows lifted inviting an explanation.

"When we were going to the ambulance. I thought I saw a man getting out of the canal. It must have been Chas. He must have run back here and erased everything. Covered his tracks and fled."

Suzanne leapt from behind the desk and ran over to the window. Looking down on the rear carpark she exclaimed, "It's gone! Dad's Roller has gone!"

We stared in disbelief at each other. "Think, Suzanne, think!" I said to her, my voice raised, almost yelling. "Where would he go?"

Suzanne contemplated my question, tugging her lip, just as I would.

"Home," She stated firmly. "He must have gone home. If I know Chas, he will be grabbing some stuff to do a runner."

"Are you sure?"

"No, but we have nothing else to go on. Come on." She left the computer running and we fled the office.

What she had said made sense. Chas would need to disappear to escape a murder charge. And he would take the memory stick with him, along with the cure. He would probably try and sell it for millions to the government. Whatever his plans were, what Suzanne had surmised seemed his most likely course of action.

We again found ourselves running through the factory to her car to make our escape.

Chapter 25

Suzanne spun the car around spraying water and dirt in an arc behind us as we screeched off towards the exit.

"Wait!" I shouted. "Ask the gateman which way Chas went."

Suzanne slammed on the brakes, and we skidded to a halt inches away from the rising barrier.

The security man leaned out of his window and asked, "What's the panic, Miss Deering? Not Henry I hope."

"No, no, it's not that, Ted. Have you seen Chas?" Suzanne tried to sound calm but the edge in her voice betrayed our urgency.

"You just missed him. He shot off in the Roller just before you arrived."

"Which way did he go?"

Ted rubbed his stubbled chin, "Bit strange that. He headed towards town."

Suzanne and I looked at each other quizzically, then she turned back to Ted and said, "What's strange about that?"

"Well, when you both went haring off this morning, you turned left, you know, away from town. And Chas, when he came back, on foot, he said him and Henry had broken down. He'd come to get the Roller to fetch Henry. But he went off in the wrong direction. Strange that; couldn't figure it out."

Suzanne rammed the car into gear and shot forward leaving Ted mumbling to himself, "Soaked he was, too. Must have been them showers; although…" The rest of his sentence disappeared behind us.

Suzanne raced out of the industrial estate and headed towards the by-pass. "It'll be quicker this way. Less traffic and speed limits."

I didn't argue with her, although it seemed to me the part about the speed limit was a bit irrelevant as we hadn't been bothered by those at all today. Still, as I didn't know where Chas lived, I couldn't offer any navigational advice. I thought it just as well as I reckoned Suzanne wasn't in the mood to listen to any.

Leaving the by-pass at the southern edge of town, we turned onto what I reckoned, from my years of experience delivering around the area, was the poshest part. Suzanne hardly slowed the pace at all. She had obviously taken this route many times in the past.

Sycamore trees, just coming into leaf, lined both sides of the avenue, the sunlight glinting off their rain soaked foliage in a myriad of colours. The area was, for the most part, quiet. The occasional driveway knew it was car-wash day and a middle aged couple were walking their dog, enjoying the sunny interlude between the downpours.

As we approached the top of the hill, Suzanne slowed right down, coming to a halt at a gateway on our left. Either side of this were hawthorn hedges, about six feet high, behind which was a small wooded area, not yet fully in leaf. Through the greenery, I could easily make out a Rolls Royce, perhaps fifty yards away, standing in front of a large, imposing house. Its shiny plastic windows and new brickwork indicated it was a recent build although a more than decent attempt had been made to design it in the Georgian style. The front door was framed by two marble pillars and fronted by about half a dozen stone steps.

Standing at the top of the hill, I imagined it was able to look down on the whole of the town; the most ostentatious house in an ostentatious street. Chas must have picked the location specifically for that purpose and had it built the way it was deliberately, I thought. Although I barely knew the man, he struck me as being just that sort of person.

While I was admiring the splendid dwelling, Suzanne took her phone from her handbag. She retrieved the card which P.C. Weismann had given her earlier and copied the number on it onto the keypad.

"Hello, Constable Weismann here, how can I help you?" The device uttered.

I could clearly hear both sides of the conversation in our quiet and peaceful surroundings.

Suzanne went on to briefly explain our situation, ending by emphasising the importance of stopping Chas. "Yes, officer, he must not get away. We believe he has the key to halting all these rage attacks. We think he may have a cure for the virus!"

"OK, we'll have someone with you as soon as possible," the police officer ended with, not sounding overenthusiastic—I supposed they are trained that way.

Suzanne pulled the vehicle off the road into the recess formed by the gateway and partially blocked the drive. "We'd be best going in on foot. We don't want to announce our arrival," she said.

I was a bit more reluctant to proceed than her as I wasn't too keen on tangling with her ex for a third time. The first two hadn't ended very well for me, and I couldn't see another clash being any better. "Shouldn't we just watch and wait for the police to get here?" I tried to reason with her.

"But he could be about to leave at any moment. He got at least twenty minutes' head start on us, and I doubt he'll be hanging about to have lunch or anything. We need that memory card, and this could be our only chance to get it. Besides, we don't know how long they'll be. They will be rather busy with the attacks."

"We could park across the entrance, maybe block him in," My fear tried to reason with Suzanne, but she ignored me, opened her door and got out.

I took a deep, resigned breath and slowly followed her. I had run out of arguments and in any case Suzanne was no longer listening to me. I once again had that foreboding feeling that I was heading to my impending doom. But I traipsed after her anyway.

We crept, crouched down, slowly up the winding driveway towards the house. The gravel crunched below our feet sounding like thunder in the stillness that surrounded us. I hoped that Chas' double glazing was the more expensive type that kept out the noise as well as the draft.

Keeping close to the trees to improve our chances of concealment, I could feel the cold raindrops dripping from the branches down my neck making me shiver. At least, I thought, that was the reason my shaking was increasing the nearer we got to the house.

Finally, we came to the end of the driveway. It opened out into an oval expanse, the length of the house and easily wide enough to turn a Rolls Royce around in without having to use the reverse gear.

I estimated, we had to cross about ten yards of open ground to the car and the same again to the house.

Suzanne had stopped and was looking up at one of the bedroom windows—Chas' I assumed. I followed her eye line and could see no movement within.

We observed for a few seconds. As Suzanne was about to continue, I pulled gently on her shoulder and said, "Stay low and keep the car between us and his window," and added as an afterthought, "When we get to the Roller, wait. I'm going to let one of its tyres down, just in case things don't go as planned. It should slow him down if the need arises."

"You've been watching too many films, Jake, but OK, it can't do any harm."

It still seemed like a good idea to me, but I was thinking on my feet here and maybe, subconsciously, I was just trying anything that would delay the inevitable.

We reached the car without apparently being seen. Remaining crouched out of sight from the house, I chose a front wheel to deflate reckoning that would have more of an effect on the steering as well as the braking.

The hissing slowed to a trickle indicating the lack of pressure left within the tyre. Suzanne looked at me, asking with her eyes if I was ready to proceed. I nodded my agreement.

We took a last glance up at the bedroom window and, satisfied it was all right to continue, raised slightly from our hunched position and prepared for the short dash.

But our attention was grabbed by a loud noise coming rapidly closer, from the side of the house. I was confused and didn't move. Suzanne had obviously realised what had caused the commotion as she tugged at my arm and whispered a yell, "Come on, run!"

I still didn't know what the noise was but thought, from Suzanne's reaction, that it wasn't a good one. She had covered nearly half the distance as I set off in pursuit, just as three Dobermans rounded the corner of the house.

They couldn't know me but their barking indicated that they were in no mood for a chat and a bit of petting. My training as a postman in dealing with such an incident didn't seem like a very conducive idea either. I had been told it was best to stand still, talk quietly but firmly to the animals and slowly back away. The other alternative, offered by an expert in canine behaviour, was to get down on all fours, head bowed in a subservient manner, and to tap the ground behind me as if I had a wagging tail.

Now, I was no expert in canine behaviour and didn't know of anyone who had put these methods to the test in a situation similar to the one I was in. For all I knew, they may well have worked. But intuition governed my actions and I just ran as fast as I could and prayed that the front door wasn't locked.

I crossed the stone steps up to the marble pillars in two strides by which time Suzanne had the door open and was through it. I managed to follow her, slamming shut the heavy wooden structure just as the first beast hurtled into it.

The thud of wood against wood as the door loudly closed and the howling of the hounds dispelled any lingering hope of an undetected entry.

Simultaneously, we turned around as echoing footfalls resounded around the large lobby we now found ourselves in, drawing our attention towards the stairs and upwards.

"Well, well, well. Look who it is." Chas stood at the top of the semi-circular marble staircase, with a tightly packed holdall in his hand. I glanced clockwise around the sparsely furnished entrance hall, looking for anything that might aid us against our adversary. There was a coat-stand to my left, then a door past which was a small, ornate oak table, its Victorian design at odds with the cordless phone that topped it. There were another two doors before the staircase and one after it. It had no other furnishings. The floor and walls were of the same sandy-pink marble as the stairs. The whole area struck me as a sort of mini replication of the factory foyer. I briefly wondered if Chas had *acquired* the materials when that foyer was under construction.

And all the time, the dogs barked and scratched incessantly at the door behind me.

"I'd have thought you'd have had enough by now, Jack," Chas sounded as though he knew he had the upper hand.

"It's Jake," I corrected him.

"Whatever. You two going to get out of my way? I was about to go away for a while." He took a couple of steps down and paused, adding, "But seeing as you're here you can save me a job. Would you mind feeding the dogs while I'm away, Suzanne?"

His self-confidence unnerved me further. We all knew that if he wanted to leave there wasn't a lot we could do about it. Our only chance was to delay him until the police arrived, and I hoped we could do this by verbal means to save me from taking another beating.

"The police are on their way. They know everything, Chas." Suzanne tried to get him to see sense, but he slowly continued down another two steps.

"I have no doubt you've called them, but I don't hear any sirens; do you?"

Chas was right and we knew their arrival wasn't imminent.

"Unless, of course, they've left them off so as not to disturb the nice neighbourhood." Chas' confident smirk had returned as he quickened his descent.

"You can go, Chas, but leave us the memory stick," Suzanne assertively bargained.

The huge man appeared to consider her request as he paused half way down and retrieved the stick from his jacket pocket. He looked at it for a few seconds, turning it over in his hand and then said, "Na, I don't think so. You never know when it might come in handy." He tossed our prize in the air, caught it and replaced it into his pocket.

Chas glowered at both of us in turn, daring us to challenge his decision. I tried my best to hold his stare but felt compelled to back down first.

"Now, if you don't mind, I've got a plane to catch. Oh, and don't forget the dogs, Suzanne."

As he came off the last step Suzanne took a half pace forward. Chas glared straight at her, tilted his head, raised an eyebrow, and just said, "Really?"

I used the distraction as a chance to obtain the only item I had found that was remotely like a weapon—an umbrella, which rested at the base of the coat-stand beside the door. Although it was a pretty large umbrella, I knew it was nowhere near adequate; but it was all I had. So I swiftly grabbed at it and weighed it in my hand as if it were a broad-sword.

Chas halted, looked at my weapon, looked me up and down and burst out laughing. Shaking his head, he continued on his way purposefully toward the exit.

I darted forward, believing my only chance against the larger, more cumbersome man, was speed of movement. I thrust the umbrella at his abdomen but he easily side-stepped my attack. Quickly regaining my balance, I arced my weapon towards his head but again he defended himself. He lifted his heavy holdall as if it were a mere carrier bag and parried my attempted blow.

Suzanne stood by watching, unable to do anything that might help me.

I regained my composure to make another assault. But Chas was already fed up with my pitiful attempts, dropping his bag and grabbing the umbrella in mid-flight at my next swing. He yanked it from my grasp with little effort and threw it into the corner by the stairs.

I shot forward again in a rugby tackle at his waist causing him to stagger backwards against the wall. But just like the battle at the canal, my attack was brief and doomed to failure.

The powerful man peeled my arms from around his midriff and raised me from the floor before hurling me across the room. The door to the left of the coat-stand abruptly halted my momentum as my shoulder collided with it. It took a few seconds for me to shake off the dizziness this caused, during which time Chas had retrieved his bag and was once again heading towards the exit.

I wasn't done yet and once more charged across the hall at him. This time he grabbed my injured arm, twisting it viciously making me howl with agony. He didn't let go but continued to screw the limb, looking straight into my eyes, unblinking, not wanting to miss a microsecond of the pleasure he was obtaining from this until the arm audibly snapped like a twig. Fire shot up it from the wrist to the shoulder and beyond, stabbing into my brain like a red hot poker.

He threw me to the ground and left me there writhing, clutching my excruciatingly throbbing, useless, limb.

Suzanne had picked up the umbrella while Chas had his back turned. Through my tears, I saw her strike him over the head with it. He hardly even flinched, but turned around and took it from her, pushing her aside. As he reached the door he paused as if a thought had struck him.

He gently put the holdall down, turned back towards Suzanne and in one swift movement knocked her stone cold with one punch to the jaw. He opened the front door and sent the dogs away with a single command, "Home!" They were not about to argue with their master.

To my surprise, he didn't go outside, but instead returned his attention to Suzanne and scooped her up off the floor as if she were a doll.

Through my befuddled haze, I realised he was taking her with him!

With Suzanne in one arm, he picked up his bag with the other and strutted out of the building towards the Rolls Royce.

I had to try and stop him!

Despite the state I was in, I managed to scramble to my feet and zig-zagged across the hall to the front door like a drunk. The need to save Suzanne far outweighed any pain I felt as I forced my battered body onwards. I stumbled down the steps and pitched forward onto the gravel below, banging the damaged arm in the process. Fire once more surged up the limb to renew its attack on my brain.

But I fought the agony, determined to save Suzanne. I hauled myself to my feet as Chas threw her limp body onto the back seat of the Roller. He was in the driver seat with the door shut before I could reach them.

I grabbed at his door handle but the ignition must have central-locked the vehicle and it would not open. Chas leered at me through his side window as he pulled away.

The tyres sprayed me with gravel as they sped off. I stood there, half dazed, half shocked, completely beaten and watched them disappear down the winding driveway. The tyre I had let down had no effect on their progress at all. I cursed run-flat technology.

Chapter 26

The sound of tyres wrestling against gravel followed by the thunderous clang of metal against metal jolted me back into action as I realised the Rolls Royce must have struck Suzanne's car. I set off running, well, more staggering, down the drive towards them.

As I neared my target, I could see the reversing lights on the Roller as it stood half on the driveway and half in the trees. It had glanced off of Suzanne's car, knocking it partially into the avenue.

At first, I thought the Rolls Royce had got stuck as the rear wheels spun sending up a cloud of steam from the muddy verge where gravel met grass.

I looked around for a weapon, a more reliable one than I had just tried back at the house. There were numerous broken branches at the woodland edge, but finding a suitable one was proving difficult. It had to be hefty enough to do some damage, but light enough for me to be able to wield in one hand. The first couple I tried looked the part were too rotten and crumbled in my hand. The one I eventually settled for was about the length and thickness of my arm. It still had a greenish tinge to it and felt solid enough as I banged it on the ground.

I weighed the weapon in my hand and confidence surged through me as I was sure it would do the trick. The adrenalin kick brought about by my renewed optimism revitalised and reenergised me as well as masking the pain from my bodily injuries. I strode vigorously towards the car.

But it suddenly gained a grip on the mud, twigs and leaves concoction and lurched backwards extracting itself from the woodland. Quickly engaging the forward gears Chas again propelled the car towards the main road, its path no longer blocked by Suzanne's Mercedes.

He had thwarted me, and this time I felt beaten for good. They were about to disappear and there wasn't a thing I could do about it. I could only watch as Chas aimed the car into the road and away from the town. Off to who knew where, taking Suzanne and the memory stick with him.

There was no wailing of sirens, no cavalry coming over the horizon at the last minute to save the day, no SAS to rescue the world.

But there was another vehicle approaching, at speed it seemed, by how rapidly its sound was nearing.

I looked towards Chas' car and realised at the last moment he would be unable to see this other vehicle as it was obscured by Suzanne's car jutting out into the lane.

The Rolls Royce emerged into the avenue and the speeding car, which I could now see was a blue Toyota, had too little time to react. The rain-slicked tarmac from the day's numerous showers made the road impossible to negotiate, especially at the speed the Toyota was travelling, and it slammed into the driver's door of the Rolls Royce, forcing the heavier car off the road.

The Rolls Royce slammed into an old oak tree, the thick trunk hardly quivering at all from the impact. Raindrops that had accumulated on its leaves sprinkled down, the sunlight shining through them in a sparkling rainbow of colours.

As the Toyota bounced off the heavier car, it veered out of control across the road and into the ditch at the side. Its impetus caused it to somersault up into the air before gravity brought it crashing back down, roof first, with a mighty cacophony of breaking glass and crumpling metal as it landed on top of the sturdy low hedge that separated the highway from the countryside. It hovered there for a split second as if deciding which way to fall. Finally having made up its mind the front end toppled over into the field beyond, the rear end remaining on the hedge. The bright blue bodywork contrasted vibrantly in the sunshine with the yellow of the rape crop beyond.

The whole thing only took seconds. The flash of action and boom of outrageous noise dissipating as quickly as it had arrived. Both cars' engines had ceased and all that could be heard was the quiet hiss from the Rolls Royce's punctured radiator, the squeak of a still rotating buckled Toyota wheel, the innocent twitter of birds of the countryside and the lazy breeze shuffling through the partially leaved trees.

I stood there gawping at the wreckage. I couldn't see how anyone could possibly have survived such a brutal collision. My thoughts immediately returned to Suzanne, and I began to run towards the Rolls Royce. As I got nearer, the strong acrid smell of spilled petrol hit the back of my throat. I realised it wasn't only a radiator that had been breached as a river of the liquid trickled down the road, away from the Rolls Royce. Its multitude of colours mixed with the rainwater producing a soft slick sheen on the tarmac.

I had covered about half the distance when, to my utter amazement, Chas' door began to move. My mouth fell open and my pace slowed to little more than a walk. Although his door was badly contorted, the powerful Chas managed to force it open, and it screeched its displeasure, metal straining against metal.

Chas slowly hauled himself clear and staggered into the middle of the road holding his bloodied head.

Almost at the same time, another figure emerged from the other vehicle and clambered over the hedge. Although he appeared much more badly injured than Chas, having been travelling at by far the greater speed and in a much lighter and less well protected vehicle, he was not staggering.

He seemed oblivious to the deep gash on his forehead, his hideously deformed right arm and the two-foot long branch that stuck right through him like a spear having entered his chest and come out through his back at the shoulder blade.

No, he was not staggering, he was running and screaming, screeching like an irate seagull. He was focused on only one thing—the person who had caused his dilemma. No injury or disability or pain was going to get in his way. He was going to rip the other driver apart, because, unbeknown to him, he was the latest victim of the raging.

The horrendous noise and speed of movement drew Chas' attention and he saw the other man just in time, managing to side-step his lunge causing him to crash at full speed into Chas's Roller. The impact forced the tree branch deeper into the man's chest until it plopped out behind him; the blood drenched dripping, gory mass resembling a freshly skinned snake as it writhed along the ground.

The man was at least six inches shorter than Chas, hardly reaching up to his chin and barely half his weight—indeed Chas' thigh seemed thicker than the man's torso; but he had the power of the rage.

He flew at Chas a second time, grasping at his throat and clawing at his face. Chas defended himself as best he could, levering the smaller mans' hands away, but not before they had ripped away sizeable chunks of flesh from his face.

Chas raised the slight man off his feet and hurled him with all his might against the Rolls Royce, shattering the rear side window. He fell in a crumpled heap to the ground. That would have been enough to finish any person in normal circumstances. But the smaller man climbed straight back to his feet, now with a large shard of glass protruding from his lower back. He was as oblivious to this as he was to the rest of his injuries.

A third time, he leapt at Chas, this time knocking the dazed and weakening man to the ground. At once, he was on top of Chas, attempting to rip as much flesh from him as possible.

Unrecognisable through the wounds and blood, Chas tried to cover his face with his arms. He continued the struggle using all the strength he had left to unbalance the man. They rolled over and this time Chas ended up on top sitting astride the Toyota driver.

Suddenly, the man went limp, and I knew, from the previous victims and my own experience, that he was succumbing to the final symptom of the rage. But Chas, whether he realised this or not, wrapped his hands around the flaccid man's throat and squeezed as long and as hard as he could, causing his eyes to bulge and face to swell up like a balloon.

The pressure forced the trapped blood within the man's head to seek the easiest exit and it began to trickle from his eyes, nose and mouth. Chas finally let go. He remained astride the corpse, his shoulders slumped and his head fell to his chest in exhaustion. His hands dropped limply to his side.

I loped across the few paces that separated us and, using this momentum, swung my hefty piece of broken tree branch as hard as I could, smashing it against the side of Chas' head with a solid pop that I was sure would have scored a home run in any baseball game. The force of the blow toppled the bloodied man off of his dead adversary and into the road where he lay, unmoving and unconscious, his flowing blood mingling with the petrol and water adding yet more colour and producing an image akin to a sixties pop art picture.

I was more than pleased with my choice of weapon and the job it had done.

The wooden cudgel, no longer needed, slipped from my grasp to the tarmac with a dull thud. I stood there looking down at my nemesis, pleased to have finally wiped that smirk from his face. He was well out of it but still breathing. I bent down, my aching body pleading against the movement, and put my hand inside his jacket, quickly locating the memory stick for which we had come. I breathed a sigh of relief and popped it into my trouser pocket.

Satisfied that Chas would no longer give me any trouble, I turned my attention towards the Rolls Royce and its occupant, Suzanne. I peered into the vehicle to where she lay prostrate on the rear seat. The side of her face was pock marked with bloodied incisions from where the window glass had exploded inwards.

The door opened easily, being almost undamaged from the collisions. "Suzanne, Suzanne!" I frantically shouted attempting to awaken her. Aside from the cuts and a red swelling on her jaw where Chas had struck her, the only other injury she appeared to have was a large lump on her forehead above her right eye, presumably from coming into contact with the car seat, during one of the crashes.

I leaned into the car, repeated her name twice more and gently shook her by the shoulder. After a few seconds a soft, painful sigh emanated from her lips, rather like the ones I do when waking up with a hangover. Her eyes opened and the pupils grew and shrunk alternately as she tried to bring the world back into focus. "Wha—?" was all she could utter as she raised a hand to her injured head.

"Shush, shush," I soothed, stroking her hair away from her face, "Just lay still, help will be here in a minute."

I could hear the distant sound of emergency vehicle sirens approaching, their blue lights coming into view as I turned in their direction.

Two police cars drew up in front of the scene of carnage, sirens silenced but blue lights still winking to warn any approaching vehicles. P.C. Weismann got out of the first car and took control of the situation, directing the other officers to seal off the road and send for ambulances. Her self-assuredness took me somewhat by surprise. She was a totally different person from the quiet lamb I had first encountered just a few short days earlier. Maybe I was wrong—first impressions might not always be the right ones.

Suzanne pulled herself upright into a sitting position and asked, confusion written across her face, "What happened?"

"Chas crashed the Roller. He's out of it. Are you OK?"

"I-I think so..." she replied shaking her head in an attempt to clear it and immediately regretted having done so, "Ow!" she yelped as the pain kicked in.

After allowing her a few seconds to recover I asked, "Can you manage to get out?"

Suzanne went to nod her head but stopped herself realising what that would do, smiled lamely, and replied, "Yes, I think so."

I helped her out from the wrecked Rolls Royce. She was still a bit dazed and unsteady on her feet but managed to climb free using my good arm for support.

Once her instructions had been issued, Weismann came over to us.

"I'm afraid that one's dead," I said pointing to the mangled remains of the Toyota driver.

"And he wants handcuffing," Suzanne said, having regained much of her awareness and gesturing towards Chas as he started to groan, consciousness slowly coming back to him. "He can be very dangerous, even in that state," she added confirming to me that she had seen past the person she used to call her boyfriend. "You'll want to be questioning him about murder."

Chas continued to moan and hauled himself up onto his elbow before attempting to get to his feet.

"If you could remain where you are, sir," Weismann instructed Chas.

But he ignored her, or perhaps didn't fully comprehend what she had said, and continued to rise.

The officer wasn't taking any chances and smoothly restrained the larger man, securely fastening his hands together in front of him with her cuffs.

While we awaited the arrival of the ambulances, the other officers took statements from us, impassively taking down every detail of our barely believable tale. I wasn't sure they were convinced by what we told them—I know I would have been very sceptical if I had not witnessed it with my own eyes.

I put my hand into my pocket. "Oh, you'll be needing this," I said handing the memory stick over to Weismann. "We're hoping this contains the cure that can bring an end to these rage attacks, so take good care of it." I attempted a smile.

"Thank you, sir, we will," her smile was about as successful as mine.

Two ambulances arrived. Chas was helped to his feet and escorted into one by a police officer. He leaned heavily onto the constable obviously in a bad way from his ordeal. I thought any one of lesser physical capabilities than he, such as myself, would almost certainly not have survived.

Suzanne and I climbed into the other ambulance, assisting each other both mentally as well as physically, and we were soon on our way. This time, I was quite looking forward to spending a few hours in a hospital waiting room, with nothing to do but wait our turn, without any cerebral or bodily exertion required.

It was finally all over, and for the first time in days, I felt I really could relax. The relief drained the energy from my body. I glanced across at Suzanne. She was sitting there, eyes closed, hands by her side and head tilted back resting against the side of the ambulance. She swayed gently in harmony with the movement of the vehicle, looking as warn out as I felt.

Now that the adrenalin rush had begun to disappear, the pain replaced it. Every part of me was once again shouting out with agony, nowhere louder than my shattered arm. I looked down at the deformed limb, closed my eyes, hoping that exhaustion would take me away from the pain, at least for a short while.

"You all right, Jake?" Suzanne's voice forced open my eyelids, her concern and smile bringing me some respite.

"I will be when I get some damn pain-killers," I wearily replied, but managed to return the smile. "You?" I asked.

Suzanne again smiled, and nodded, closing her eyes, tiredness taking over.

We arrived at the hospital what seemed like seconds later. I realised I must have dozed off. As we were wheeled into reception, I could see Henry, seated in the waiting area, along with about half a dozen other people, still awaiting attention. Behind him was the coffee machine.

As I scanned the area, my eyes fell upon Margaret at the reception desk, looking exactly as she had done ten days ago. Then Lisa-Anne called out Henry's name as the next in line to be seen.

So many things had changed in my life in such a short period of time, but others, like that which was around me, seemed to be eternal, and I drew immense satisfaction and reassurance from this.

Suzanne's wheelchair drew up alongside me as we waited to be logged in. She put her hand in mine, and I gently squeezed it, keeping hold of her, drawing even more comfort and strength from the moment. She leaned across allowing her head to rest on my shoulder.

Chapter 27

Six weeks later…

"Beeep!" my mobile phone had loudly informed me of an incoming message. *'Lunch? Xxx'* was all it had said. Suzanne didn't need any more words to get across to me.

'Great idea. Cricketers Rest @ 12.30 OK? Xxx' had been my reply as I tried to be just as succinct, but didn't quite succeed. Still, I think I got my idea over.

'OK xxx' Suzanne had ended the exchange.

It would be good to see her again. It would be nice to talk to her under more relaxed circumstances now that the rage attacks were just a memory. Admittedly, a very vivid and horrendous memory, but now firmly in the past.

The Cricketers Rest was an excellent establishment that provided above average pub cuisine at more than acceptable prices. But what made it my preferred choice was that it was just up the road from my home and within easy walking distance. As my arm was still in plaster I was unable to drive. You don't realise how much you need a car until you don't have access to one. Even the simplest tasks like shopping, or going to the bank, or hospital appointments, or even out for a meal become a bit of a military operation.

Luckily, the weather was also in my favour that day as I set off for my dinner date. I had been to this particular pub quite frequently in the past, but this was the first time I hadn't driven there.

It's really surprising how much you don't notice when you are manoeuvring a motor vehicle or perhaps how much more you are able to take in when leisurely strolling instead. The first thing that hits you is the sounds. The occasional passing vehicle goes by almost unnoticed as the rustling trees in the light breeze vie gently for attention with the sedating singing of a variety of our feathered neighbours.

The air smells so much fresher than the artificial atmosphere of the car cocoon, and the breeze plays gently and satisfyingly against the skin.

Spacious driveways, some flanked by vibrant green hedges, others by brightly painted wooden fences in a variety of colours and yet more by expensively constructed brick and stone walls. Only a few had vehicles occupying their gravel or tarmac frontages as most would have whisked their owners off to their places of employment. After all, these things had to be paid for and the bigger and better they were the more they cost both in terms of money and time.

My delightful daydreaming quickly transported me to my destination.

The entrance from the road was flanked on either side by two Lombardy Poplars that seemed, at such close quarters, to reach right up into the clouds, like Jack's giant beanstalk. The spring sunshine glistened through their partially leaved slender branches, spangling like jewels as the soothing breeze whispered lazily through them. I must have looked like someone in serious need of help as I gawped up at them, admiring and appreciating the wonderment that nature is able to produce.

I quickly shook off my child-like amazement and looked around self-consciously, hoping nobody had been watching me. Satisfied I had remained undetected, I once more cloaked myself in the expected adult, almost macho disguise and strutted through the main entrance and into the bar area.

As the name suggested, the Cricketers Rest was a themed pub. The front of the oak effect bar was adorned at intervals with sets of cricket stumps. On the walls were black and white photos of long since retired players; most of the names attributed to them meant nothing to me although I recognised a few, like Darren Gough, Fred Trueman and 'Sir' Geoffrey Boycott. Pride of place went to a battered old 'Duke' ball which had apparently taken a hat-trick some years earlier.

I by-passed the bar and went in search of Suzanne. I knew this wouldn't take long as the place wasn't overly crowded and, sure enough, I soon spotted her by the window in the Larwood Suite—the three separate dining areas were also named after cricketing legends of yesteryear; Holding and Jardine being the other two.

"Hi, Suzanne; good to see you again," I called and waved as I strode across the plush carpet in the sparsely populated pub. A one armed bandit flashed and winked at me as I passed it, perhaps empathising with my disability. Behind me, I could hear the clink of pool balls and low-key laughter as a group of lads enjoyed their early start to the weekend. Otherwise, the place was pretty much quiet, the ambience perfectly reflecting the sport the establishment represented.

"Thanks for inviting me. How are you doing?" I asked as I approached her table.

Suzanne was casually dressed in blue denim jeans and loose fitting same blue tee-shirt with the logo *one life and living it!* It also carried the maker's name—some Italian guy I had never heard of. Her attempt at casual probably cost more than any suit I had ever bought; in fact, more than all the suits I had ever bought.

"I'm great, thanks; and you?" She said as she rose to meet me.

We embraced, and her luscious aroma wrapped itself around me. It wasn't the same stuff I remembered her wearing the last time I saw her but smelled just as expensive.

She looked her usual immaculate self, "You're looking gorgeous, as always," I said, "What's the special occasion?"

"Thanks," she replied, "Nothing really. I just thought it would be a good idea to catch up; to see you again."

"It's only been a fortnight since I last saw you…" I started to say.

Suzanne cut me off, "Oh, I'm sorry. I didn't realise you were fed up with me already. I can go if you want." She smiled playfully.

"I didn't mean it like that. Besides, you've been away, haven't you? Where was it, erm, America?" I played along with her couldn't-care-less game, pretending I had hardly given her a second thought, glad to see that the chemistry was still there between us.

"You know it was. I had to go, for Dad's sake. He really needed the break. Missed you though." She pecked me on the cheek and sat back down.

"What are you drinking?" I asked, pulling my wallet from my faded jeans pocket (not fashionably faded, more age-worn and lived in but smart enough for a pub meal).

"You can put that away," she said.

It was my turn to interrupt, "Not this time. You're not using the 'expenses will cover it' line again. I'm paying; it is my turn."

Suzanne opened her mouth to protest but my raised hand silenced her.

"Just a Coke. I'm driving," she said, letting me win for once.

I nodded and went to the bar, soon returning with her Coke and a pint of bitter for myself.

"How's the arm?" Suzanne asked as I sat down opposite her.

I turned it over and back, looking at it like you do, "It's not too bad now. Still aches a bit and feels very weak, more through lack of use I think. I've only had it out of the sling a couple of days."

The cast was a bit tatty, frayed at the edges and its original off-white colour was now even more off-white, but it would have to remain on for a few more days yet. I didn't go on about it though as I didn't want it to sound like I was whinging too much.

"How is Henry?" I continued with the niceties, but genuinely concerned.

"Yeah, OK, OK…" She didn't sound too sure as the sentence trailed off.

My brow furrowed quizzically inviting her to continue.

"His health is fine but he seems, well, a bit broken, I suppose. What happened with Chas really hit him hard. I worry about him…" She had a distant look in her eyes and just allowed the sentence to hang there.

I leaned forward and put my good hand on hers, "It'll take time, but I'm sure he'll be all right," I tried to ease her anxiety, "He's a tough cookie you know." I smiled and gently squeezed her hand.

Suzanne seemed to appreciate this and visibly refocused on her surroundings as she pushed her concern for her father to the back of her mind.

"Thanks. He's shutting the business you know." She adjusted the subject slightly.

I nodded my head in acknowledgement.

"We were in bad enough shape as it was, but the publicity from it all kind of made us unviable. I think it allowed dad to make what he knew was the only decision. Even without what Chas did, we wouldn't have survived much longer."

"You'll be OK though, won't you?" I asked.

"Oh, yes. Dad could see this coming and had made sure we will be all right financially. And with the sale of the land we'll have nothing at all to worry about. He's already considering a very reasonable offer, you know. It's a large area in a prime position and won't take much selling."

I didn't know what to say. On the one hand, like Suzanne said, they would be all right for money, but on the other, her father's life work had ended so acrimoniously. There really wasn't anything I could say I suppose, so I remained silent.

Suzanne ended the brief void by changing the topic of the conversation to me. "And what about you. How's work; still hassling you?"

I smiled, "Of course. I wouldn't expect anything less from them. They keep trying to persuade me to come back on *light duties*," I demonstrated these two words with bunny ears (inverted commas made with the first two fingers of each hand). "But I know their idea of *light* will differ too much from mine. I suppose, I'll give it another couple of weeks then have a try. I should be bored enough by then."

"Speaking of work, what do you plan to do?" As the factory was closing I assumed she would need to find something.

"Haven't really thought about it yet. Besides admin for Dad, I've not done much else. I've a degree in politics so I should be able to talk my way into something. I don't need to work, financially, and I'd like to make sure Dad's OK first. But eventually I'll need to fill my time with something."

"Shall we have a look at the menu? I'm starving." It wasn't just an attempt to lighten the mood; I actually was ready for something to eat.

We each scanned a copy of the brightly coloured menu with its pictures supposedly representing their fabulous food. I have generally found these national restaurant chains' actual offerings rarely live up to the promise suggested by these depictions. However, that provided by the Cricketers Rest was usually well above the average in quality, I had found.

I didn't know what I had expected of this day. Ever since I had known Suzanne, because of the circumstances, all our conversations had been fraught with worry, despair, negativity or desperation. Now that the virus threat appeared over, I, naively perhaps, expected things to be different; a fresh start, maybe. But now I realised that, although the threat might be over, you can't just wipe away what had happened. You can't merely consign it to the past and continue as if nothing had happened. The physical scars were there for all to see but the mental ones tend to get ignored, especially by others. This realisation made me feel a little bit guilty. I had been happy to escape with my life and return to life pretty much as before. Suzanne's life, on the other hand, had been much more profoundly affected; hers would be changed for ever.

"The steak's excellent here," I said.

Suzanne stopped perusing the menu and appeared to be considering my opinion for a few seconds. "Yes, that sounds good. Medium rare with salad, please. What are you having?" She said, replacing the menu into its rack alongside the special offer leaflets, children's menus and other paraphernalia.

"Mmm, I think I'll have the steak and ale pie." I didn't fancy trying to cut through an inch of beef with my dicky hand. And I would be having chips and veg with mine. The health kick I had promised myself in the heat of battle would have to wait, at least until my injuries were completely better. Or until I could find another excuse.

I ordered the food, and as I re-joined Suzanne, my phone interrupted us. It was Sharron. I pressed the accept button without hesitation.

"Hello, Sharron, what can I do for you?" My tone was friendly and relaxed.

"I was just wondering what time you would be round tonight. 'Bout eight all right?" she asked.

"Eight's fine. See you then."

Sharon ended with, "OK, see you then. I love you."

I ended the call without responding.

"Sharron," I said to Suzanne.

"I know, I heard," she responded in a non-committal tone.

I was unable to read her reaction and decided to expand on my situation. Besides, I felt I owed her an explanation. I firmly believed Suzanne had been instrumental in saving my life, and I wasn't about to start making things up. There was clearly chemistry between us—an attraction of some degree. She deserved to know the truth; where we stood.

"She wants us to give it another try."

I paused for a second, but Suzanne said nothing, her expression remained unchanged, giving nothing away.

So I continued, "She's thrown *thing* out. Apparently, he was also, err, shall we say, *interested* in the fitness and well-being of other clients."

Suzanne smiled at that. I knew then this would be easier to do than I had feared.

"Anyway, I thought maybe I owed her that much; to at least give it a try. I've not moved back in or anything like that, yet. I want to take it steady and see how I feel as things progress."

Suzanne placed her hand on mine, "I think it's a good idea. You can't just throw away twenty years. You can't erase two decades of feelings as if they didn't happen. I hope it works out for you, Jake, I really do; you deserve it."

She squeezed my hand a little tighter and smiled at me. I could tell she genuinely meant the words she had just uttered. But that smile and those eyes didn't make my resolve for a reconciliation any easier.

"She hurt me a lot. Only by trying will I find out how much. I suppose that's why I don't want to move back in, not yet." I was totally unsure whether I was doing the right thing. I had strong, very strong feelings for Suzanne but, well, I reckoned I could only deal with one of the situations at a time, and it had to begin with Sharron. Furthermore, I realised, this was likely to deal with any Suzanne situation as it would most likely end any possibility of taking things with her any further if Sharron and I didn't work out. Unfortunately, (or fortunately?), real life doesn't work out like a soap opera.

We finished our meal in silence.

"Pudding?" I asked.

"Oh no, I couldn't. I'm full," Suzanne answered.

I thought that was that then. I certainly knew how to end things on a bad note. Damn, I didn't want us to part that way.

It was as though Suzanne had read my thoughts, "But I'll have another Coke, though, if that's OK?"

I breathed a sigh of relief and said, grinning, "I think the budget can stretch to another drink apiece."

The atmosphere lightened considerably after that, and we chatted about nothing in particular for nearly another hour.

Our afternoon drew to its natural conclusion, and I rose to leave. "I will stay in touch, you know. I mean it." And I did.

Suzanne left her seat to join me, took a hold of my hand, looked deeply into my eyes and said, "Oh, I know you will. I'll make sure of it."

She planted a lingering kiss on my cheek and we embraced, for ages, knowing it was a parting embrace, neither of us wanting the moment to end.

Over her shoulder, I could see the news on one of the several TV screens dotted about the pub. The sound was down but the captioned live item informed me that a peace rally in Manchester wasn't going very well. Rioting had broken out, bricks and other debris were flying about and police in riot gear were attempting to disperse the mob using tear gas.

I somehow found the whole thing strangely quite comforting. It seemed to confirm that everything had returned to normal.

"Can I give you a lift home?" Suzanne asked as our clinch finally concluded.

"Thanks, but no thanks. It's a lovely day for a walk," I smiled, "And besides, every time I get into a car with you, things don't, how shall I put it, seem to run smoothly."

Suzanne smiled that gorgeous smile of hers that lit up her entire face, and the sun danced rainbows off of her immaculate hair. It was a perfect image for me to remember her by.

We parted, and Suzanne called out to me as she went to her vehicle, "Call me, soon. If you don't, I'll call you." And then she was gone.

I needed to use the gents before setting out for home.

As I came out, I glanced at the TV screen. The riot was still ongoing. In the bottom right hand corner, I could see several police officers restraining a young woman. As they attempted to put handcuffs on her, she struck out at one of them, knocking him clean off his feet. Her face contorted in a horrendous scream which I actually thought I could hear from the soundless TV.

As another hand attempted to get a hold of her, she bit it taking the little finger straight off and sending the officer reeling away in agony. A policewoman cracked her over the head with her baton, but it seemed to have no effect.

The young woman broke free, blood and spittle frothing from her mouth as she staggered wild-eyed towards the camera. She stared straight at me, and collapsed lifeless to the ground.

The End